The Legacy of Mrs. Cunningham

The Legacy

of Mrs. Cunningham

a novel

Marian Rizzo

WordCrafts Press

*To my daughters, Joanna Jones and Vicki Christensen,
the joys of my life.
In memory of baby Rachel, who's waiting in heaven.*

Judy Cunningham

February, 1984

Adele Cunningham had died. And, she had lived. Two hours of personal testimonies had proved as much. Multiple individuals had stepped up to the pulpit to share what Mrs. Cunningham had done for them, either through prayers or through advice. The truth was, Adele Cunningham left a legacy that would never die.

After the service and a brief time at the gravesite, family members and several close friends gathered in the Cunningham living room. They mingled with drinks in their hands and continued to talk about how Mrs. Cunningham had changed their lives.

Overwrought by the loss of her mother, Judy Cunningham needed a place where she could grieve alone. She sought a path through the swarming crowd. Arms fell like gates at a railroad crossing and blocked her way. She endured the body hugs, the wet kisses on her cheek, and the suffocating mix of heavy perfumes, halitosis, and body odors. Mumbling her apologies, she broke free and passed from the living room into the kitchen.

Aunt Connie stood at the counter arranging a platter of cold cuts, her back to Judy, her round bottom outlined beneath the decades old black dress she'd worn to every funeral as long as Judy could remember.

A couple of Adele's friends huddled together at the sink, prepping vegetables, their high-pitched chatter rising above the splash of water and the clank of silverware. Judy snuck past them and headed for her mother's bedroom at the rear of the kitchen. She slipped inside and eased the door shut.

Then, breathing a sigh, she drank deeply of the quiet.

A hint of winter's daylight filtered through the lacy curtains at the window and sprinkled shimmering dots on the antique chest of drawers, its scroll-shaped latches flashing tiny bursts of light into the atmosphere.

A sense of nostalgia took over as she swept her eyes across the four-poster bed, the hand-crocheted, pink and green granny quilt, and the lacy pillow shams, everything neatly arranged as if Mother had just left the room. On the little bedside table sat a Tiffany lamp, a worn leather Bible, and a box of tissues, remnants of Adele Cunningham's daily meetings with God.

Judy set her purse on the floor, slipped out of her overcoat and tossed it on the bed. She approached her mother's rocker and ran her hand over the curved back.

"Mom's prayer chair," she whispered.

This was where Adele Cunningham met God every morning and every night, plus at needed times throughout the day. Judy settled into the chair, shut her eyes, and imagined her mother's arms enfolding her.

"I'm gonna miss you, Mrs. Cunningham."

Mrs. Cunningham. That's what everyone called Mother. By the time Judy and her brother, Paul, had reached their teenage years, they'd started calling her that too.

"You need prayer?" people often said. "Ask Mrs. Cunningham. You need advice? Mrs. Cunningham will know what to do."

She pulled a tissue from the box and dabbed at a sudden spill of tears.

"I could use some of your advice right now, Mrs. Cunningham," she murmured, and a surge of panic rushed to her heart.

She set the rocker in motion and thought about the many notes her mother had left behind for her to deliver. She'd hand-written more than two dozen of them during her last week in the hospital. One of those little blue envelopes had Judy's name on it. She'd slipped it, unopened, in her purse along with the one Mother had addressed to Judy's boss, Parker Addison. *Why on earth had Adele Cunningham written to that man? He hadn't come to the funeral, and with good reason.*

Judy caught her breath. Had her mother suspected? Had that wise woman been aware of her daughter's emotional struggle? Perhaps her own note contained the answer. She reached for her purse.

A knock on the bedroom door caused her to freeze, her hand mere inches from her purse.

She waited. The door opened a crack.

"Judy, are you in there?" Aunt Connie cooed.

She pressed her lips together, then said, "Yes, Aunt Connie."

"People are looking for you, dear. Will you please come join us?" There was a pause. Then she added cheerfully, "Food's ready."

"All right, Aunt Connie. Give me a couple more minutes."

The door clicked shut. Judy opened her purse and withdrew the envelope that bore her name. She stared at it for a moment, a shiver of anxiety traveling through her. Then, holding her breath, she slid her fingernail under the flap and opened it.

PART I

TWO DAYS BEFORE THE FUNERAL

ONE

ALICIA CARTER

The shrill call of the alarm clock pulled Alicia from her dream. She rolled out of Butch's arm and struck the alarm button. It was 5 a.m., way too early to get into an argument. Nevertheless, she set her jaw, determined to at least tell him her plan.

She swiveled toward him. "I've made up my mind," she said with as much confidence as she could muster.

He let out a sleepy grunt.

"I'm going home," she went on. "I'm gonna attend Adele Cunningham's funeral, and while I'm there, I'm gonna reconnect with my daughter."

She raised her eyebrows and waited for his response.

His eyes half open, Butch eased himself up on one elbow. He looked like he was struggling to join the real world.

A flash of blue peered back at her, and he sat upright. He frowned. "Are you sure you want to do this, honey? The kid's got to be ten years old by now. She won't even know you."

"I'll know her." She raised her chin.

He shook his head. "I don't know—"

"Listen, Butch, this emptiness inside me will never go away, not until I do this one thing. No matter how busy I stay with all my decorating projects and lunches with the girls and shopping trips—nothing fills the void—not even you."

He drew back from her, a wounded expression on his face.

"Sorry, Butch. You've been wonderful." She sought the right words. "But you must know, the relationship between a man and a woman is different from that of a mother and her child. Ten years ago, I left a part of myself in that hospital. The nurse carried my baby out the door, and I couldn't stop her. Not then. Not at seventeen and with my parents and grandparents in control."

She let out a huff. "They had given me two options—adoption or abortion. Hah! Some choice. Either my baby lives with someone else, or I kill her."

He straightened, and his brow knitted together in what looked like concern.

"Abortion?! It was barely legal back then, and certainly not morally right."

He shook his head, then rested a gentle hand on her shoulder. It amazed her how Butch remained calm in every situation, no matter how emotionally upsetting it was for her. As a commercial airline pilot he was trained to make split-second decisions. Years of such training had kept him strong and exceptionally cool, even in his personal life. Why couldn't she be like that? Why did she have to fall apart every time things didn't go her way?

Now, she was asking him to understand her need to reconnect with the child she'd given up more than a decade ago.

"I'm telling you, it's a mother-daughter thing," she repeated with emphasis. "I bonded with my baby long before she was born. I carried her inside me for nine months. Nine months of waiting, and dreaming, and imagining what my baby might look like. Would it be a boy or a girl? Would the child have my blue eyes? My blond hair? My turned-up nose?"

He smiled and appeared to be trying to understand. But how could he? Butch never cared whether they had children or not. He simply wanted her, or so he'd said many times.

Alicia continued her plea. "The moment my baby was born, something rose up inside me. I can't explain the feeling. Love, I think." She released a troubled sigh. "They allowed me to hold her for two minutes. Two minutes, Butch, and then they whisked her away. One second she was in my arms. The next she was out the door with someone else."

Sobs erupted. They started in her chest and moved upward into her throat.

Butch released a long sigh and stroked her arm. "Gosh, Alicia. Except for the one time you told me you had a baby out of wedlock you mentioned it only once or twice over the years. I figured you'd gotten over it a long time ago. Now, out of the blue, you're bringing it all up again."

He paused and let out a little chuckle. "Are you sure this isn't like every other senseless project you've come up with over the years?"

Had he really said that? Speechless, she glared at him.

His face colored. He shrugged. "I'm sorry. I didn't mean that, honey. They weren't senseless. But come on, think about it. You keep trying to fill the void in your life by trying new things. Remember the time you decided to refinish our furniture? The living room was a cluttered mess for six months. In the end, you gave up and we had to buy new furniture to replace the ones you'd demolished."

He chuckled again, but she saw no humor in his joke.

"Okay, how about the ceramics class you joined last year?" he persisted. "Didn't I support you in that? I even bought you your own kiln. It's still sitting in the basement collecting dust. Then there was the time you purchased an expensive sewing machine and started making your own cl—"

Alicia brushed his hand off her arm. "Stop it, Butch. Just stop! This is different. We're not talking about furniture or ceramics or clothes. We're talking about a living, breathing human being."

He smiled sweetly. "I'm not trying to hurt you, honey. I'm trying to protect you."

He seemed sincere. She fell against him and rested her head on his shoulder. Was he at least *trying* to understand? He stroked her hair. His slight show of compassion moved her. Perhaps she might be able to get his approval. It would be so much easier with his support.

She tilted her face toward his. "I want to know her, Butch. No, I *need* to know her." She searched his face, now void of expression.

Fearing she'd lost his attention, she straightened. "I *need* to make sure she's all right, that she hasn't been mistreated."

He responded with a slow shake of his head. "I don't know, honey. It's been so long. What if she believes the people she's living with are her real parents? Do you want to disrupt that child's life? And theirs too?"

"I've thought about all that. It's not fair. Not to her or to me. People deserve to know their roots. They deserve to know who their biological parents are, no matter what kind of life they've had—good or bad."

"Look." He let out a long sigh. "Let's take a step back and consider all that's happened since you gave up your baby. You've had three miscarriages, and the last one really set you back. Counseling didn't help. Neither did those pills you took for a while. You need to give yourself time to heal, Alicia. In another month or two, you'll look back at all this and realize healing takes time."

"You don't understand, Butch. I've struggled with this for years—long before the miscarriages, but even more after each one."

He managed a compassionate smile. "Think about it, Alicia. You did the right thing. You were too young to raise a child. You allowed someone else to raise her and to love her. You gave her a chance to live, and you went on to live the life you were meant to have. Now what's happened? Instead of moving ahead, you want to go back. You want to relive the past or something. What's the matter? Aren't you happy here? With me?"

"Of course, I'm happy. But something's missing." Tears filled her eyes. "I walked away from my daughter. My flesh and blood. I walked away, but she's stayed with me every day of her young life."

He released another sigh. "Okay, what about the couple who raised her? You told me they were childless. You entrusted your baby to them. Now you're threatening to pull her out of their home. Can you imagine how many lives you're going to disrupt with this one decision?"

"Yes, I've thought about all those things. For years I stayed away from my hometown. Except for wanting to see my daughter, I didn't have any other reason to go back." She stared into his eyes. "Until now."

He nodded like he understood. "Mrs. Cunningham's funeral."

"Yes. Her passing has revived all those memories. It's as if they happened yesterday. All I can think about is, *I have a daughter, and I want to see her again.* This funeral gives me the perfect reason to go back and do that." She sought his face for any sign of understanding. "Is that so wrong, Butch?"

He narrowed his eyes, a flicker of distrust in them. "It's not wrong if all you want to do is get a look at her. But what happens after you've seen her?"

She gave a quick lift of her shoulders. "Who knows? I'll take it slow. Once I see her I'll know what to do. If it means letting her know I'm her mother, so be it." She ignored the shock on his face. "Don't you see, Butch? It's fate. Mrs. Cunningham's spirit is telling me to go home and connect with my little girl."

His face screwed up in disbelief. "Oh, right. The stars conjoined and paved the way for you to ruin someone's life. Are you trying to tell me that woman died so you could hurt a whole lot of people? And do you think that couple will sit back and let you take their child away from them, that they're not gonna give you a fight?"

Alicia snickered. "They don't have any legal claim to her. My baby's father never signed the adoption papers. The jerk went off to college and left me to deal with the whole mess. His parents paid for everything, then they turned away. They never even asked to see their granddaughter. So, you see, there's no official document, no court decree that says that couple legally adopted my child. We shook hands and everyone kept their mouth shut. They got a baby, and I got to keep my self-respect."

He shook his head and let out a heavy sigh. "I have to get to the airport." He moved away from her.

"Butch, please—" She grabbed his arm. He jerked it away.

"That's enough." An air of authority had returned to his voice. In an instant, he'd stopped being her husband. He was in the cockpit now. Big captain. Spouting orders at his crew. "I'm going on an international flight. I have to be in operations three hours before departure." He set his jaw. "I'm gonna take a shower." He gazed into her pleading eyes and the lines on his face softened. "We'll continue talking about it over breakfast. Maybe we can come up with something else you can do to fill the lonely hours."

So, that's it. the most important issue in my life is merely a discussion that could be finished over breakfast. She watched him disappear into the bathroom.

With the thunder of the shower placing a final barrier between her and her husband, she reached for her terrycloth robe and slid into her fluffy pink slippers. The getup looked an awful lot like the one she wore to the hospital ten years ago. Why had she purchased the exact same bathrobe and slippers? She pressed her hand to her abdomen. In seconds, she was back in that delivery room, counting the minutes between contractions.

It was December of 1973, three weeks before Christmas. Alicia Davis was sixteen years old and painfully aware that she was three months pregnant. She waited until Christmas Eve to break the news to her parents. *Merry Christmas, Mom and Dad.*

From that moment, Sandra and Elliot Davis took over and made all the decisions for her.

"We think it's best if you stay with your Nanna and Poppa and deliver your baby at the hospital there," her mother said, a firmness in her voice. "You'll be sheltered from all the small-town gossip. No one else will ever know. You can live on your grandparents' farm and attend the Christian school near their home. If your dates are accurate, you'll have the baby in the middle of summer. Then you can stay there and finish your last year of high school. We don't want you coming back here where everyone can ask questions. Not until you've taken care of this problem."

Alicia's head spun with all of the instructions. She couldn't argue. But, problem? Was that what she was—a problem? She couldn't wait to pack up and move out of there. But she knew what living on the farm meant. It meant she'd have to attend her grandparents' church every Sunday. It also meant she'd have to listen to her grandfather read Bible passages to her every evening before bed. She'd have to endure her grandmother's lectures about the proper behavior of a young lady, and what she should do and not do from then on. A swell of claustrophobia consumed her, and she thought she wouldn't be able to take another breath.

Months passed. Alicia turned seventeen. Her grandparents arranged for a local doctor to monitor her pregnancy. Summer drew closer, as did her delivery date.

That day in the hospital, she thought she might die. A part of her had left with someone else. She resented everyone. Her parents. Her boyfriend and his folks. Her grandparents. Even the old doctor who promised to keep his mouth shut.

After the baby was born, she enrolled in the Christian school her grandparents had chosen. She finished her last year of high school, and immediately after graduation, she ran off to flight attendant training and left her former life behind.

In a way, the excitement of being on her own served as an escape of sorts. She'd entered a whirlwind that left no time for reflections or remorse.

After three weeks of training, she was placed on reserve status. The guys in crew scheduling assigned her a trip nearly every weekend—no surprise, for that was when regular block holders called in sick. Anyway, she didn't mind working weekends. Those were the best trips. Overnights in Vegas and San Fran, lots to do, and extra per diem pay.

Then Alicia snagged the most sought-after, unmarried copilot on the line. Her girlfriends envied her. Her rivals hated her. It didn't matter. Butch Carter was tall and muscular, and he had a full crop of brown hair and the bluest eyes she'd ever seen, even bluer than her own. They almost looked fake, like those clear marbles in a kid's game bag.

On top of all that, he was getting ready to check out as captain, which meant his paycheck was about to double.

They married in a quiet ceremony in a little chapel in Las Vegas. From then on their work trips served as mini vacations. They even traveled on their days off and used their pass privileges to run off to exotic places like Spain's Costa del Sol and the French Riviera. They took cruises, went on ski trips in the Alps, a trail ride in Wyoming, a camera safari in Africa. Alicia's escape from her former life continued. She dove into activities that helped her forget about the past, enjoy the present, and look forward to a better future. Life was good.

Until she had her first miscarriage. Though she survived the physical trauma, she fell into a terrible state of depression. She quit her job, went to counseling, and moped around the house for the next three months.

With a promise to make things better, Butch purchased a five-bedroom home in the Chapel Hill subdivision of Lexington, Massachusetts. His trips flew out of Logan International Airport in Boston, a sixty-minute drive to work, depending on traffic.

Alicia turned her attention to decorating their new home. And though she rarely talked about it, she began to ache for the baby she'd given up. Their home certainly had enough bedrooms for several children.

After six months, she became pregnant again, but like before, she miscarried during the first trimester. She read books on fertility, took mega doses of Vitamin E, and considered fertility injections. The cycle repeated with still another miscarriage, again within the first three months. Every loss was followed by several months of depression and more counseling. Butch went beyond the call trying to comfort her, but to no avail. She'd look into his cool blue eyes and see only sympathy there, never a solution. Ultimately, her gynecologist shook his head and suggested they consider adoption.

Adoption? Years later, the word came thundering back at her. Now she kicked it aside like she did every time a doctor had suggested it in the past. How absurd to consider adoption when she already had a child who lived less than three hours away. With those bitter memories still running around in her head, she scurried into the kitchen to make breakfast.

While she pulled out the pans and the items from the fridge, her mind sorted through various arguments she might use to convince Butch to go along with her plan to go home. She started frying bacon, scrambled some eggs, dumped in a handful of shredded cheese, and got the coffee going. Then she ran to get the morning paper off the front stoop. Still, she wasn't sure what she might say to that stubborn man.

Butch surfaced—showered, shaved, and dressed in a fresh, clean uniform. He kept three uniforms and rotated them every week. One was at the dry-cleaners, the other two hung in his closet, ready to go at a moment's notice. The same was true of his shirts, at least a dozen of them, freshly laundered, with starched collars, and crisply folded inside plastic bags.

His thick hair was gelled and slicked down enough to accommodate his captain's hat. He looked like he'd just stepped off a magazine cover, and he smelled like the men's cologne counter at Macy's.

Ignoring Alicia's troubled gaze, he sniffed the aroma of fried bacon and smiled his approval. Then he grabbed a chair and dove fork-first into his plate of scrambled eggs. He didn't say a word about their little talk. It was as if she'd never brought it up. Alicia glanced at the clock over the stove. He'd be leaving soon, and she wasn't ready to let him go, not without giving her a word of support. For some reason she couldn't explain, she wanted his blessing. Needed it, no matter how forced it might appear.

He avoided looking at her, grabbed a triangle of toast, and scooped up the remaining eggs. He reached for the morning paper, glanced at the front page, and continued chewing. His eyes were on everything except Alicia. He took a couple more bites and washed it all down with a long draught of coffee. It was obvious he was trying to ignore the issue, perhaps hoping it would simply fade away. If she didn't say something soon, he'd finish his breakfast and be out of there before she had a chance to lay out her entire plan.

Summoning courage, she leaned across the table toward him. "I'm going to that funeral, Butch. I want you to know that. Mrs. Cunningham was like a second mother to me."

He lowered the newspaper.

"You know what else?" she said, glaring at him. "I haven't seen my friend Judy since she came to visit us, two years ago. I need to talk to her."

"You two talk on the phone a couple times a month. You catch up on each other's life, and you make plans to get together— plans that never seem to work out." He finished off the toast.

"Yes, but now I really do need to see her—face-to-face. I need to offer my condolences over her mother's passing, and I need to talk about—well, things."

He rose from the table and refilled his coffee cup from the carafe on the counter. "Do you honestly think talking to Judy about this *plan* of yours will help?" He'd said "plan" like it was a dirty word.

"I want to tell her the truth about why I left. She never knew."

"I thought she did." He settled back in his chair, his question-ing eyes glued to her face.

She shook her head. "Her mom advised me to keep it a secret. I left home before I started to show. After that, Judy and I rarely saw each other. Then my baby was taken away from me, and I was simply this old friend who had moved away from Fall River to live with her grandparents. Judy never knew the reason. She must have thought what we wanted her to think—that I wasn't getting along with my mother and needed to go away for a while."

He began to take a sip of his coffee, but paused and lowered the cup. "What good will it do to tell her now?"

She shrugged. "I don't know. Maybe she'll be able to give me some advice, like her mother used to do. After all, Judy *is* the daughter of one of the wisest women I've ever known. Maybe some of Mrs. Cunningham's wisdom rubbed off on her."

"You mean, maybe she'll encourage you to go after that little girl, right?" He shook his head. "What if she says the opposite? What if she tells you to leave well enough alone?"

She shrugged.

He reached across the table for her hand. "Look, why don't we do like Doctor Pearlman said and consider adoption? We're both young. I have a good job. We can afford to pay all the fees. And we have this big house. Fill it with all the kids you want. Wouldn't it be nice to give some homeless child a nice place to live?"

She slid her hand out of his grasp and leaned back. "I don't *want* someone else's child. I want my own. I've made up my mind, Butch. While you're in Europe or wherever you're running off to this time, I'm going home, like I planned. But don't worry yourself over it," she said this with a touch of sarcasm. "I'll be there for only a couple of days. I'll attend the funeral, spend some time with Judy, and then—we'll see. By the time you get off your trip, I'll be home again—maybe with some good news."

He frowned at her. "Good news, Alicia? For you? Or for them?"

"Good for everyone."

She looked down at her plate. She hadn't taken a single bite. She grabbed a knife and spread strawberry jam on a piece of toast, then she nibbled at a corner. Their conversation was going nowhere. She hardened her gaze and searched his face for some inkling of understanding.

His frown dissolved, and he gazed at her with compassion.

"You did a brave thing, giving up your baby." His voice was soft, even kind. "You were thinking of her welfare."

She melted a little then. "I wasn't as brave as you think. I couldn't have gotten through that time without Mrs. Cunningham. Shouldn't I at least go and pay my respects?"

He shrugged. "I suppose," he offered and finished his coffee.

So, that was it. She'd have to be satisfied with that little crumb. It was time to move ahead with her plan.

"Don't worry, Butch. I won't do anything rash. If it doesn't seem right, I'll walk away. I did it before, and I can do it again."

He nodded. Was that approval? Or acquiescence?

Encouraged, she opened her heart to him. "If I sit in that church and pray like Mrs. Cunningham taught me to, maybe I'll be able to think the same way she did. Maybe then I can make the right decision. I only need to be near that woman again, alive or dead. It'll be like she's actually there, guiding me."

He stared at her with those authoritative captain's eyes. He had the power to stop her, if he wanted to.

He pushed away from the table. "No matter what I say you're gonna do what you want. All I can tell you, Alicia, is, be careful. Consider the feelings of everyone involved. Pray about this decision, and for goodness' sake, have some compassion. Isn't that what Mrs. Cunningham would say?"

She nodded. "I'll take it slow. If it looks like this might hurt the child, I'll back off. Believe me, I'm not about to destroy anyone."

She walked with him to the front door. Waiting in the foyer were his suitcase and flight kit—two symbols of the job that regularly separated them for days at a time. She wrapped her arms around his neck, kissed him, and then backed away. Forcing a smile, she opened the front door and stood aside.

"Don't worry, Butch. I'm a big girl. I can handle this."

His blue eyes glinted with skepticism. He picked up his bags and walked out. She stood in the doorway, chewing her bottom lip. She hadn't told him everything, hadn't told him she'd hired a lawyer and had already started the necessary paperwork. Hadn't told him she was willing to go to court if necessary.

As she shut the door of the house, she also shut the door on the guilt that was pressing against her heart. She'd have plenty of time to deal with it later. Her spirit lifted, she turned away and hurried to the bedroom to pack a bag.

TWO

Pastor Robert Goode

Robert Goode tiptoed into his daughter's room and approached her bed. He sucked in his breath and gazed at the tiny form curled up in a ball. Mindy's puppy-dog quilt had slipped off her shoulders. Robert pulled it up where it belonged, then he stepped back and stared down at his precious angel. Tears filled his eyes.

"Real men don't cry," his father had drummed into his head from the time he could walk. "Let the women make fools of themselves, blubbering and sobbing. Don't *you* ever do that."

Though he'd always tried to follow his father's directives—and there were far too many to count—Robert had shed tears on many occasions without his father ever knowing. Like the day the class bully knocked him off his bike on his way home from elementary school. He doctored his scraped knees and bawled like a baby in the privacy of the bathroom. He cried till he thought his stomach might rupture when his dog, Rusty, got hit by a car, and again when his little brother ended up in the hospital with pneumonia. And when he failed to make the Bible quiz team, he let the tears flow while walking home from school, then dried them quickly before stepping inside the house.

His father never witnessed Robert's fall from manhood, never had the opportunity to berate him for failing to *act like a man*. That's how Robert had grown up. Hurting, but unable to share his pain, not even in front of his mother, for she, too, lived under her husband's domineering rules.

Robert didn't begin to take charge of his life until after he graduated from high school. When his father pressured him to follow the men of the family into the medical field, Robert chose the ministry.

"You'll be sorry one day," Alex Goode had scoffed. "Don't expect to earn much of a living in a job like that. People don't appreciate their pastors, not like they used to. But they treat doctors like gods. Doctors have the power over life and death. But pastors? What is *their* great calling? They merely guide their flock into the unknown. You'll be lucky if you get a Sunday morning thank you."

Alex Goode showed even more disdain for Robert's choices when he started dating Jennifer Bishop, a kindergarten teacher and the daughter of a telephone repairman. With a grunt and a shake of his head, Alex tried in vain to arrange a date between Robert and another doctor's well-bred daughter. He refused to go. The closer he and Jennifer got to a wedding date, the thicker the tension grew in the Goode home.

When the day finally arrived, even a two-edged sword could not have cut through the animosity that had risen between Robert and his dad. He stood at the altar with his father's narrow-eyed glare piercing the back of his head. His desire for a career in ministry and his choice of a bride served as the two final nails in his coffin.

Alex cornered him after the service. "Okay, so you want to go your own way? Here's your wedding gift." He shoved a legal size envelope in Robert's hand. "It's the last bit of financial help you'll ever get from me. You're on your own now."

Then the older man walked away in a huff.

Inside the envelope, Robert found a thousand dollars in fifty-dollar bills. He shrugged off the insult. God would take care of him. That was one time in his life when he didn't shed a single tear.

Most of the time, however, tears came easily. He'd shed happy tears when Jennifer accepted his proposal, and again when he caught sight of her, adorned in white and haloed by a glow of light in the church doorway. He'd wept tears of gratitude when he received his ordination, and again when the board at First Street Christian Church called him as pastor, and most recently when the congregation celebrated his twenty-fifth anniversary of service with a surprise party on his behalf.

Then there were the sad times, still difficult to forget. He'd sobbed along with Jennifer when their doctor told them they wouldn't be able to have children—a physiological problem on his part, which caused him even more grief. He couldn't give his wife what she desired most in life—children of her own.

"It's okay, Robert," she'd said, though tears had gathered in her eyes. "I love you more than anything on earth. Children or no children, we'll keep going together."

In a magnificent turnaround, he flooded a handkerchief with tears of joy the day Mrs. Cunningham told them she'd found a baby for them. He'd cried again when Alicia Davis gifted them her newborn child. The distraught teenager had said she wanted her daughter to be raised in a Christian home. He'd promised to fulfill her wish.

Now, as he stood watching Mindy sleep, more tears flowed. This time, they came out of fear that he might lose his little angel. Still in shock over the letter he'd received from Alicia's attorney, he wrestled with the challenges he and Jennifer were facing, both financial and legal, if they wanted to fight for little Mindy. He didn't know if they could win. They had no legal right to the child, no contract, no official decree. And like his father had warned, he had a limited income, which meant he couldn't afford the court costs and other fees required to wage a decent fight. There was no way he'd beg the old man for help.

The scent of lilacs alerted him to his wife's presence. Jennifer had tiptoed into their daughter's bedroom and had drawn close to his side.

"She's ours isn't she?" Jennifer whispered. "Please, Rob, tell me we won't have to give her back after all this time."

"I don't know." His voice broke. "I hope not."

"That girl—why on earth is she coming here now?"

"Mrs. Cunningham's funeral."

She nodded. "Of course. Alicia hasn't been home in ten years. All of a sudden, Adele Cunningham dies, and she's going to storm into town and take her baby away from us."

He wrapped an arm around his wife. "If not for Mrs. Cunningham, we might not have had the last ten years with Mindy."

"Yes, we were finally able to get a baby, and Alicia could get on with her life." Jennifer's voice carried an unmistakable bitterness. She stomped her foot. "She can't take her away from us, Robert. I won't let her."

The tightening of his throat kept him from answering.

"What about her promise?" Jennifer pressed. "She said we could raise her as our own, that she wouldn't interfere. Tell me, Rob, what right does she have to take her now? Mindy thinks we're her real parents. She—"

"We *are* her real parents, Jen. We're the ones who took care of her when she got sick. We're the ones who changed her diapers and paced the floor with her at night when she couldn't sleep. We soothed her when she was scared, doctored her scraped knees, taught her how to read and to ride a bicycle, played board games with her, did everything biological parents do. And what did Alicia do? She got in trouble and gave birth to a baby. That was *her* contribution. Then she was gone."

Unexpected seeds of hatred had entered Robert's heart. He could feel them growing out of control. He was the pastor of a church, a man of God. How could he have allowed such an emotion to take over? He knew what could happen. His hatred for Alicia Carter threatened to destroy him and his ministry, yet he was powerless to stop it.

Tears were streaming down Jennifer's face. The sight of her anguish triggered more animosity for the child's natural mother. He took a deep breath and tried to temper his voice. "Now, now. I'm gonna take a close look at the law. Maybe there's a statute of limitations or some other legal recourse. We haven't yet begun to fight."

She gave him a weak smile, though more tears flowed. "I knew we should have gotten a lawyer back then. Why did we trust a teenager, Rob? Why didn't we make everything legal so she could never pull something like this?"

"Well, for one thing, the father was still around—somewhere. Though he wanted nothing to do with the child, his parents had paid all of Alicia's medical expenses. So, in a way, the boy was still in the picture."

"He didn't want the baby. His family had money. They could have taken her, but they didn't want her."

"No, they didn't. But for some reason he didn't sign the release. Maybe it was pride. Or perhaps he expected to show up one day and claim her for himself. Like the mother's doing now."

"At least Alicia's parents didn't interfere. They wanted the scandal to go away. Do you remember how relieved they were when we agreed to raise their grandchild?"

He nodded slowly, pensively. "Yes, I do remember." He let out a snicker. "They disappeared for good when we showed up in town with Mindy in our arms. They stopped coming to church. Never came to visit their grandchild, never remembered her on her birthday or at Christmas. It was like she never existed, at least not to them."

Jennifer stroked his arm. Her touch soothed his angry heart if only for the moment. "Well," she breathed. "It worked out fine as far as I'm concerned. I didn't want our little girl to grow up confused about who her parents were. She was ours. Period. Now we're being forced to get a lawyer in order to hang onto what is rightfully ours." Her voice had gotten louder, more pronounced.

He shook his head. "Oh, Jen, we couldn't afford a lawyer back then. What makes you think we can afford one now? Or the court costs?" A feeling of hopelessness overwhelmed him. "I'll tell you what. I'll do whatever it takes to keep our little Mindy, but it might mean losing everything else."

At the sound of her name, the little girl opened her eyes for a second. Then her lashes fluttered shut, and she rolled to her other side.

"Let's go," Jennifer whispered. "We might wake her. We can talk out in the living room."

Reluctantly, Robert pulled away from his precious angel. He followed his wife to the door and turned for one last look at the sleeping child. His throat ached, and his eyes burned with fresh tears. Then, he slipped out in the hall and eased the door shut behind him.

At least he didn't have to fight this battle alone. As always, Jennifer had stuck by him like glue since the day they married thirty-two years ago. Robert had started calling her *Mrs. Krazy Glue*, but always with a twinkle in his eye and adoration in his voice.

From the beginning, Jennifer fit the mold for the perfect pastor's wife. She kept her teaching job and supported him through his last two years of seminary. She followed him from one church position to another until they settled for good in Fall River. Weeks before they moved into the parsonage, she developed relationships with the women in their new congregation. She counseled the younger ladies, comforted the elderly, became a second mother to teenagers. She started a women's Bible study, oversaw the church Sunday School classes, cooked meals for the sick, and, beyond all that, she oiled the wooden railings inside the sanctuary, spot-cleaned the carpet, and brought order to the pile of papers on her husband's desk. In more recent years, she helped start the church's elementary school.

No one else worked as hard as Jennifer did to keep the church going—no one, that is, except for Mrs. Cunningham.

Now *that* was a woman who could put a team of work horses to shame. Apart from her secretarial job in a real estate office, she spent much of her free time helping out at the church—dusting, cleaning bathrooms, maintaining the nursery, and making sure the weekly bulletins were printed and stacked on a table near the entry door. Most of all, Mrs. Cunningham had a reputation as a true prayer warrior. People called on her at all hours of the day and night. Jennifer kept a log of Adele's answered prayers—the ones she knew about. The list filled two notebooks, and she'd gotten halfway through the third when Mrs. Cunningham died.

What's more, Adele Cunningham had counseled dozens of people with a ninety-nine percent accuracy in positive outcomes. Numerous individuals, couples, and families had sought her out for guidance and prayer intervention. Was his church large enough to accommodate the number of people expected at her funeral? While he was feeling pressured over the possibility of losing Mindy, he had to come up with a eulogy for Adele. How could he say all he knew about her in twenty minutes?

Why shouldn't he offer a praiseworthy message for someone who had changed his life? He warmly recalled the day he and Jennifer went to Adele Cunningham's house and confessed that they'd never be able to have children.

"We've known for years," Robert admitted. "But we still haven't gotten over the truth."

Mrs. Cunningham wasted no time. She sat them down on her front porch and sent up a fervent petition to God. One of her statements gripped Robert's heart like a security blanket and still stuck with him to this day.

"What is the answer, Lord?" she'd said. "What can help this childless couple fill their home with love and joy? Perhaps their hearts can make room for a child in need. Guide them, Lord, for you know what's best."

She went on to pray about the virtue of waiting on the Lord, but Robert didn't hear much beyond her mention of "a child in need."

He came away from their prayer huddle confident they had found an answer. Adoption.

It turned out a traditional adoption cost several thousand

dollars. And there was another problem. Robert had turned forty-four and Jennifer was two years behind him. Many of the child-placement services topped the parental acceptance age at thirty-five, especially where newborns were concerned.

Months passed. They were about to give up when Mrs. Cunningham phoned them with a lilt in her voice and a promise of good news. Robert invited her to his office the next morning.

It was the early summer. The outside temperature had hit 95 degrees. Robert's office vacillated from stifling heat to a momentary blast of cool air emitted from a vibrating window air conditioner. The worthless contraption rattled the pane every time it clicked on.

Jennifer and Mrs. Cunningham settled in armchairs. Robert paced in front of the tumbledown air conditioner.

Adele smiled at the two of them. "My dear friends, a close friend of my family is having a baby."

Robert stopped pacing and held his breath. Jennifer raised her eyebrows and leaned toward Mrs. Cunningham.

"Did you hear what I said? A close friend is having a baby." Mrs. Cunningham grinned like the cat that swallowed the canary. "She's an unwed mother—a teenager—and she wants to find a suitable home for her child."

Robert reached for his wife's hand. "A baby, Jen." He choked out his joy over the clatter of the air conditioner. "A baby."

Jennifer calmly rose from her chair and walked to the window. She turned off the noisy box, then, her eyes wide, she faced Mrs. Cunningham.

"Did we hear you correctly, Adele? Did you say you've found us a baby?" Jennifer's tone was soft yet hopeful. Tears rimmed her eyes. Robert wanted to engulf his wife in his arms to protect her from more disappointment.

But Mrs. Cunningham stood up and walked to her side. "The young woman told me she wants her child to grow up in a Christian home. I immediately thought of you two."

Noticeably shaken, Jennifer returned to her chair and choked out a relieved sigh. Robert walked up behind her and rested his hand on her shoulder. He kept his eyes on Adele.

"If you're interested I can tell the girl I've found the right couple," Mrs. Cunningham offered. "When I spoke with her several weeks ago, she wasn't ready to make a decision. The good news is, she didn't want to have an abortion. I was happy to hear her say that."

Jennifer nodded in agreement but said nothing. Tears spilled from her eyes. Robert bent close to his wife and pressed his cheek against her face.

"Our prayers are answered, Jen," he whispered in her ear.

"A baby." Jennifer lifted her face toward the ceiling. "Thank you, Lord."

Robert gathered his wife in his arms, and they wept openly together, unaware when Mrs. Cunningham tiptoed from the room.

They found her outside, standing beside Robert's dilapidated old Ford, a wrinkle of concern on her forehead.

"It's a two-hour drive to the hospital," she said with trembling voice. "Will this thing make it?"

"With God's help it will." Robert could hardly contain his excitement. How could he worry about a silly car at a time like this?

Adele chuckled and gave a nod. "The baby is due in a few weeks. I'll give you a call when the contractions start. Meanwhile, get some work done on this thing. You need to get it in good running condition for the trip."

A thought struck Robert. "Doesn't the girl want to meet us first? Won't there be legal documents to sign?"

Adele shook her head. "I'm afraid this will have to be done without the paperwork. The father's parents are paying for everything. For some reason they want to maintain control."

The information left Robert ill at ease. But when he gazed at his wife and the elation on her face, he dismissed his discomfort and vowed to trust God with the outcome.

Almost three weeks to the day, Adele phoned them with the news. It was 7 a.m. Robert ran from the bathroom to grab the phone. He'd scraped only half the shaving cream off his face. Jennifer was in the kitchen preparing breakfast. He rushed in to tell her the news. The baby was coming.

Jennifer turned off the stove, left the eggs and toast on the counter, and ran to the spare bedroom. Barely looking in the mirror, Robert finished his shave and threw on some clothes. Jennifer emerged carrying a bag she'd filled with baby items.

Fifteen minutes later, they honked the horn outside the Cunningham house. Adele came bounding out the front door, swinging her purse. Her eyes widened, and she stared at Robert's face.

"Did you cut yourself?" She started chuckling and handed him a handkerchief.

He patted his cheek with the linen cloth. It came away dotted with drops of blood. "Guess I was in a hurry." He giggled nervously, then pocketed the handkerchief. "I think I'll live. Let's go, Adele."

With a shake of her head, Mrs. Cunningham slid in the back seat.

Jennifer turned around in the front and faced her friend. "What if the girl changes her mind? Once she sees the baby she might not want to let go. They do that, you know."

Robert shook his head over his wife's innocent remark. The good Lord hadn't let them down yet.

Adele clucked at her. "You're a minister's wife. Do I have to remind you what the Bible says about needless worry?"

Jennifer let out a sigh. "You're right of course."

Robert patted his wife's hand and sent her a silent message of encouragement. Then he pulled the car away from the curb and headed out of town. Within an hour they were crossing the county line. Every rut, every bump in the road sent his vehicle jostling from one lane to the other. He silently prayed that the old rattletrap would get them to the hospital and back home without breaking down.

While the two women chattered happily about baby toys and nursery items, he let his mind wander to visions of a child brightening up their home and tried to focus on the road ahead.

"I'm not at all prepared for this," Jennifer admitted. She patted the bag on her lap. "I bought a few things for the baby, but I'm not sure I thought of everything."

Mrs. Cunningham rested her hand on the back of Jennifer's seat. "Don't you worry about that. The ladies of the church are giving you a baby shower after the service on Sunday. Believe me, you'll get more items than you need."

"A baby shower?" Jennifer's voice carried a hint of concern. "Whatever did you tell people?"

"The truth. That you've received a baby from an unwed mother. They don't need to know the girl's name or the circumstances."

Several minutes of silence followed. Jennifer wiped tears from her eyes. Mrs. Cunningham settled back in her seat. Robert glanced in the rearview mirror. "Is something wrong, Adele?"

"I'm pretty sure you know the mother."

He kept his eyes on the road. "Who is it?" His throat tightened with apprehension.

"Alicia Davis."

Robert nodded. "That explains the girl's disappearance from church and her absence from choir practice. Such a good singer, too. She can hit those high notes like no one else. I wondered what had become of her."

"Does it matter?" Mrs. Cunningham said.

He shook his head. "No, no, not at all. I just wish I could have helped her through this."

"Alicia is a strong young woman, both physically and emotionally."

"And what about the father?"

"The young man comes from a well-to-do family. As far as I know, he's never gotten into any of the bad stuff. No drugs or alcohol. He doesn't even smoke pot. It seems he wanted to get on with his life without being tied down by a baby."

Robert frowned. "Sad. Kids sometimes take risks without understanding the consequences."

He glanced at Jennifer. She dabbed at a few more tears, but her lips were smiling. At last she was going to have the one thing she'd always longed for—a child of her own. His heart throbbed with joy for her.

He turned his attention to a mileage sign at the side of the road. "Twenty miles to go."

The two women went on to chat about things that were more interesting to females than to men, such as blankets and cribs, feeding schedules, and baby toys. For the time being, he blocked it all out and kept looking for another mile marker. He couldn't stop smiling. A kind of electricity had filled the old Ford, and he was reveling in it. For the first time in years, his wife was laughing out loud. Her face was aglow, and her eyes sparkled with anticipation.

When they arrived at the hospital, they learned Alicia had gone into labor and had been moved into the delivery room. Then came the pacing, the sitting, the rising, the checking of watches, the drinking of as much coffee as they could hold, plus a good deal of hand-holding prayer.

It was late afternoon when the doctor emerged, a broad smile on his lips and a twinkle in his eyes. "It's a girl, a beautiful baby girl," he announced.

Mrs. Cunningham let out a hoot. Jennifer flung herself into Robert's arms.

"She's perfect," the doctor said. "Seven pounds, three ounces."

"And Alicia?" Mrs. Cunningham asked.

"She's fine." He nodded toward Robert and Jennifer. "Are these the adopting parents?"

"We are," Robert proudly responded.

Adopting parents. Parents. Robert hadn't used the term until that moment. He was about to become a father. Jen was going to be a mother. It was a dream come true.

They met briefly with Alicia in the delivery room. She

acknowledged them with a nod, reiterated her desire for her child to grow up in a Christian home. Then, satisfied with Robert's voiced assurance, she turned her tear-stained face toward the wall and Jennifer received the baby in her arms.

Now, here they were, ten years later, and their dream was about to crumble. Robert ran his hand through his hair. His eyes blurred with tears, and his father's words came back with a vengeance. *"Real men don't cry,"* the old man had said. *"They're supposed to take charge of a situation and fix it."*

But how could Robert fix something that was beyond his ability? A flash of anger rekindled within him. Why did God have to take Mrs. Cunningham? He sure could use her strong spirit right now.

As though reading his thoughts, Jennifer made a similar remark. "I wish Mrs. Cunningham were here."

He took his wife's hand and drew her to the sofa. Except for the ticking of the clock on the mantel, the room had settled into a pensive quiet. He slid his arm around Jennifer's shoulder.

"Did I ever tell you that woman influenced a great many of my sermons?"

Jennifer's eyebrows went up. "Really?"

"I'd catch her straightening up the nursery, or scrubbing toilets, or some other thankless job, and we'd have the most profound conversations. Remember that sermon I taught on the armor of God?"

"It was one of your best."

He nodded. "Mrs. Cunningham."

"Is that right?" Jennifer's eyes widened. "What about my all-time favorite—your message on the Lord's Prayer. Please tell me that was yours."

He shook his head. "Hers, too."

"So all your best sermons came from Mrs. Cunningham?"

"Right. I'm ashamed to admit it, but I don't have a clever bone in my body. For years I depended on my talks with Mrs. Cunningham to jumpstart my Sunday sermons. Remember that time she had a bad cold and didn't come to the church for a week?"

"Not really."

"Well, if you think back, that Sunday I gave the worst sermon of my career. It was an insipid, lifeless muddle of thoughts. Later, I figured it out. I needed Mrs. Cunningham."

"Oh, come on, dear. Surely, you had lots of good ones."

"Well, okay, but, even then, *she* created the springboard. A prayer. A word. A verse of Scripture. She always said *something* that got me thinking beyond the mundane. Then, I simply kept going with it."

Jennifer let out a heavy breath. "I had some marvelous talks with her myself."

They sat quietly for a few minutes, then he shifted away from her. "Tell me, how are you going to handle losing Mindy—I mean, if it happens?" He rested his hand on her knee. " We've got to be ready, Jen."

She shook her head, and a tear dropped to the back of his hand. "I won't handle it. I won't. I'll do whatever it takes to convince that girl to leave Mindy with us. For now, I have no idea what I'll say. Tell me, Robert. What would Mrs. Cunningham do?"

He didn't have to think long. "Pray," he said. "That's what she'd do."

"That's right. I've been praying ever since you told me Alicia was coming home. I prayed that you'd be able to find a lawyer who can help us keep our little angel. I prayed that Alicia will change her mind, and we can move on as though none of this ever happened."

"There's something else we need to pray about," Robert said. "We need to pray that we'll keep our testimony, that no matter what happens, we'll be Christians first. And we have to remember God is in control."

"That's a given, isn't it, Rob?"

He shook his head. "Not always. I have to admit, resentment

has started boiling up inside me. I'm afraid I've started hating that girl for wanting to take Mindy." He turned his upper body toward his wife. "Think about it, Jen. She turned her back on that child ten years ago. Now, for some reason I don't understand, she's developed a kind of maternal instinct. She's going to hurt us, and not only us, but Mindy too. That's what makes the hatred rise up within me. I want to be able to protect you and our little girl, but a thankless woman has more power over our lives than I have."

Jennifer eyed him sheepishly. "She doesn't have more power than God."

He bent over and allowed the tears to flow. *He* should have been the one to bring up trusting in God. Yet, his wife had reminded him of his position as a pastor and a believer. Why did he crumble under such pressure? Why did he need Jennifer and Mrs. Cunningham to tell him what he already knew in his heart?

"Jen," he said, raising his head, his face moist with tears. "I'm going to have to depend on you to keep me from lashing out at that woman. When I see her again, I'm afraid I might blurt out something that will ruin everything. I never thought I would say this, but I despise Alicia Davis—or Carter, or whatever her name is now. I have hatred in my heart, and, God help me—I don't know how to get rid of it."

THREE

BEN MICHAELS

The news of Mrs. Cunningham's death created an immediate time warp for Ben Michaels. In an instant, he traveled fifteen years back in time to a Saturday morning baseball game. He was ten years old and in love with the sport, not quite ready for the tragic accident that would keep him out of the game for a while.

An early morning fog had settled on the ballpark. It was too thick for him to even see first base. As expected, the coach called the game and Ben started for home, swinging his mitt and hoping for a better day tomorrow. He was lost in thought, not merely intent on tomorrow, but on a whole bunch of tomorrows and a possible future in the big league. His coach had said he had potential.

Suddenly, two dim lights, like the eyes of a cat, emerged from within the fog. They moved toward him at such a high rate of speed, he didn't have time to jump out of the way. The impact flung him over the car's hood and hurled him onto the pavement on the opposite side of the street. For a brief moment, he raised his head and looked around. A man exited the car and raced toward him. Then he dropped back against the hard pavement and lost consciousness.

He awoke in a hospital room, his head aching, his pitching arm in a sling, and both of his legs in casts. A blur of white bustled about his room, checked the tube that ran to his left arm, fluffed his pillow, and scooted out the door without a word. Still in a daze, he turned his head slightly, despite the throbbing in his temples, and caught sight of his mother asleep in a corner chair. He tried to call out to her but every movement, even the simple opening of his mouth, hurt like the dickens.

Moments later, Doc Kramer came in and stood next to his bed, staring down at him. The old man's forehead was lined with concern.

"Sorry, son. I'm afraid you've had a wicked accident." The doctor's usual gruff manner had mellowed since the last time Ben got sick. Two years ago, he contracted the flu. Kramer came to the house and gave him a shot of penicillin in the butt. Feeling like he was, Kramer was the last person he wanted to see.

His head still swimming, he tried to open his mouth in protest, but all he could do was cough, which made his whole body tense up.

"Don't try to speak, Ben," the doctor said. He pressed a cool hand to Ben's forehead. "The way things look right now, you're lucky to be alive. Both of your legs are broken, and your arm is fractured in three places."

Ben shook his head. "No shot, okay?"

Doctor Kramer smiled down on him. "No shot. I promise."

"I–I need to play ball," he managed, his voice barely a whisper. "I need to finish the season."

Doc Kramer let out a grunt. "Listen, son. You need to concentrate on getting well." He released a sigh. "No baseball, but you'll be able to do lots of other things," he said, nodding like he was offering good news.

Ben's mother flew out of her chair and came to Ben's bedside. "Don't tell him that, doctor. Don't tell my boy he won't play ball."

Doc Kramer shrugged. "I'm merely relating what the X-rays showed."

Ben turned his head toward his mother. She smiled sweetly, though concern wrinkled her brow. She placed a hand on his good arm. "You're gonna walk again, darling," she murmured. "And you're gonna pitch too. Don't let anyone tell you that you can't."

Doc Kramer grunted again but said nothing.

Tears puddled in his mother's eyes. "I've called Mrs. Cunningham," she said, a glimmer of hope in her voice. "She's promised to come and pray for you. Do you know what happens when Mrs. Cunningham prays?" She paused and faced the doctor. "Things happen," she said, her voice firm. "Things that have confounded the best doctors."

Doc Kramer left the room shaking his head. His mother moved to another part of the room to a table that had a lot of flowers on top. She was humming a familiar song she used to sing to him when he was young. He recognized it from the movie, *The Sound of Music*, and it had something to do with raindrops and kittens and brown paper packages. His brain was so muddled he couldn't recall the exact words, but the melody she was humming had a lilt to it that gave him a ray of hope. If his mother believed he'd play ball again, why shouldn't he believe it too?

"Look who's here," Ben's mother called out. She hurried to the doorway.

Mrs. Cunningham was standing there, a straw purse in her hands, a smile on her lips. Even as she embraced his mother, she never took her eyes off of Ben. His mother whispered something in Mrs. Cunningham's ear. The woman nodded with understanding. Then she was at his bedside.

"Do you know what we're gonna do, Ben Michaels?"

He gazed into her shining face.

"We're gonna pray for *complete* healing, that's what we're gonna do. Not only are you gonna walk again, you're gonna pitch again."

Then she plunged into a prayer that was so intense it had him thinking she had a direct line to God. His Sunday school teacher had said that God hears the prayers of a faithful servant. Though he'd said his share of bedtime prayers, hearing Mrs. Cunningham's plea made his own petitions seem weak.

Here she was, talking to God like he was right in the room with them. She even went beyond his injury and mentioned his dream to be a pro baseball player one day. She was shooting for the moon.

That first prayer in Ben's hospital room kicked off a whole string of prayer sessions. Mrs. Cunningham returned every day for the next two weeks. After he was released, she showed up daily at his home. Sometimes she brought cookies. Most of the time, they sat and talked about his love of baseball. And, she always ended their visits with a prayer.

"The strength to heal often comes from within," she told him one morning. "Miracles do happen, Ben, but sometimes you have to help them along. Think positive thoughts. Imagine yourself running and playing. Like it says in Philippians, you can do all things through Christ who strengthens you. You just have to believe."

At first, Ben had doubts about all Mrs. Cunningham expected of him. After all, what did she know about mangled legs? She had two good ones to walk on. With such thoughts circling around in his head, Ben sank into a terrible state of hopelessness. He peered out the living room window as his friends walked by wearing baseball caps and carrying their bats and mitts. He longed to join them, to stand on the pitcher's mound, hurl a ball at Tommy Waters, and watch him swing and miss. As his teammates walked by, their cheerful voices sailed through the windowpane and plunged him deeper into despair.

Eventually, his head stopped aching, his arm came out of the sling, and the casts came off his legs. He started to think maybe Mrs. Cunningham was right. Maybe he *would* play ball again. Then one morning, he wriggled his toes.

He hollered for his mom.

She scurried into the room, a dishtowel in her hand, lines of concern on her forehead. "What is it, son?"

He grinned at her. "I have feeling in my legs, Mom. I have *feeling.*"

She phoned Mrs. Cunningham. "It's time we got Ben out of bed."

Mrs. Cunningham must have flown there. Panting, she burst

into his bedroom and flung her purse on a chair. Then, with the two women bracing him, Ben slid his legs over the side of his bed and lowered his bare feet to the floor.

He couldn't contain his excitement. "I can feel the linoleum. It's cold."

He took a few shaky steps and leaned hard against his mother. They walked him across the room and back to his bed, then got him settled there and stood back. His mom started sobbing. Mrs. Cunningham let out a whoop and a loud thank you to God.

A week later, with Doc Kramer's blessing, Ben returned to school, but he had to wear leg braces. The good thing was, he no longer had to do his school work in bed. And when his friends walked by the house on Saturday mornings, he followed after them, though he knew it would be a long time before he'd play again—if at all. In time he ditched the braces, and though his steps were awkward, he managed to limp the couple of blocks to the playground where he'd watch the games from the sidelines.

"Your legs can improve," Mrs. Cunningham told him one afternoon while they were seated side-by-side on the living room sofa.

She placed her hands on his knees and prayed. Then, she leaned so close he could smell the rose water on her neck. When she raised her head, her tender blue eyes locked with his.

"Don't give up, Ben," she whispered. "God can heal you completely. You don't have to settle for limping around on weak legs. He can help you walk and even *run* again. You only need to draw on the strength that's sleeping inside you. Wake it up, Ben. Tackle the ant hills, and before long you'll be climbing mountains."

Mountains? Ben couldn't picture himself climbing mountains. He'd be happy if he could ride his bike up the hilly streets at the edge of town.

The kids at school eyed his limping with a mix of fear and puzzlement on their faces. Some of the older boys wanted to know what it felt like to have legs that wouldn't work for you. The girls smiled with pity and, embarrassed, turned away.

Only one person treated him like there was nothing wrong. Elizabeth Adams, the prettiest girl in the fourth grade. Whenever she passed him in the hall, she smiled at him, but it wasn't a sympathetic smile, like the other girls offered. Her smile was sincere, even friendly. She said hello, and she even asked if she could walk home from school with him one afternoon. When they reached his porch steps, she ran her hand over his pitching arm. Then, she tilted her face, swept back the ebony curl that had fallen across her cheek, and stared at him with admiration swirling in her dark eyes. Ben nearly fell over backward.

"You're gonna play baseball one day, Ben," Elizabeth said. "And, I'm gonna help you. We'll go to the park and you can toss a few balls to me. We'll go every day after school and on Saturdays after the games. After a while, you'll be out there with the other guys. You'll surprise everyone."

She drew closer until their faces were inches apart. Ben's mouth went dry and his heartbeat quickened. Ten years old. He went snake hunting with the guys and let daddy long leg spiders crawl up his arm, but he was afraid of a girl. It was a strange, almost welcome fear, and he didn't know what to do with it.

With Mrs. Cunningham's encouragement and with Elizabeth's image always before him, Ben increased his regimen beyond the basic exercises the physical therapist had ordered. He spent most of his waking hours on his feet, even paced his bedroom floor while doing his reading assignments so he could work his legs. And he surprised his mother by offering to haul out the trash and pull weeds in her garden—anything to strengthen that pitching arm of his.

Several months passed. Then, one afternoon, Ben limped home from school, went into the kitchen, and approached his mother at the stove. Her cheeks were flushed from the steam rising out of a kettle of beef stew. The aroma of gravy and vegetables stirred his taste buds, but he had something more important than supper on his mind.

"I'm gonna play ball again," he said with conviction. "I'll be eleven years old soon. I want to join a Little League team while I'm still eligible."

She set aside the soup spoon and placed both hands on his shoulders. "I believe in you, Ben. I'm so proud of you and the progress you've made." Her sudden pause disturbed him. Her eyes clouded a little and she scrunched her lips, like she was trying to find the right words. "Just in case," she said. Another pause and Ben stepped back from her. "In case you don't play ball, your father has another plan for you."

Ben started shaking his head.

"Listen, son. You've done extremely well in school, particularly in math. Your father said if you keep your grades up you can join his accounting office when you graduate from high school."

Ben stared numbly at his mother. *Accounting office?* That wasn't his dream.

"I'm gonna play ball," he repeated. "Professionally. Do you remember what Mrs. Cunningham said? She said I can do anything I set my mind to, that I only have to believe. Well, I believe I'll play baseball."

He read the doubt in her eyes, and a touch of sadness swept over him. It saddened him that all his mother had wanted was for him to walk. But, he didn't want to settle for mere walking. He wanted to run. He wanted to pitch. He wanted to play ball. Mrs. Cunningham had said he could do it. Why had his mother given up the dream?

The following spring, Ben did what he'd told his mother he wanted to do. He joined a Little League team. He couldn't run as fast as the other guys, but he was a decent batter and he could pitch better than anyone else in the league.

Time passed, his limp grew less noticeable. In his second year of middle school, Ben tried out to pitch for the junior baseball team. He announced it to his folks over supper one night.

"I don't know, Ben," his father said. "You've come a long way, but you still can't run fast enough to make the team. You know you have to be able to do it all. You have to be able to field and run and do all the things the other players do. I don't think you can keep up, son."

Ben came away from the table more depressed than ever. The truth was, he didn't have a chance of getting picked, not with *real athletes* vying for the position—kids like Tommy Waters, Tim Blakely, and Paul Cunningham. The coach could only choose one of them for first string pitcher. The others would have to take other positions or settle for warming the bench. He couldn't bear such humiliation.

The Sunday before tryouts, Ben sought out Mrs. Cunningham after the church service. He caught up with her in the nursery doing a job most people thought was beneath them—cleaning out diaper pails and spraying little plastic toys with disinfectant. When Ben entered, she looked up, smiled at him, and set aside the spray bottle and the rag in her hand.

"I want to sign up for the youth baseball team," Ben blurted out. "There's a lot o' kids tryin' out. My folks say it's impossible, but I'd like to at least try."

She frowned at him in the way she had when she thought someone had said something ridiculous. "What do you mean impossible?" she said, her hands on her hips. "That word isn't in my Bible, except where it says, *nothing is impossible with God.*"

He looked sheepishly back at her. "Will you pray for me, Mrs. Cunningham?"

Without another word, she took both of his hands in hers and went right to God. When she finished, she looked Ben in the eye, like she did when she had some corrective teaching on her tongue.

"Listen, young man," she said. "You have as much right to be on that team as every one of those other boys."

He lowered his gaze. "I've gotta tell ya, one of them is your son, Paul."

"So?"

"So, we're both trying out for the same position. Pitcher. So are a few other guys. I guess you know, only one of us can get picked for first string."

"Don't you worry about my Paul. He can play other positions and other sports, maybe basketball. And get your eyes off of the other guys. Concentrate on what *you* can do. Keep your mind on your goal, and then go for it. Now, I want you to show up at that field tomorrow after school. Hold your head up and get right in your coach's face. That way, he'll know you mean business."

Ben couldn't believe Mrs. Cunningham was rooting for him, even while her own son was in the running for pitcher. He searched her face for some sign of regret. There was none.

"But, my leg, Mrs. Cunningham. I'm just a stupid gimp. I can't run the bases like the other guys. I might ruin things for the team."

"First of all, you're not stupid. And a gimp? I don't think so. Look how far you've come. Two years ago, you couldn't even get out of bed. You've done more in two years than most people accomplish in a whole lifetime."

Ben shrugged. A flush rose to his cheeks.

"Don't you dare let anyone talk you out of going after what you want," Mrs. Cunningham went on. "Why, Ben, you can throw a ball like nobody's business. I caught sight of you practicing at the park the other day with that girl. I think her name is Elizabeth, right?"

He nodded and tried not to smile too wide.

"Let me tell you," she went on. "I was impressed. Your coach will be impressed, too. So what if you're not a fast runner? Stop worrying about what you *can't* do, and show the coach what you *can* do."

She ended their chat with a wink and a pat on his back. As Ben left the church, he sniffed his hands. They bore a trace of disinfectant. He didn't wash it off right away—not before dinner, not even before going to bed. When he went to sleep that night, the fresh, lemony scent brought Mrs. Cunningham right into his bedroom, her words of encouragement still ringing in his ears.

As it turned out, Ben made pitcher and the other guys were relegated to second string or other positions. No one complained.

Even Paul Cunningham gave him a friendly punch in the arm and wished him well. The achievement gave Ben the boost he needed. He went to the park every morning before school and practiced skipping around the bases. His legs grew stronger. By the time the season started, he was able to hit and run almost as well as the other guys. He pitched several no-hit games that year. And the next. When he got into high school, he moved right into the pitching slot for the varsity team.

Elizabeth Adams followed him through all the grades. She became a cheerleader. During the games she shamelessly sent every spirited shout in his direction. The other guys noticed and kidded him. But he didn't mind. Their childhood friendship had evolved into steady dating, and one was rarely seen without the other.

At the end of Ben's senior year, a baseball scout singled him out and signed him to a farm team in another state. Elizabeth promised to wait until he sent for her. But he was caught up in a whirlwind. Two years later, he was called up to the majors as a relief pitcher, but by that time his romance with Elizabeth had cooled, and they both had looked elsewhere for love.

Now, here he was, looking back on several years of successful seasons, during which time his team had come away with two World Series championships.

At 25 years old, he was in the midst of his career when his kid sister, Ruthie, telephoned with bad news. Mrs. Cunningham had died.

"I thought maybe you'd want to attend her service," Ruthie said. "If you can't leave right now, maybe you can send a flower arrangement or a sympathy card."

A sense of urgency brought tears to Ben's eyes and a lump to his throat.

"No," Ben said, aware of the gravel in his voice. "No flowers. No card. Mrs. Cunningham meant far too much for me to do something as mundane as that. I have to pay my respects in person."

In the quiet of his home office, Ben scanned his shelf of trophies, a row of little golden men frozen in various poses, swinging a bat or pitching a ball. He wouldn't have acquired any of them had it not been for Mrs. Cunningham.

If she hadn't given him the incentive to keep trying, he'd be pushing a pencil in his dad's accounting office and wishing he had followed his dream.

More tears surfaced. Ben blinked them back, but a few stubborn drops trailed down his cheeks. There was no question. He needed to fly home and attend Mrs. Cunningham's memorial service.

It made no difference that spring training started tomorrow. Mrs. Cunningham had dropped everything when he needed her. That was the least he could do for her.

True, a whole new crop of pitchers had been called up for training, and he'd ended the last season with a less than stellar performance. But he couldn't think about that right now. He had one thing on his mind. *Mrs. Cunningham had died.*

He went right to his desk, picked up the phone, and dialed his pitching coach. He quickly explained about the funeral.

"Spring training will have to start without me," Ben said, keeping his voice firm. "I'll only miss a day or two."

He pictured Marty rising from his desk, glaring at the phone in his hand. His coach's gruff voice came over. "Ben, you're skating on thin ice. After the way the last season ended, you're gonna need as much practice as I can dish out. You need to prove your worth to the team."

"I can handle it, Marty."

"I don't know. I might not have any choice, but to—"

"I'm going, Marty." He'd actually interrupted the one person who had the most control over his life. "If you don't like it, just move up Johnny Peppi in my place. It's *that* important to me."

A few uncomfortable seconds passed. Then there was a long

sigh at the other end. "Ya better get back here in two days," Marty growled. Then the line went dead.

With that settled, Ben had one more hurdle. He had to tell his wife he was going home. And he was going alone. He had a pretty good idea how Candy might react. She wouldn't like him leaving so soon after they relocated to their Florida home. Then there was Billy. Five years old and the most precious thing in Ben's life. He'd promised to take his son to Disney World. Now he'd have to disappoint him—again. Another let-down. Another promise put off until later.

Ben headed for the kitchen. The moment he stepped through the door, young Billy leapt from his chair at the table and lunged into his father's arms.

"I had a dream," the boy said, and his face lit up as though it were Christmas morning.

Ben settled his son back in his chair, bent over to eye-level, and gave him his full attention. "A dream? Tell me about it."

Candy slid an empty cereal bowl on the table in front of Billy.

"We went to Disney World," Billy said, his little voice going up an octave. "You and Mommy and me. And Mickey Mouse got in the cart with us and went on the ride."

"I'll bet that was a lot of fun," Ben said, ruffling his son's hair. "What else happened?"

Billy shrugged. "I woke up."

Ben broke into chuckles. Candy was smiling. He was glad the morning had kicked off on a positive note, making it easier to break the news of his trip.

He straightened and faced his wife. Her blue eyes sparkled back at him.

He let out a breath. "Mrs. Cunningham passed away."

A cloud swept the smile from her face and her eyes lost their sparkle. She didn't speak, merely waited for him to say more.

"I need to go home, Candy. I need to attend her funeral."

She took a step back and crossed her arms. "I don't understand. You're about to start spring training. Remember?

Pitchers and catchers first? What about your coach? What did he say?"

"Marty didn't give me an argument," Ben said, aware of the weakness in his voice. "Actually, I didn't give him a chance to. Anyway, I'll only be gone for a couple of days—no longer."

"What about Billy and me?"

"You'll stay here. I can travel easier by myself. It's a funeral, Candy, no place for a little kid. Remember how he reacted at my Dad's funeral last year? I don't want to put him through that again."

A vertical line appeared between Candy's eyebrows. Ben turned away and walked to the counter where he poured himself a cup of coffee. Though Candy hadn't said a word, the heavy breath she exhaled told him everything he needed to know. She was furious.

Her next movements confirmed it. She stomped to the cupboard, pulled out a box of cereal, and slammed the cupboard door. Then she did the same at the refrigerator, stomping and slamming. She came to the table with a bottle of milk, dumped a pile of cereal in Billy's bowl and sloshed the milk over the side. Billy sat very still, his round eyes darting back and forth between them.

Ben's heart melted. The youngster had witnessed far too many marital arguments in his five short years. He shook his head with disgust. Disgust at his wife's behavior and even more disgust at himself. He took a sip of his coffee and tried to ignore her scowl.

Don't marry a trophy wife, the older team members had warned him. *They're 'cleat-chasers,' self-centered prima donnas who'll bleed ya'dry financially and make you wish you'd gone from your mother's womb straight to heaven.*

But, Ben had known a lot of players who'd married beauties and were perfectly happy. So how was a guy to know? Anyway, the older players' sage words of advice had faded into oblivion the first time he laid eyes on that little blond vision of loveliness sitting in the stands during a practice session. A glimmer of sunlight lit Candy's hair like a halo and her sky blue eyes seemed to gaze right into his soul. Stunned, he froze on the field, unmoving until the other guys nudged him back to life. Somehow, he got his heart back in rhythm and went on to complete his worst practice game ever. Afterward, he found out her name. Candice Parsons.

Now he sat at the table and stared at his wife, wondering, like he always did these days, what had become of the soft-spoken beauty queen he'd married?

He took careful sips of the hot liquid, and glanced at Billy. The kid was a perfect blend of his parents' genes. His shock of blond hair matched his mother's golden mane and his blue eyes were a duplicate of hers. But, his body frame, tough jaw, and love of athletics were all Ben, and the little guy had inherited his father's easygoing demeanor, a stark contrast to Candy's spontaneous outbursts.

Instead of picking up his spoon and digging into his cereal, Billy stared at his mother, his blue eyes floating in tears.

"It's okay, son," Ben said. "Mommy and I are trying to decide something important. We're not mad." Did Billy buy that lie? He wasn't sure.

He sent Candy a silent plea. To his relief, Billy picked up his spoon and dug into his cereal.

Candy clammed up, but she stood there, her eyes aflame and her hands balled into fists. Her feet were firmly planted, like she'd assumed a fighting position.

He took a deep breath and lowered his tone. "Candy, you must understand. I need to go to that funeral. I've told you before, if not for Mrs. Cunningham, I wouldn't be where I am today. She was the only person who believed in me, the only adult who supported my dream to play baseball. Unlike my mom and dad, she never faltered."

Candy pressed her lips together and narrowed her eyes. Flashes of blue poked through her long lashes.

"Please, understand," he said. "I have to go."

"Well, it sounds like you've made up your mind." Candy's tone was sharp enough to cut his throat.

He struggled to remain calm. "I have," he said. "Please, don't try to change it."

"And what about us? Why do Billy and I have to stay here? By ourselves. Why can't we go with you?"

"As I said, I can travel easier alone. I'll catch a flight tomorrow afternoon, rent a car, spend the night at the inn, and come home the next day, right after the funeral. I'll pay my respects to the family and then I'll leave."

The truth was, he didn't want Candy to go. She'd never gotten on with his sister, and what's worse, Candy could flare up at a moment's notice. All he had to do was say the wrong thing at the wrong time. No, as much as he loved her, he sometimes didn't like her at all.

Candy's icy blue eyes stared him down. He knew what was coming next. He didn't want to hear it. Not again.

"Tell me," she said, lifting her chin. "Is there some other reason you need to go there by yourself—someone else you're planning to look up?"

There it was, that touch of jealousy that surfaced whenever he mentioned his hometown. Ben regretted the day he told Candy about his first love, Elizabeth Adams. The girl's name came up again, two months ago, when Ruthie wrote and told him his old flame had gotten a divorce.

"Isn't Elizabeth a free woman now?" Candy snapped. "Won't that be cozy, the two of you using a woman's funeral as an excuse to get together again."

Ben looked her in the eye. "Yes, Elizabeth's divorced. But like I said before, it makes no difference to me. She's an old friend, and that's all. I didn't marry her. I married you, Candy. I love you."

He rose to his feet, drew close to his wife, and wrapped his arms around her.

"You have nothing to worry about, honey. I've stayed faithful to you all these years, and that's not gonna change."

Billy hadn't budged. He was still sitting like a statue, anxiety written on his young face. With his parents hugging right in front of him, he began to relax. Then, apparently satisfied, he shoveled another spoonful of cereal in his mouth, scraped up a few stray kernels, then leaped from his chair.

"I'm goin' out back an' play with Ginger," he announced, and ran out the door.

Candy slipped out of his arms. She grabbed a dishcloth and wiped up the mess on the table. With angry swipes, she sopped up the spilled milk, brushed the crumbs into the palm of her hand, then tossed Billy's bowl and spoon in the sink with a noisy clatter. When she turned around and faced Ben, her eyes were aflame.

Through his entire pitching career no batter had ever stared him down as effectively as Candy did at that moment. With mounting discomfort, he walked to the kitchen window and looked out at the backyard. Billy ran across the lawn. Their golden retriever leapt from the stoop and charged after him. The boy picked up a ball and tossed it. With her tail wagging, Ginger appeared to be smiling as she lunged after the ball, then scampered back to Billy and dropped it at his feet. They repeated their little game several times allowing Ben a momentary diversion from the storm that was brewing in the kitchen.

But he couldn't ignore Candy forever. "Honey," he said, turning from the window. "We have got to try to get along better—for Billy's sake."

Candy's girlish pout and flashing eyes didn't have the same appeal they'd had when they first started dating. These days, the beauty queen had vanished, and in her place was man's worst nightmare, a hysterical shrew. Her mouth had been moving but he hadn't heard a word she'd said. Over the last few years, he'd trained himself to block out the worst parts of their conversations. But now he had to listen, had to somehow convince her the trip was necessary.

" ...and you'd better have a good reason to drop everything for a trip like this," Candy finished. "You have a lot of people who are counting on you. Not just me and Billy. Your coach. Your teammates. You can't go running off by yourself. Back home. With an old flame waiting to get her claws into you. Tell me, what do you think is going to happen when you show up there?"

He raised a hand. "Settle down, Candy. I'm going there to pay my respects to Mrs. Cunningham and to her family. Paul's an old friend of mine. I want to see him again, that's all. As for Elizabeth, I couldn't care less what she does."

Her scowl softened, but only a little. Beneath her wrinkled brow, a tempest was still stirring. "Can't you just send a sympathy card?" she whined.

"I've told you before. I owe my career to Mrs. Cunningham. It would be wrong for me not to show up."

This wasn't the first time he and Candy had had words. Their marriage started taking a downward turn right after the honeymoon. About the time they were ready to call it quits, Billy came along. He'd become the glue that held their marriage together. What a huge responsibility for a little boy to have. Even now, with their emotions clashing, Ben didn't want their marriage to depend on his son. Maybe it was a total loss, after all.

"So?" Candy said, her jaw set firm.

"So, I need to go."

"You won't see Mrs. Cunningham. She's gone."

"I can let the family know I'm there. That should mean something to them."

She shook her head and her blond curls fell in cascades to her shoulders. In spite of her tirades, she was still one of the most beautiful girls he'd ever seen.

"It's a memorial service, for Pete's sake," she said. "A memorial service doesn't seem like a good reason to drop everything and spend a fortune on a last-minute airline ticket. You know the prices go up during the last couple of days before a flight."

"We can afford it."

Candy ran a hand through her golden locks. The movement

once tantalized Ben, but not these days, and certainly not at this moment. He stared into her icy blue eyes.

"What about Elizabeth?" she said, and he winced. "She's gonna be on the prowl for you. If you think I'm gonna sit quietly down here while you meet up with your old girlfriend—"

"You have nothing to worry about. Years ago, I had the chance to marry Elizabeth, and I didn't. I left home without her. I let a lot of time pass between letters. She got tired of waiting, and she married Matt Jenkins."

"And now she's divorced. Now she's Elizabeth Adams again. You can't tell me she hasn't been on your mind."

"No, she hasn't. Not until you mentioned her name this morning." He shook his head. "I want you to know, Candy, since my sister told me Adele Cunningham died, I've thought of nothing else. I loved that woman. I need to go to her service and say a final good-bye."

"Listen to me, Ben. I'm telling you right now, if you go back there, you can forget about coming home."

"You don't mean that."

"I do. Either you forget about your hometown girlfriend, or you can find somewhere else to live. In fact, you can stay right there and move in with Elizabeth, for all I care. You're gonna have to choose. Billy and me? Or your former life?"

Candy stomped out of the room. How unfair of her to ask him to choose. Ben clenched his jaw and returned to the window. Billy spotted his dad and stopped running. The boy's smile sent a tender ache into Ben's heart. Billy raised his hand. He smiled back and returned his son's wave, then he stepped away from the window.

He walked out in the hall, took the stairs two at a time to the second floor, and pulled a suitcase from the top shelf of the bedroom closet. He was going home.

FOUR

Frank Peebles

The ear-splitting ring of the phone on Frank Peebles' desk had given him a royal headache. First thing, his wife called and told him to pick up a gallon of milk on his way home. After that, the phone didn't take a breath. Two of his customers telephoned looking for their shipments. The head of a local charity pestered him for a donation. The secretaries of multiple firms called about orders, delays, and manufacturing problems. More calls and more headaches.

He passed the complaints to his plant manager, Burt Rhinehower, then he handled the orders and bills himself. He was able to silence the charity person by claiming he'd already given *at the office*. Before the morning ended, he popped an antacid in his mouth and turned his attention to the growing pile of paperwork on his desk.

At that moment, Miss Smith tiptoed in with another handful of bills. He gave her a nod. "Bring me some coffee, Alice. Strong and black."

He barely got the words out of his mouth when the phone shrilled again. The gravelly voice on the other end got Frank wiping his balding head with a wrinkled handkerchief. It was Harvey Pennant, the president of the firm's board of directors. Frank reached for another antacid.

"What is it?" he snarled. "I'm busy here."

"The meeting's scheduled for ten o'clock tomorrow morning," the president said, his tone equally gruff.

"Can't make it."

"What do you mean, you can't make it? The board expects a fresh budget report."

"I can't be there. It's as simple as that." With the phone propped on his shoulder so he could have both hands free, he leafed through the stack of old bills. A noticeable silence built up on the phone. He set aside a couple of bills to pay later and shifted his attention to the new stack his secretary had brought in.

The board president huffed out a loud breath. "What's going on, Frank? What is so important that you can't be there?"

Frank shrugged at nobody in particular. "A funeral."

Another few seconds of silence passed. Then Harvey softened his tone. "Sorry, Frank. Someone close?"

"Used to be." He wasn't prepared for the lump that came to his throat. It happened whenever he thought of the Cunninghams. He missed that family. Especially George. Five years ago, he experienced the prick of regret when he learned his best friend had died. This time the pain went even deeper. Adele Cunningham had passed.

Harvey broke the silence. "I don't understand, Frank. You want to skip out on the board when we're in a budget crisis so you can go to the funeral of someone you *used* to know?"

He swallowed the lump and continued to leaf through the pile of bills without really seeing any of them. "That's right."

"So what do I tell the board?"

"Tell 'em anything, and reschedule the meeting. I'll be back in a couple of days."

"The delay will only make things worse. The board is already upset about what happened last month."

Frank had been trying to forget the canceled order. They'd lost one of their biggest accounts simply because he couldn't control his temper.

"I'll deal with it."

Harvey let out a sigh. "Okay, Frank, I'll tell them, but they're not gonna like it."

"Tough doo-doo." Frank slammed the phone in it's cradle, catching his index finger between the two pieces of plastic.

"Ow! Great. I'll lose a fingernail over this," he moaned.

He clutched his sore finger with the other hand and stared out the wall of windows at the warehouse below. Forklifts ran back and forth transporting skids of finished products from the work area to the dock. Crews of denim-clad workmen bustled about like their lives depended on finishing the day's work. Nobody lay down on the job. They knew they were being watched. And he was the watcher, a multi-millionaire with a stomach ulcer, a headache, and now a sore finger.

When the throbbing eased, he went back to sorting through the bills. After several minutes of staring at numbers that had begun to blur together on the pages, Frank put his face in his hands. He'd fallen under just as much pressure as his workmen had encountered. The question was, when had his business dropped into the hands of shareholders and board members? When had he lost control? He raised his head and gazed around his office at the oiled oak furniture, the row of file drawers, the wall of photographs depicting each product line that reached the market. And on his desk, a framed dollar bill, the first one he and George Cunningham had earned when they started out.

He shook his head and let out a sarcastic chuckle. What he wouldn't give to go back to the day when he and his best friend teamed up and started their plastics business in Fall River. The two buddies had kept an eye on the plastics industry during World War II, when synthetic materials were used for everything from parachute chords to cockpit seats. Then came a wave of public demands for household items constructed out of materials that wouldn't rust or rot or fall apart.

"It's the material of the future," George Cunningham had said. The big man with the rosy cheeks smiled like he'd struck gold. "Synthetics will help to preserve our natural resources," George boasted, his green eyes sparkling with excitement. "Manufacturers will no longer have to cut down trees to make household items. Plastic offers a tough, resilient, easy-to-clean alternative. Just think, Frank, if we pool our money we can set up a plant right here in Fall River. We'll hire a few local guys, pay a reasonable wage—not as high as the big city rates, of course, but fair—and we can begin production in a matter of weeks. We'll produce everything from unbreakable dishes to furniture."

It didn't take much convincing to get Frank to kick in his life savings, which, for a 23-year-old, was a lucrative 15,000 bucks. George did the same, and they began to look at properties on the edge of town. They settled on an abandoned barn, a sturdy construction that had a loft and several horse stalls that could be turned into offices and work stations. They spent two months cleaning up the place, nailing down loose boards, and tossing out unusable debris. They furnished their offices with discards from a real estate office that was going out of business.

Down the center aisle they set up a line of production machines and a conveyor belt. George hired a dozen guys right out of high school, and Frank trained them the way he wanted things done. Within the first year their work crew increased to twenty, and a middle-aged woman took a desk in the front office and handled the books and the telephone orders.

By that time, DuPont had introduced a line of non-stick cookware, adding yet another winner to a growing list of products. Of course, the manufacturing giant was more widely known than the fledgling operation of *Cunningham and Peebles*. Frank expressed concern that the big conglomerate might force them out of business. If they wanted to survive, they needed to expand their product line.

"They're miles away from us, in Delaware," George said with a toss of his head. "We're not competing with them. Not directly. We're doing something entirely different, and we're staying local. You have nothing to worry about, Frank."

As George had predicted, their business took off. A few years later, they tore down the old barn and built a larger, more modern facility on the same property. They hired more workers and began shipping products all over the country.

Now, nearly forty years later, Frank stared at the pile of orders on his desk and tried to imagine how different things might have turned out if he'd stayed with George. Back then, they were the sole owners. No stock holders, no board to trample down their decisions. It was just the two of them, meeting over coffee or discussing their next project while fly-fishing on the river. How he missed those days. How he missed George.

Frank's troubles began the day he ran off to start his own business. He didn't realize it back then, but that's when he planted the seeds of frustration in his life. At the time, he didn't feel any remorse over taking the bulk of the collateral and leaving George with less than half of their resources, plus a few die-hard employees who chose to stay behind instead of heading out with Frank.

Too bad George couldn't have dreamed bigger, Frank mused. He had wanted his friend to share his plan and move their plant to a bigger and better playing field. He'd read magazine articles about corporate moguls and their lifestyles—overflowing bank accounts, fancy women, expensive clothes, cars, and houses. He wanted that lifestyle. George didn't. He was content to marry Adele Baker and settle down in a three-bedroom bungalow right there in Fall River.

The day they settled up, George was sitting at his desk in the far corner of their joint office. Frank paced the floor from one side of the room to the other, his Western boots clunking against the hardwood floor, the smell of melting plastic wafting up from the factory below. Frank made one last attempt to convince George to join him.

"I like owning a small business," George persisted. "We can focus more on quality instead of quantity. When you increase volume you can't help but diminish the value of the product."

"With my plan we can have both," Frank argued. "Quantity *and* quality—volume *and* excellence—just a lot more of it." He paused in front of George's desk and frowned at his longtime friend.

George shook his head. "Look, Frank. We've established a solid client base. We know the people we sell to. They're like family. If we get too big, we could lose our hometown image."

"Family?" Frank snorted. "Hometown image? Listen, George. Those people buy a *product*. That's all. Other than that, we don't really know them."

"*I* know them. Why just last week, Gerald Feinmester—"

"Oh, forget about Gerald Feinmester. We can expand our so-called *family*, if that's what you want. We can go international. I've got some ideas that will give those big-wigs at DuPont a run for their money."

He slammed a fist into his palm and began to pace again.

George let out a burst of laughter that stopped Frank in his tracks. He whirled around and returned to the front of George's desk. He crossed his arms and narrowed his eyes at the guy he once called his best friend.

George sat back with a silly grin on his face. He was the one guy—probably the only one—that Frank couldn't intimidate with his notorious scowl.

This riled him all the more. "You think it's funny? To dream? To make our lives better?"

George's smile faded. "Relax, Frank." A wave of concern clouded the deep green of his eyes. "Don't you want to take a step back and think more clearly about this flight of fancy?" He raised his eyebrows and leaned across his desk until they were face-to-face. "How about we drop everything tomorrow morning, close the plant for the day, and just go fishing?"

Frank took a step back. "*You* can go fishing. I don't want to sit in a row boat and watch the world pass us by. We close the plant for one day, send the workers home, and do you know what will happen? We'll slide back to last place in the plastics industry. That's how intense the competition is getting these days."

George dropped back in his chair and frowned with sympathy.

"Well, Frank. It looks like we have different plans. I like my life the way it is. I work hard during the week, but when Friday afternoon rolls around, I lock my office door, go home, and spend time with my family. I relax on the weekends. I fish. I play golf. You don't seem to enjoy those activities anymore."

"That's right, I don't." Frank moved closer to the desk and placed both palms on the worn surface. "I've worked hard to make this business what it is today. I don't have time for marriage and family. I want to make my first million. After that I'll think about a personal life." He straightened. "You're right, George. We do have different plans—so different, in fact, maybe we should split everything right down the middle and go our separate ways."

That was 1950, more than 30 years ago. With George's blessing, Frank took the bulk of the machines, a huge chunk of their savings, and most of their workers, and he set up shop in another part of New York State, closer to the big city where he could make use of the Atlantic ports o' call. True to his plan, Frank grew his business into one of the most prolific plastics manufacturing companies in America. His business branched off to include several more departments that handled Teflon cookware and nylon threads. By 1965, he hit the international market with a wave of new products, exactly like he'd dreamed of doing.

Maybe his business wasn't as big as DuPont, but it did well enough to earn Frank his first million, then his second, and his third. He married a flashy showgirl—a gold-digger with a big appetite—who also happened to be a lush who ate and drank herself into size eighteen dresses she bought at Bonwit Teller and other high-end stores. Meanwhile, Frank put in an unreal amount of hours at work, leaving him no time for golf or fishing or any of the other pastimes he used to enjoy with George.

He frowned at the pile of papers on his desk. His business now belonged to a board of directors. He lost sleep over errors that had to be corrected before their next meeting. He spent the few free hours he had in a doctor's office. He took pills for high blood pressure, high cholesterol, ulcers, and insomnia, and he began to feel like a prisoner to a business he no longer controlled. Most of all, he missed his old friend. If he could go back in time, if he could do it all over again, he might do things differently. He sometimes dreamed about what it might have been like if he'd stayed with George, contented with that little two-bit factory and a measly income that provided enough left-over cash to enjoy the simple life, with far fewer headaches than he had now.

Sadly, the two of them never spoke again. Frank regretted their split from the day he left. Then, five years ago, he learned from a mutual friend that George had passed away. He packed a bag and headed home to pay his respects to the best friend he'd ever had.

Frank watched George's service from a shadow in the back of the church, afraid to face the icy stares of the Cunningham family. Surely, they hadn't forgotten the day he split and left George with a mess to clean up.

After the funeral, when everyone congregated at the cemetery, Frank stood behind a large elm tree so no one would notice him. But one figure broke away from the crowd and walked straight to his hiding place. Though more than thirty years had passed, he recognized her. George's wife, Adele Cunningham. She hadn't changed much, still had that striking blond hair, though it was cut shorter and had strands of gray running through it. She still had that confident stride that set her apart from other women her age. She drew close, and his heart began to flutter with uncertainty.

"Hello, Frank. Why have you stayed away so long?" Her tone was genuinely sweet. She stepped closer and wrapped an arm around him.

Frank frowned in puzzlement. He'd expected an attack of some sort, but what he got was a welcoming hug. "I–I didn't want to—I mean, I just thought—you know—that I wouldn't be received well."

She leaned away from him and smiled into his face. "There is absolutely no reason for you to feel that way," she said. "We all missed you, Frank. Especially George."

"But–but, George?" He frowned in disbelief.

Adele reached for Frank's hand. He choked up for a moment. When he was able to speak again, it was with sincere remorse.

"I'm so sorry, Adele. I should never have left George holding the bag. I was selfish. Downright selfish."

She shook her head, and a sweet smile drew up the corners of her mouth. "Frank, dear Frank. Don't you know? George forgave you a long time ago. He figured the two of you were two people with different goals. He never held a grudge. In fact, he would have welcomed you home with open arms. He honored your decision, so he kept quiet. He didn't want you to think he was trying to hold you back."

Frank bowed his head, ashamed to look Adele in the eye. "I–I thought—"

"What? That George cursed you for leaving? He wasn't like that. You know he wasn't. In fact, he always hoped you'd write or call. You never did, so he assumed you wanted to cut off all the old ties, that you wanted to forget the past and move on."

"Forget? Forget my best friend?" Frank blinked against a rise of tears. "Impossible."

"Then why did you stay away?" She tilted her head, her eyes questioning.

He shrugged. "I was a self-centered young man. Money and power and success. That's what I wanted." He gazed into her eyes, two sympathetic orbs of blue. "It wasn't what George wanted," Frank admitted. "Sadly, my heart became like the plastic I produced—hard, strong, and lifeless. I thought if I didn't look back, I didn't have to face the truth that I'd made a huge mistake. Then, the other day, when I found out George had died, I didn't care how things looked anymore. I had to come and say a final good-bye."

Adele sighed, and her eyes flooded over. "It was an untimely death, quite unexpected."

"Was it—was it his heart?"

She nodded. "It was a genetic thing. Something about the valves and the arteries. George had an attack the year before. Then he caught a bad case of the flu, and his heart couldn't take it."

"I'm sorry," Frank said. "I wish I could have seen him before he passed. I wish I could have talked to him, made him understand why I left and how sorry I was to have done that. He must have been devastated—"

Mrs. Cunningham broke him off with a laugh. "Devastated? You dear man. My George didn't let the split stop him. He earned a decent living with his little factory. He loved his business, but he didn't let it control his life. He was home every night, and on weekends he relaxed with friends and family. When he shut the door at five o'clock on Friday, he turned his back on his business, at least for the weekend. And he went to church on Sunday." She looked him in the eye. "Don't you see? George worked hard, but he also enjoyed his time off. He might never have had such a life if he'd gone off with you. And he probably would have died a lot sooner."

"Then he didn't resent me?"

"Lord, no. If you had come around, he would have *thanked* you."

"What?"

"Sure. He knew you wanted to grow the business. If you'd stayed here and done that, you might have dragged him along— kicking and screaming. As it turned out, your leaving was the best thing that happened to him. And to us."

Adele gestured toward the family, still hovering beside George's casket.

Frank wiped his eyes. "I wish I had known."

"Listen, Frank, I want to thank you for coming today. It means a lot to me."

Frank stepped back and eyed Mrs. Cunningham with fresh admiration. While the Cunninghams had found contentment in the little things, Frank had piled up debts he might never be able to pay off. He owned a house too large for just him and his wife, plus three cars, a pleasure boat, and a closet full of the most expensive clothes Daphne could buy—most of them purchased with plastic credit cards that would very likely outlast him.

Mrs. Cunningham slipped her hand inside the crook of his arm. "Look, Frank, why don't you join us at the house for the reception? You might see other folks you used to know."

Reluctantly, he followed the cavalcade to the Cunningham home. Once inside, a wave of memories engulfed him. The smells were still there. The residue of pipe tobacco in the air. The scented potpourri to cover it up. The coffee waiting in the kitchen. For the moment, Frank relived the mornings when he came for George in a pickup truck with no floorboard and one wheel bent so crooked the thing wobbled all over the road. The lamp in the corner reminded him of the evenings when they sat around a folding table in that same living room, playing cards until midnight. He couldn't help but zero in on the mantel and a picture of the two of them in flannel shirts and blue jeans and holding their fishing rods and a mess of fish like trophies. The image brought back the weekends when he and George made time for one of their early-morning jaunts on the river. Then there were the many Sundays and getting together for lunch after church, with Adele's fried chicken and biscuits warming his stomach. Back then he didn't have to take an antacid to ease the burning that was all too familiar now.

Frank let out a contended grunt. That was the lifestyle George had settled into until the day he died. Now Frank wished he had stuck around, that he'd shunned the urge to get rich and had kept their friendship going.

What's more, George had a loving wife and two great kids. Frank and his wife had no children, no legacy, no joy, no real future for the Peebles, except for two bored and lonely people. George may have died first, but, Frank had to admit, his own life ended the day he left Fall River.

After George's reception, Mrs. Cunningham cornered Frank again and placed both hands on his shoulders. Then she murmured a prayer for his well-being. She didn't mention his business, or his finances, or his future plans. Instead, she focused on his health and his peace of mind. At the end of her prayer, she added a request that Frank might seek *the better thing*. He'd walked away wondering how on earth he was going to do that.

"Don't be a stranger," she called from the doorway as he got into his car.

But as soon as he drove away, he began to shed the memories and the regrets and once again focus on the work that awaited him back home. He had a bunch of orders to get out, phone calls to make, and a board of directors to appease. Sadly, he never again found the time to go fishing or play golf.

And, he didn't even think about going back home again. Until now. For another funeral. Adele Cunningham's this time. For the first time in years, tears flooded to his eyes.

Board meeting or not, nothing was going to keep him from making that trip. He glanced at the clock on the bookshelf— five p.m. His flight was scheduled to leave in three hours. The red-eye would get him there in time to crash at the hotel. He pushed the button on the plant's public address box and leaned in to give a rare announcement.

"It's five o'clock," he said. "Put everything away and close up shop. I've got a plane to catch."

It was amazing. The farther Frank got from his business, the more relaxed he felt. He caught himself smiling, even as he wove through rush-hour traffic with horns blaring and lengthy red lights at nearly every intersection.

With a fresh surge of enthusiasm, he burst through the front door of his house and headed straight for the spare room, pulled a suitcase off the top shelf of the closet and laid it open on the bed.

His wife was at his side in seconds.

"What are you doing?" she said.

"Packing."

"Where's the gallon of milk I told you to pick up?"

"Oops!" He ignored her glare, chuckled, and packed a pair of pajamas. He thought about their situation, how he earned enough money to buy a whole dairy farm if he wanted to. "Why didn't you send your maid out for the milk?"

"She had to go home. Sick kid or something."

"Tough doo-doo, Daphne. I'm in a hurry."

Then he darted past his wife, still chuckling.

"It's not funny, Frank. I told you to stop for a gallon of milk. One thing. One lousy thing, and you couldn't even do *that*?"

"Nope."

She backed away from him. "What's wrong with you?"

He placed his grooming kit in his suitcase, then added one dress shirt, packaged by the dry cleaning service, and his favorite tie, the one with the chevrons all over it. Ignoring the look of puzzlement on his wife's face, he added a flannel shirt, a turtleneck sweater, and a pair of blue jeans, perfect for a day of fishing on the river. He rummaged around in his underwear drawer and came up with three pairs of boxer shorts, a couple of T-shirts and two pairs of heavy socks.

In a duffel bag he stuffed a pair of rubber boots, fur-lined gloves, and a box of flies and hooks.

"Looks like you're going fishing," Daphne said with a smirk. "Thought you said it was a funeral."

He looked up at her. "I'm doing both." He checked the contents of his two bags, satisfied he hadn't forgotten anything. "I'm goin' to the funeral tomorrow. Then, I'll stay an extra day and work in some fishing."

Daphne remained in the doorway, blocking his exit. She was a big woman, easily twice his size. He glanced at their wedding photo on the bureau. She was beautiful in her white dress and demure veil while standing next to a scrawny guy with a hook nose and receding hairline. He'd often wondered how that gorgeous showgirl had so quickly morphed into the incredible she-hulk. Frank had settled for the first woman who showed an interest in him. He'd regretted it ever since.

She glared at him from the doorway. "Have you lost your mind, Frank? Fishing? At this time of year? That's Fall River in the middle of winter. Why, the river will be iced over."

"No it won't. It's almost the end of February. Spring is just around the corner. The river's got to be flowing pretty steady now. But, if the water's frozen, I'll break through the ice. Surely, somebody in town must have a pickax."

"Don't be ridiculous. There won't be any fish."

"Oh yes, there will. George and I used to go ice fishing every winter. You'd be surprised at the size of the fish we caught."

She placed her hands on her hips, and spread her feet in a defiant stance. "This is senseless, Frank. What good will it do to catch fish when we can buy them at the supermarket, boned, cleaned and ready for the frying pan? Our housekeeper can cook up a mess of fish anytime you want."

"It's the sport of it, Daphne. Something you know nothing about. Besides, to be honest, I can use a couple of days of relaxation. By myself. Alone. Think about it. I haven't had a vacation in years."

With that, he gave a sharp yank on the zipper, put on his overcoat, and swept the two bags off the bed. With determined steps, he strode into Daphne's path, forced her out of his way, and marched down the stairs to the foyer.

Then, he hesitated, set down his bags, and turned to face his wife. She was coming down the stairs, several steps behind him, moving as fast as her two little legs could carry her shifting blubber. When she reached the bottom, he flung both arms around her as far as they could go and planted a big, wet kiss on her lips.

"That should keep you until I get back," Frank said. "See you in three days."

"The milk—" she started.

He left her standing there with her mouth open, her eyes like two big saucers. In seconds, he was inside his car, backing out of his driveway. With a smile on his lips, he peeled out and headed for the subdivision exit. He drove to the airport, a wave of contentment filling every bone and sinew in his body. He was like a prisoner who'd been released into society, a kid on Christmas break from school, a fish that had wriggled off the hook and had escaped the ruthless frying pan.

He hadn't had this much freedom in years, and he loved it.

FIVE

Brenda Schwartz

Brenda Schwartz sat at her kitchen table with a cup of herbal tea and the morning newspaper spread open in front of her. She scanned the front page, shrugged off the mundane headlines, and turned to the local section. She read a few paragraphs in a story about animal adoptions, then she flipped to the obituary page and gasped. Adele Cunningham had died. Why hadn't anyone told her?

Of course, most of the people in town probably expected her to respond with a smirk or a snide remark, like *the world's a far better place.* Wasn't that the aura she'd given off over the past few years? Hadn't she openly battled with Adele over decorations for the Christmas pageant and what they should do about the worn hymn books in the church? She should be gloating right now. Adele was gone, and she was still around.

Instead, she blinked hard against a sudden stinging in her eyes and tried in vain to swallow the lump in her throat. A tear oozed out. She swiped it away. Why didn't she feel at least a little smug? Her greatest adversary was gone. Adele Cunningham had taken everything of importance from her from the day they started high school until she beat her out in the pie-baking contest at the fall festival last year.

Mentally, Brenda counted her losses. In ninth grade she tried out for the cheerleading squad. She didn't make it. Adele Baker did. The girl was more agile. She could do cartwheels and flips, and Brenda couldn't even bend over and touch her toes. In tenth grade, Brenda campaigned for class president. She lost to Adele. In eleventh grade, Brenda joined the school newspaper staff. She was delegated to soliciting ads. Adele became a reporter and won a statewide award for a piece she did on the town's new parks system. Finally, in twelfth grade, Brenda sat home alone while Adele Baker went to the senior prom with George Cunningham, the one man who unknowingly had stolen her heart. To make things worse, Adele graduated with a perfect 4.0 average, beating out Brenda to become valedictorian at the final commencement ceremony.

Brenda's conflict with Adele didn't stop with high school stuff. After graduation, they competed in the arts-and-crafts show at the county fair. Adele's appliquéd nosegay blanket beat out Brenda's granny square quilt. They joined a bowling league. Adele took the final trophy. When a photographer came to town looking for models for a clothing advertisement, Brenda starved herself for a week, but she didn't lose a single pound. Meanwhile, Adele, who was tall and shapely, joined several other local beauties for the one-time photo shoot.

Most of the other girls in town didn't appear the least bit offended by Adele's many accomplishments. They lavished her with praises, patted her on the back after every success, and invited her to their sleepovers. Brenda watched their huddles from a distance, chewing her fingernails and wishing she possessed whatever it was that made Adele so popular.

Even sadder, Brenda lived next door to the Bakers. Every Saturday, she sat at her bedroom window while a parade of teenage girls marched up the front steps of the Baker house. She could have joined them if she wanted to. Adele always sent her an invitation. Instead, she chose to grumble in the quiet of her bedroom, while a recording of big band music mingled with the girlish chatter pouring from the open window next door.

In truth, she could have survived all of it had it not been for the one ache in her heart that overshadowed all the other offenses. Adele had won the attention of George Cunningham, and for that Brenda hated her all the more.

Brenda had fallen in love with George when they were in the fifth grade. Like a hero on a white horse, he came to her rescue after another boy rushed past her and knocked the books out of her hands. George quickly gathered them up and handed them back to her. His dimpled smile and twinkling green eyes sent a shiver down her spine. In that instant, he no longer looked like any other boy in school. He looked like a prince. She mumbled a weak thank you, then stared after him as he ambled off with his friends. After that first contact, she looked for George in the halls, tried to sit next to him in class, even waited outside the school while he finished basketball practice.

Brenda could hardly believe her eyes when the Cunninghams moved into the house next door on the opposite side from where the Baker's lived. There she sat, flanked by Adele's house on her left and George's house on her right.

It didn't matter that Brenda was plain as cottage cheese and George had a suntanned, muscular physique. Didn't matter that he played sports while she played the clarinet. Somehow, in spite of the fact they had little in common, Brenda and George got to be good buddies. She supposed it helped that their fathers played golf together. Their parents gathered at one house or the other to watch the Friday night fights on TV. Their moms made pizza and salads, and their fathers smoked Camels and drank beer. And Brenda and George sprawled on the living room carpet with popcorn and Cokes and a game of Monopoly between them. They shared family dinners, met at the park for Sunday picnics, even sat together in church. From the time they were teenagers, Brenda and George looked like a couple. At least as far as she could see.

She loved the way George's hair tumbled over his ears when he needed a haircut. She stared with heart-stopping admiration at his long-legged, confident stride. His lopsided smile set her heart aflutter. And she lay her head on her pillow at night, unable to sleep with George eighty feet away in his own bedroom. To Brenda, no other boy measured up to George Cunningham.

While Brenda merely dreamed of a future with George, her parents had already been eyeing him as a potential son-in-law.

"George Cunningham is the nicest boy in town," her mother said one day. "He's so polite. He'll make a fine husband for some lucky girl." Then she winked at Brenda as if she knew a secret.

Brenda held onto her mother's words. Though she and George were supposed to be *just friends*, she also hoped their relationship would develop into something more. But, the truth was, he'd never kissed her. Never even held her hand. But she could dream, couldn't she?

Then George took a job delivering newspapers to the neighborhood, and their afternoon get-togethers dwindled to none. He spent most of his free time in school sports—first baseball, then basketball. Brenda volunteered in the school library and joined the committee to decorate the gym for the school dances, though she never got to go to any of them. When Adele made the cheerleading squad, George started walking her home from practice. That's when things took a drastic change and it looked like Brenda was about to lose the only guy she could ever love.

Toughest of all was every Saturday morning when George jogged right past her house and bounded up the steps to Adele's front porch. She spent the rest of the day on the window seat, sobbing into a handkerchief, and waiting for George to emerge from the Bakers' front door.

It came as no surprise when George invited Adele to the senior prom. Brenda stayed home, mourning over his yearbook photos and glaring at the pictures of Adele. The final dagger plunged into Brenda's heart shortly after graduation when George and Adele announced their engagement. She refused to go to the bridal shower, and was relieved to find out the wedding was put on hold when George and his friend Frank enlisted in the

Army. George and Adele were married four years later when the two guys came home from their time of service. Frank was George's best man.

Brenda stayed home and sat on her bed sobbing when her mother entered the room and begged her to go to the church with her.

"They're your friends," her mother pleaded. "You should be happy for them."

But how could she summon even an ounce of good will when her heart had been shattered? She lay on her bed that day and prayed that death would take her. When death didn't come, she allowed her resentment to grow into a nightly plot to rid the world of Adele Cunningham. Some people count sheep to get to sleep. Some recite verses of scripture. Some mull over their to-do list for the next day. Such tactics didn't help Brenda get to sleep.

Instead, she pictured Adele Cunningham hanging by a noose from the rafters in George's garage, or she imagined her being swept away in the river after a heavy rainstorm. How about a cup of tea laced with rat poison? Or being struck by lightning? Those images satisfied Brenda's ego enough to put her to sleep. The next day, however, she arose to the truth—Adele Cunningham was alive and well and was happily married to George.

Of course, Brenda was never the perpetrator in her imaginings. She was too sweet and innocent to wield a knife or a gun or a bottle of rat poison. No, it had to be a villain from another town. Better yet, a natural disaster or an accident of some kind. But, Brenda knew what the Bible said about her secret plots. If she entertained such thoughts in her mind it was as if she'd already committed them. She'd also read that out of the heart proceeds all kinds of evil, including murder.

With those convictions running around in her mind, she stopped planning Adele's death and got on with her own life.

The truth was, Adele never knew she had stolen away Brenda's only chance at happiness. Eventually, Adele gave birth to

George's children—the children Brenda had wanted—a boy and a girl—beautiful, smart, perfect kids. Of course, they had to be perfect. Adele had the man, the house, the car—and now the kids—everything Brenda needed to be happy for the rest of her life.

Now her wish had come true. Her adversary was dead, and she needed to decide if she should go to the funeral and gloat, or if she should stay away and let Adele Cunningham rest in peace. After all, George was already gone. There existed no reward for Brenda Schwartz.

She mulled over the long list of accolades in Adele's obituary.

"You can't take a U-Haul to the grave with you," Brenda scoffed.

But then, another thought struck her. In fact, several thoughts surfaced and interrupted her moment of gloating.

From out of nowhere, she recalled the day the class bully, Jenny Bosco, cornered her in the girl's restroom, and was about to punch her face when Adele walked in. Though Jenny had the physique of a fullback, Adele was fearless and surprisingly strong. She stepped between them, grabbed Jenny's raised arm and flung her backward.

"You don't mess with my friend," Adele said, narrowing her eyes. "If you do, it'll be no different than if you messed with me."

Jenny never bothered Brenda again.

That wasn't the only time Adele came to her rescue. Once, when Brenda hid under a tree in front of the school during a thunderstorm, Adele showed up with an umbrella and walked her home. She taught her how to dance, how to make a quilt, and how to apply makeup. Though they were the same age, Adele acted like the big sister Brenda had longed for most of her life.

Later, after Adele married George, the two women were thrown together on church committees and civic projects. Though Adele, a talented, confident young woman, usually was put in charge, she never talked down on Brenda. In fact, she often gave her easy duties that put her in the spotlight. When it came time to solicit donations from the town leaders, Adele sent Brenda knocking on their doors. As a result, she got to know the local politicians which later set her up for a job in the mayor's office.

It was Adele who encouraged Brenda to take college classes, Adele who showed her how to fix her hair in a more flattering style, Adele who got her to join a dance club. Adele even introduced her to Arthur Welch, a career soldier who lived on a nearby Army base and often attended the Saturday night dances. The shy young man wasn't much to look at, except when he was in uniform. Otherwise, he looked as washed out and rumpled as any of the other losers in town. But dressed in his well-fitted khaki pants and shirt, with a row of medals on his chest, the young Army captain got some heads turning. Including Brenda's. The night Adele introduced them, he immediately invited Brenda to the dance floor.

Though Arthur had not been her first choice for a husband, she would have married him, if not for the war in Korea. They parted tearfully at the bus station, and she never saw him again. As soon as the news came out that Arthur had been killed in action, Adele was at her house in minutes. She sat quietly while Brenda sobbed into a pile of tissues. It meant a lot to Brenda to have someone sit beside her and not say a word, even if it was Adele.

From that moment, Brenda resolved never to love again. Love was too painful. She'd lost one man to the most popular girl in town and the other to a senseless war.

Too embarrassed to let anyone know she had been wrong about Adele Cunningham, Brenda went on with her life and allowed people to continue thinking she resented that woman. To Brenda, their relationship had turned into a sort of love-hate scenario that could never be resolved.

With the obituary still before her, Brenda gazed at the photo above the rectangle of text. Adele had put on a few pounds after birthing her two children. She'd lost her girlish figure, had taken on a matronly appearance. And her blond hair had faded beneath a shower of gray. She even looked a tad shorter in recent years.

Meanwhile, though Brenda had always been a bit frumpy and was a few pounds overweight, she hadn't changed much over the years, hadn't gained a single pound, and her hair was the same color it always was—mousy brown. The fact was, she had stayed the same, and Adele Cunningham had aged.

She gazed at Adele's photo and a wave of compassion flooded through her. Then she uttered the words that could set her free.

"I forgive you, Adele Cunningham. You never knew how much it hurt me to see you and George together. Never knew how much I hated losing to you, how much I hated *you*. But that's over. I forgive you. In fact, I love you for the wonderful person you *really* were, the one my pride never allowed me to get to know."

The obituary said the funeral would take place in two days. She smiled to herself. For years she had lived next door to a truly special person. Adele Cunningham had portrayed the Christian life. She'd demonstrated how to love one's neighbor. While others had looked right through Brenda as though they didn't see her at all, Adele Cunningham had treated her with respect, like she had value. Go to the woman's memorial service? She wouldn't miss it for the world.

SIX

SAMMY POWERS

The newspaper lay open to the obituary page on top of Sammy Powers' bunk. He knelt beside his cot and reread the text. The lines filled a vertical, three-inch rectangle, each letter clearly defined and with a black border around the perimeter. Above them was a black-and-white photo of the only person who ever believed in him. The ink blurred together as several tears struck the page.

Sammy had to admit, the typesetter had done a good job. He recalled how the machinery worked with all its intricacies, right down to the ninety-character keyboard, the composition stick, the lingering aroma of ink, and the clicking of tiny metal letters that produced the article now before him. *The Fall River Daily Chronicle*, the town's only newspaper. He'd worked in the back room of that small-town publication when he should have been finishing the eleventh grade.

He sniffed the residue of ink. The aroma took him back to a time when that same odor hung heavy in the stairwells and clung to his clothes at the end of the day. He stared at the name in bold print.

Adele Baker Cunningham, *62, longtime resident, mother of two, and faithful volunteer at First Street Christian Church. Preceded in death by her beloved husband, George. Survived by a daughter, Judy Cunningham, a son, Paul Cunningham, and three grandchildren.*

The article went on to list Adele's many accomplishments —county fair ribbons, bowling trophies, and several certificates of service for her work in the church. To Sammy, none of those accolades compared to what he personally knew about Mrs. Cunningham, how she had tried to help him turn his life around, how she'd paid more attention to him than anyone he'd ever known, including his own mother.

It musta broke the poor woman's heart to learn she'd failed. Another tear struck the page.

But had Mrs. Cunningham failed? Or, had *he*? Sammy had to admit the truth. That woman had done everything a person could to help him get on the right track. If only he'd stayed there. If only he'd listened to the nagging of his conscience. One night, one slip-up, one stupid mistake, and Mrs. Cunningham's plans for him were smashed for good.

It was Mrs. Cunningham who nudged Sammy into a job in the first place, right after he quit school in his junior year. He was eighteen years old and he didn't want to repeat that grade again. Mrs. Cunningham found him on the street, begging for change. She invited him to have lunch with her. They sat on a park bench eating hotdogs she bought from an outdoor vendor.

They talked for nearly an hour. Sammy opened his heart to her, shared things from his youth that could make the hairs stand up on the arms of the worst criminals—how his drunken father had beat him close to death, how his mother had turned her back so she didn't have to witness the killing of her son, how his two brothers had left home after getting the same treatment. Then he admitted his own faults, that he'd broken a bakery store window one night and had run off with a fistful of cookies, and that wasn't the first time he'd taken what didn't belong to him.

Except for a wrinkle of her brow, Mrs. Cunningham showed little emotion while he told his tale. She said nothing, just kept nodding and encouraged him to go on. When he finished, he slumped over in exhaustion. She rested a hand on his back and prayed over him.

She prayed like he was worthy of prayer, though he believed he wasn't. Out of that woman's mouth came the most heart-rending pleas to God, and he began to feel like someone believed in him, that he could make a new life for himself. And all he had to do was try.

Then came the first of many lectures.

"You can't change your past, Sammy, but you *can* control your future. You need to turn your back on the ways of the street. Stop stealing. Return what you can, *if* you can, and then look ahead."

But Mrs. Cunningham didn't merely give lectures. She took action to help him get on his own two feet. The first thing she did was move him out of the dysfunctional home where he'd been barely existing and into a homeless shelter in town. With her persistent supervision—he jokingly accused her of nagging him—over the next few months, he managed to stay out of trouble long enough to take a few jobs mowing lawns and running errands for people. But Mrs. Cunningham didn't let it rest. It was time, she said, to apply for a real job.

She arranged for an interview with Jack Cartwright, a supervisor at the *Fall River Daily Chronicle*. Though nervous as all get-out, Sammy showed up on time for the interview wearing new pants and shirt, compliments of Mrs. Cunningham. For some reason beyond his expectations, Cartwright hired him on the spot.

He couldn't wait to tell Mrs. Cunningham. He ran from the newspaper office on flying feet to her front porch, where he found her sitting on the porch swing as though she'd been waiting for him to show up.

"I got the job, Mrs. Cunningham," he shouted and stumbled up the front steps. Breathless, he stood before her, grinning like a kid with a new bike. "I got it. I'm gonna work as a kind of go-fer between the newsroom and the pressroom."

"That's wonderful," she said, rising. She gave him a big hug, then stepped back and looked him in the eye. "Now the challenge is to hold onto that job and maybe move up to higher levels." She paused and invited him to sit beside her on the porch swing. "The secret," she told him, "is to let the boss know you intend to work hard. Do whatever they tell you and go a step further. You know what they say. *Idle hands make mischief.* If the boss sees you doing a good job, he's bound to promote you."

Those first few days in the layout room awoke his senses to a strange, new environment. The aroma of fresh ink stung his nostrils, the rumble of the presses got his heart thumping, and the flurry of activity drew him into the excitement of daily deadlines. It turned out to be the right job for him. He loved the energy that surged throughout the old brick building, away from the public eye. While the readers saw the finished product—a few pages of text, photos, and a bunch of ads—Sammy got a taste of what it really took to put a newspaper together. He roamed freely about the building from the reporters' den on the top floor to the basement where the finished and folded publications came off the belt. He was hooked. He envisioned himself as a newspaperman for life.

As the new guy, he spent a lot of time running errands up and down three flights in a stairwell that echoed the thumping of his speeding footsteps and the panting of his breath. The excitement picked up at about five o'clock when the top floor came alive at deadline. Reporters rushed in with their notebooks in hand, hit their desks and pounded out their stories for the next day's paper. The whole building jumped with phones ringing and keys clicking. Editors shouted for copy and laid out photos, measured the pages, cursed aloud when the collection of pieces didn't fit, then started all over again.

On the noisy second floor the presses spit out the copy, page after page after page of printed text and a blur of photos. After a while, the publisher poked his head out his door and demanded a printout of the front page, which, Sammy quickly learned, was the most important section of the newspaper. It's what drew people to the storefront boxes where they'd slip in their quarters and get to read the latest news, fresh off the presses. On the boss' command, Sammy pulled a copy off the belt and rushed it to the publisher's office. Then, he scurried down to the basement and helped the guys slip advertisements inside the local section as it passed by on the conveyor belt.

The foreman didn't give him a minute's rest. "Stuff those flyers in there, Sammy, and hurry up about it," the foreman shouted, a cigarette bobbing between his lips. "An entire row of newspapers flew by without a single insert. Move it, you guys. Move it. You too, Sammy. Get a move on."

Being part of the whole experience sent a wave of adrenaline through him. At the end of the day, he'd leave the building, smelling like ink, but whistling, with his hands in his jeans' pockets, and feeling like he'd done a pretty important job over the last few hours.

In time, several of his co-workers left for other positions, *anything but the newspaper business*, they said. But Sammy stayed. What else could a high school dropout do? He began to think he could have a longtime career with the *Daily Chronicle*. He could take those GED classes, go to night school and get a diploma. Then, maybe college. As he slid the advertisements inside the local section, Sammy's dream kept growing. He looked at the loud-mouthed foreman. He could do that job as good as that blowhard. Maybe better.

But things hadn't worked out, and here he was, stuck in the state prison with another four years left before he'd be eligible for parole.

Mrs. Cunningham stared back at him from the black-and-white photo in the middle of the obituary page. She was smiling, and her eyes seemed to look right into his soul. Had she seen the blackness that resided there? Maybe. But Mrs. Cunningham never mentioned his mistakes again. Instead, she talked about how good things could be if he would only try. Another tear surfaced and spilled onto the page. More of the text blurred.

He'd wanted to go to her memorial service. *Needed* to go there. Not only for her, but for himself.

He hadn't been inside a church in more than three years. Back then, Mrs. Cunningham had him going to First Street Christian every Sunday. She even bought him a suit. Brand new, straight from the men's section in a high-class department store.

"If you're going to sit beside me, I don't want you wearing second-hand clothes," she'd said with a twinkle in her eye.

Sammy proudly wore that suit every Sunday. He'd sit there in Mrs. Cunningham's pew, his head held high, ignoring the critical stares of the hypocrites who belonged to the Ladies Aid Society. They didn't bother him. Not while he had Mrs. Cunningham by his side.

One would think the sermons that poured from the pulpit, combined with Mrs. Cunningham's prayers, might have made a difference for Sammy. But his bad luck had begun the second he dropped from the womb, and it rarely let up. Sammy came from a whole family of losers, beginning with an alcoholic father who beat his three sons regularly, a mother who drowned her miserable life in one bottle of gin after another, and two brothers who took identical paths to prison several years ahead of him.

When you start out with that kind of family history, a life of crime inevitably follows, he reasoned. He didn't know how to rise above it. No matter how many positive thoughts Mrs. Cunningham pounded into his head, he always came up knowing what he really was—a loser. One look in the mirror confirmed it. The disheveled, scarred-up face looking back at him had no place in a decent society.

Not even Mr. Cartwright could change his destiny. That man gave him every opportunity to prove himself. He moved Sammy into an apprenticeship long before most of the other teenagers who worked there. When the others quit, Sammy stuck it out for another two years. Then came his big fall.

It was raining the night Sammy made the biggest mistake of his life.

Most of the crew had gone home. All that remained were the press operators and the delivery drivers. Sammy helped load the last of the bundles in the back of a van, then he returned to the building to get his lunchbox. Right about then, the devil kicked in with an idea that sounded pretty good.

Mr. Cartwright had already left the building. The press people had shut down their machines. The delivery vans were pulling away. It was only Sammy now, with an open back door that would latch shut after he left.

He didn't stop to consider how great it was that Mr. Cartwright had trusted him to be the last one out the door. All he knew was, the situation presented an opportunity beyond his wildest dreams.

Whistling under his breath, he ignored his lunchbox and lumbered down the hall to Cartwright's office. The safe stood in the corner, its padlock glistening under a dagger of moonlight streaming through the window. He'd memorized the combination one day when Cartwright didn't know he was watching over his shoulder. *What luck.* Not that Sammy had plotted anything, but it was as if the opportunity had been born at that very moment.

He hesitated while two inner voices vied for his attention. One urged him to flee the building. *Get out of here. Do what you were told and go home.*

The other taunted him with that glistening padlock. It was like those comedies where Satan and an angel sit on a person's opposite shoulders, each vying for his attention.

Come on," one voice taunted. *Nobody's gonna know it was you. All you gotta do is turn that combination, open the safe, and take the loot.*

Don't do it, the other warned. *Cartwright will figure it out, and then you're up a creek. Literally.*

And so the scene went, back and forth, with Sammy getting more confused by the minute. He froze in front of the safe. Should he or shouldn't he? He was about to turn around and leave, when he heard one final plea.

Think about your poor mother. Winter's comin' and she needs a new coat. You'll be doin' something bad, but you'll accomplish so much good. Kind of like Robin Hood—steal from the rich and give to the poor.

Within ten minutes, Sammy had several hundred dollars in his pocket, the safe was shut and locked, and he was out the door and heading down the street in pouring rain, pedaling his bike as fast as he could make the dang thing go. He didn't look back, didn't even breathe until he was halfway home. He bumped his bike over the railroad tracks and was almost to his street when he heard the siren closing in from behind.

He'd been in enough trouble during high school—petty things like graffiti and shoplifting—to know this meant he was in big trouble. For those misdemeanors, he'd gotten a slap on the wrist and suspension from school, plus another whipping from his dad.

But this was grand larceny. If he got caught, it meant a trial. And prison.

Sammy Powers got caught.

Even with Mrs. Cunningham speaking up on his behalf, the judge didn't waver. He sentenced Sammy to ten years in the state prison with a chance of parole in seven. He returned all the money. After all, he didn't get a chance to spend a dime of it, didn't have time to buy his mother a coat.

Mr. Cartwright came to the trial and told him never to come back to the newspaper. His career was shot. His life was over.

Mrs. Cunningham began her visits the day he was incarcerated. She walked through that steel door and picked up the phone on the other side of the glass. Sammy couldn't look her in the eye.

Then she said the most profound thing.

"I don't care what you did, Sammy, you have a goodness inside you that's going to come out someday."

"I don't know, Mrs. Cunningham," he said, raising his eyes like a wounded puppy. "My folks have given up on me. They said I'm exactly like my brothers. Bad to the bone."

"Don't listen to them. *I* haven't given up on you. I still believe you're going to do great things someday. You just have to find your place in life, that's all. Once you find it, don't let anybody tell you you're no good or that you can't do anything worthwhile. *I* say, you can make it. And you know what? The Apostle Paul said so too. He wrote that a person can do all things through Christ who strengthens him. That's where you can get your strength, Sammy, along with a new plan for your life."

He broke down in front of her and could hardly say another word for all the choking and sobbing that came out of him.

She eyed him through the glass with sympathy. "Tell me, Sammy, how did you get caught?"

"Mr. Cartwright was hiding in the building. Turns out, he was testing me."

She nodded. "I see."

"I messed up, Mrs. Cunningham. You had faith in me. Mr. Cartwright gave me the chance of a lifetime, and I disappointed both of you."

"Sammy, there will be other chances. You have a whole string of them waiting down the road. The thing is, you have to learn from your failures. Once you do, then they're not failures anymore. They're stepping stones."

"Well, this stepping stone sure landed me in a big hole."

She laughed, and it brought a twinkle to her eyes. Sammy found the courage to smile back at her. How was Mrs. Cunningham able to accomplish that in him? He could be down one minute and up the next. He gazed into her eyes and found a ray of hope there. If she still believed in him, why shouldn't he believe in himself?

"Will you pray for me, Mrs. Cunningham?"

"Of course. It's what I do best."

There in the middle of that brick-and-mortar prison with razor wire running around the top of the outside walls and guards at every door, Mrs. Cunningham and Sammy Powers had a Holy Spirit prayer meeting. With his eyes closed, he temporarily forgot where he was. He could have been in a church, or in a park somewhere, free as a bird, talking to God.

They repeated that scenario at least once or twice a month over the next few years, usually on the first and third Fridays. But Mrs. Cunningham didn't show up last week. Or the week before. She didn't call, the way she had whenever she expected to miss their regular date. He'd been pacing the floor in his ten-by-eight foot cell this morning when a guard shoved the newspaper through the bars.

"Here's something that might interest you, Sam." The voice was gruff, but there was a strange sadness in the man's eyes.

Sammy looked at the page. The paper had been purposely folded with the list of obituaries showing. When he spotted Mrs. Cunningham's picture, he lost control.

"No!" he cried. "She can't be gone. No. No. No."

Tears spilled down his cheeks. It was as though he'd been drowning and now had lost his only lifeline. He flung the paper on top of his cot and fell to his knees.

Now, still on his knees, he reread the text, like he couldn't believe it the first time. An ache started deep inside his gut and rose with a wrenching pain equal to the last time his father pummeled him senseless. He wept without restraint and without any concern for his hulk of a cellmate lying on the cot a few feet away. The big guy sat up.

"Aw, what's the matter? Did somebody hurt our little Sammy?" he mocked.

With that, Sammy flew across the cell like he'd been flung from a catapult. It didn't matter if the hulk was twice his size and three times as strong. Sammy pounded him, climbed on him, and tore at the guy's hair. Then two big hands pulled him free and tossed him to the other side of the cell. Sammy's back struck the concrete wall with a resounding whack. He slumped over and spilled a gusher of tears and snot onto the tile floor.

Two guards were on him in seconds.

"Maybe a couple of days in solitary will teach you guys a lesson," one of them said.

The guards hauled them both off to separate compartments.

Sammy ended up in a four-by-six cell with only a straw mattress on the floor, a latrine in the corner, and a small opening in the door for passing in meals. Surprisingly, he welcomed the dark solitude. Alone, he could mourn there, undisturbed. He could pour out his anguish, and no one would hear. No one would be there to mock him.

"Mrs. Cunningham," he murmured. "Why, oh why, did you have to go and die?"

The most important person in his life was gone, and he couldn't even go to her funeral. He chewed on his bottom lip until he tasted blood. With Mrs. Cunningham gone, so was his only hope.

PART II
THE DAY BEFORE THE FUNERAL

SEVEN

JUDY CUNNINGHAM

Judy Cunningham paused before her closet and frowned at the array of colors. She hadn't purchased anything black since her father died five years ago. After his funeral, she stuffed the outfit in a bag and donated it to the church mission barrel.

She never wore black, not even to dinner parties. The color washed out her already pale complexion. It drew the lines of her face down and left her looking older than twenty-seven.

Now she was facing another funeral, and on top of feeling miserable over losing her mother, she needed to go out and purchase a black dress.

"You *have* to wear black," Aunt Connie had insisted. "It's tradition. People always wear black to funerals."

Judy knew better. People dressed in other dark colors. Mostly navy blue, but also brown or deep gray. She gave her aunt one of her pleading expressions that had always worked when she was a child.

But Aunt Connie shook her head and crossed her arms. "You don't want to disrespect your mother, Judy. And think about all those people who will be attending her memorial service. They'll all be wearing black. You don't want to stand out like a sore thumb."

Mother was gone, and Aunt Connie was in charge now. And so, twenty-four hours before the funeral, Judy drove to the shopping mall, walked the hallways, and fought the urge to flee. Nearly every store window had at least one manikin dressed in black, sometimes two or three. It was as if the buyers in those shops had collaborated with Aunt Connie.

She needed to make this quick—hurry inside, pick something off the rack, and get out. At the third store, she tried on several outfits in the fitting room, scowled at her reflection in the mirror, and tossed each of them aside.

"I look like an old schoolmarm from the 1930s," she scoffed.

In the end, she settled on a stylish dress with a tucked waist and a scooped neckline. With the right jewelry and a colorful scarf she could even wear that outfit to work.

A surge of guilt jolted her back to the reason she'd gone shopping in the first place. Her mother's funeral. Adele Cunningham wanted everyone to show up in a bright color. Sunshine yellow. Or brilliant green. Or, her favorite—cherry red. She'd mentioned her preference in the hospital last week. But Judy thought she was joking. Just like she never expected her mother to die.

Of course, Aunt Connie had insisted that her sister didn't *really* expect everyone to dress like they were going to a Saturday night social. "Don't even mention it to anyone," she'd told Judy. "Your mother couldn't have been serious. No, no, no. We need to wear black."

Shoving the memory to the back of her mind, she hurriedly purchased the dress she'd selected and drove home. After hanging her purchase in her closet, she went to the living room to see how she might be able to help.

Keep your focus on the funeral, she told herself. *Help Aunt Connie get the house ready for guests. Forget about the black dress. Forget about Parker and the problem he's given you.*

Forgetting came easier when she entered the living room. Her mother's spirit was everywhere. Embroidered wall hangings. A handmade quilt draped over the sofa. A ceramic angel on the end table. All of them creations by Adele Cunningham's nimble fingers. Then there was that photo of Adele and George on their wedding day, perched on the fireplace mantel for as long as Judy could remember and removed once a week for dusting.

She drew closer and gazed at her mother, a typical 1940s bride in a long, white, clingy gown and holding a humongous bouquet of flowers that concealed most of her torso. Her heart fluttered a little as she realized how much she resembled her mom. Her tall, willowy figure, her pale hair and glassy eyes. Even in a black-and-white photo, anyone could tell she was a blond-haired, blue-eyed beauty.

Sometimes, when she looked in the mirror, she was startled by the image of her mother looking back at her, when all the while it was her own reflection.

She looked about the living room and discovered several remnants from Christmas that her mother had left undone. A basket of ornaments stood in the corner of the room along with several strings of colored lights all bound up with string. Here it was, almost two months after the holiday and her mother hadn't put it all away. Adele Cunningham had more important things to attend to. Like doctor visits and then a hospital stay that lasted two weeks. What's more, she'd left the nativity scene on the table by the window long after the holiday had passed.

"It won't hurt to remember the real reason for Christmas," Adele had said.

As always, no one argued with her. Not Judy. And especially not Paul. He was Mother's favorite son—her only son, actually—and her pride and joy.

Judy wasn't the least bit jealous of her brother. Paul was a wonderful guy. He was considerate of others, willing to step back so someone else could take first-place—like the time he messed up his game so Ben Michaels could be pitcher. Over the years he'd excelled in other ways. High school and college basketball trophies. A master's degree in architecture, a lucrative career, and, on top of everything else, a wife his mother had received with open arms, and, in recent years, three wonderful grandchildren.

Judy, on the other hand, had not married, couldn't promise any grandchildren in the near future, and was about to mess up her life big time. She knew this, yet she'd already boarded that high-speed train to nowhere, and she didn't know how to get off.

Parker came to mind again. His ghost was always hovering in front of her, taunting her, confusing her. Then followed the inevitable guilt.

In an effort to keep busy, she went straight to the manger scene and began to take it apart. She located the storage box on the floor against the far wall, a sign Adele had brought it out for the final dismantling after New Year's Day.

There was something final about taking down her mother's last Christmas. Something terribly painful about having to face next year's holiday without her. Judy hadn't expected her mother to die. No one did. She'd thought there'd be plenty of opportunities to open her heart to the one person who could help her. Somehow, she'd let far too many of those moments pass, and now it was too late.

She should have suspected something wasn't right when her mother asked for a couple boxes of note cards and a pen. That simple request should have alerted her to the truth. Adele Cunningham was preparing to die, and she had something special to say to a few select individuals.

A mix of feelings rolled around inside her head. She should have confided in her mother. Should have told her about Parker. Now she felt trapped, and the only person who could have shown her how to get free was gone.

In a clandestine way, Parker Addison had convinced her to trust him. A dimpled smile. A wink of the eye. A brush of his hand against her arm. All seemingly innocent gestures that quickly evolved into secret lunches and a promise that he'd soon be free to pursue her openly.

From what Judy knew about her boss, he'd grown up in a trailer park outside of Albany. The only son of a single mom, he rose above their impoverished existence. He was a track star in high school, maintained a 4.0 average, and earned a full college scholarship. He acquired a master's degree in finance and landed a job with Ventura Brothers Law Firm immediately after graduation. The three brothers paid for his post-graduate law school. Their investment paid off. Once licensed, Parker helped expand the company's client base into a multi-million-dollar enterprise. As a junior partner, he'd hired Judy straight out of business school. She recalled with a touch of embarrassment how he'd made the decision without once looking at her resume. Instead, his eyes had moved from her face to her legs and back to her face again.

She blushed as she remembered the moment, how she'd yanked the hem of her skirt down and tucked her legs out of sight under the edge of her chair. In time, she began to relax around her handsome boss and even welcomed his admiring glances. He was easy to look at. Athletic build that spoke of regular exercise and perhaps a marathon or two. Dark hair, graying at the temples. Piercing green eyes, like her father's.

She stopped what she was doing and hurried back to her parents' wedding photo on the mantel. As she thought, Parker Addison resembled her father. She turned away, frowning with puzzlement. It had been nice being Daddy's little girl. His dying had left an emptiness she hadn't yet resolved. Was Parker merely filling the void her father left behind?

Aside from Parker's likeness to her father, she couldn't recall anything else that had drawn her to him.

Still puzzled, she turned her attention to the stable and began taking it apart. The walls and roof came off easily and went into the storage box with little effort. It was kind of like dismantling her life, one piece at a time. Since she met Parker, her good sense had gone by the wayside, then her propriety, then her self-respect. If things kept going the way they had been, it was only a matter of time before her reputation went down the toilet too.

She was having lunch with Parker a few days ago, while her mother was lying on a hospital bed, writing notes whenever she had the strength to sit up for a while. Judy expressed her concern.

"I think Mother's trying to do too much. She should be resting."

"You're mother's going to be just fine," Parker had said. "Operations like this have become very common. You'll see, Judy, she'll be out of the hospital and on her feet before you know it."

They were seated across from each other at their usual table. She'd placed her hand in the comfort of his palm.

"My mom's not as spunky as everyone thinks," she'd told him. "Like everyone else, she has a vulnerable side. She gives and gives and gives until she has nothing left. I'm afraid this time she's sacrificed far too much." She shook her head despondently. "I'm worried, Parker. When my mother prays for others, things happen. But now, with her lying there, looking helpless, I wonder if she's able to pray for herself."

"Then, *you* pray for her."

"Ha!" Judy pulled her hand out of his grasp and leaned back. "Me? I don't have my mother's gift."

"Do you think you're so bad that if you prayed for your mother, God won't hear you?"

She nodded. "That's exactly what I think."

"Well, I for one believe otherwise. What I know about Judy Cunningham would fill a hymnbook."

He shook his head and glanced at his watch. Seconds later he was on his feet. He backed away from the table and quickly paid their bill. It was the same as always. A quick lunch. And a fast escape.

They parted at the door, and moved to their own cars, the way they always did.

A heavy conviction hung over Judy. Did Parker really think she was like her mother? The thought had never crossed her mind. Her mother was a godly woman who had a direct line to heaven. For most of her life, she'd stood back while that woman helped one person after another. *Be like Adele Cunningham? Impossible.*

The thought of her mother lying helpless in a hospital bed brought her to a decision. While Parker went back to the office, she took the rest of the day off and went to the hospital. She sat beside her mother's bed for the rest of the afternoon. Adele

Cunningham lay there, sleeping restfully. Except for the steady hiss and click of an oxygen tank and the rhythmic beep of a heart monitor, the room had settled into a quiet lull.

Judy stayed while her mother slept, though the opportunity for counsel had long passed. She chewed a hangnail, twirled a lock of her hair, and kept glancing at her watch. Two-thirty, then three, then four. She remained frozen to her chair, unable to leave the room, but desperately aware of another missed opportunity.

A nurse glided in, checked her mother's vitals, injected something in the IV tube, and slipped out of the room without a word. It was as if Judy were invisible. Or perhaps the nurse had sensed that she wanted to be alone.

Then, in a moment of impulse, Judy fell to her knees beside her mother's hospital bed.

"Heavenly Father," she murmured. "Please heal my mother. I may have inherited her good looks, but I didn't end up with her godly character. I never learned to communicate with you like she does. I've never helped a single person other than myself. If I ever needed my mother before, I need her now. Please make her well."

She rose off the floor and planted a kiss on her mother's cheek. Then she left the hospital and drove back to the house. Aunt Connie was in the kitchen baking something that smelled like cinnamon and apples.

She went straight to the phone in the living room and dialed Parker's direct line.

When he answered, her heart flipped, but only for a second. She caught her breath and quickly got her emotions in check.

"I need to take a few days off," she said.

"I understand. Your mom's not any better?"

"No. She's the same."

"Take as much time as you need."

"Thanks, Parker."

Her heart was in her throat. What more could she say? He was at work, and she was at home with Aunt Connie.

That was the last time they spoke. Now, as she continued to take down the manger scene, she turned her thoughts to the funeral, one day away. Aunt Connie had made all the arrangements, so there was little for her to do except be there.

She collected the bits of straw and pine cones and gingerly placed them around the inside walls of the box, the way her mother always did. She arranged the shepherds and the tiny sheep on one side. Then she added the magi and their camels, followed by the stable animals—two donkeys and a cow. Last of all, she placed the holy family on top, with the babe in the center staring up at her.

A chill went through her. She'd grown up in the church and had known for years why Jesus came to earth. It wasn't to be born. It was to die. And with the choices she'd made lately, she'd given him one more reason to do that.

She added a layer of tissue paper on top of the collection, the way her mother used to do, to protect the contents. There was something symbolic about putting away Christmas. Something terribly final this time. Slowly, with tears streaming down her face, she lowered the lid in place and sealed it shut along with the final chapter of her mother's life.

EIGHT

ALICIA CARTER

Alicia set out on her trip, a thermos of hot chocolate propped inside the center console and a medley of Frank Sinatra's hits oozing from her radio. Icy rain pelted her windshield. Slick roads and heavy traffic lay ahead of her. She crept along the highway and grew more and more anxious.

She had wanted to arrive in Fall River before school let out so she could get a look at her little girl. That is, if she could even recognize the child. All she knew about her was a name—Mindy. She imagined the child looked like she did as a little girl. Blond hair maybe, and blue eyes. She was ten years old. That much was certain.

According to the lawyer she'd hired, Mindy attended school at the Christian Academy connected to Robert Goode's church.

She continued to inch along with the rest of the traffic. The windshield wipers kept a steady beat with Sinatra's "Chicago," whisking away the sleet the moment it hit the glass. With a deathlike grip on the steering wheel and a pumping of her right foot from gas to brake and back, she maneuvered her car in and out of the traffic.

Butch had phoned her that morning, a couple hours before she left the house. It had to be lunchtime in Munich.

"I woke up worried about you," he admitted. "I wanted to make sure you're doing the right thing. Remember, the child belongs to someone else now."

"Are you telling me to stay home?"

"No, I'm merely cautioning you to think closely about what you're doing."

"So, do I forget about the funeral?"

A full minute of silence passed. Alicia held her breath.

Butch let out a sigh. "Look, Alicia, you do whatever you want. But remember, your decision is going to affect other people besides yourself. Think about that couple and the child. Will you be able to look at yourself in the mirror knowing you've hurt them?"

Even now, tears came as she recalled her husband's warning. Was she making a mistake? If so, how could she live with the consequences?

A surge of determination took over. Pressing her foot against the gas pedal, she pulled into the passing lane and went around a slow-moving car.

"I need to know the truth," she said aloud. "Otherwise, I'll never get over the loss."

As she moved onto the turnpike, the icy rain diminished to a wet drizzle. She slowed the wipers, but her anxiety had increased. The closer she got to her hometown, the more pronounced was the throbbing in her chest.

She arrived in Fall River a few minutes after 12 o'clock. Her husband probably was heading out to dinner with the rest of the crew, and afterward he'd likely take a walk around town. If there was one thing Butch liked to do while in Germany, it was hit the streets in the evening, maybe do a little window shopping. Inevitably, he'd bring home an expensive piece of jewelry or a pretty blouse as proof he'd been thinking about her. But she knew what those trinkets really were. They were meant to be distractions to keep her from dwelling on being childless. How on earth could he think those worthless gifts could replace the feel of a child in her arms?

The drizzle had lessened to a mist, and the sun broke through a scattering of gray clouds. Patches of melted snow lined the familiar streets. Memories surfaced of her own innocent childhood, escapades with her best friend, Judy, and private chats with Mrs. Cunningham on the front porch of her house. How she needed that woman now.

She turned off the wipers and began to search for the road that led to the church. Jennifer Goode ran the school. Mindy was most likely in the fourth grade. If she'd guessed right, the kids had already eaten their lunch and were coming outside for recess.

Alicia turned a corner, then another, maneuvering through the streets. The church rose up ahead, like a monument amidst a cluster of 1950s boxlike homes with front porches, each one looking exactly like the next except for the color of paint on the siding. A wave of claustrophobia passed over her. She'd been away so long she'd forgotten what this place was like with its web of streets and the suffocating trappings of small-town life. What did these people do on Saturday nights? Movies? Bingo? The local Grange?

Leaving was the best decision she'd ever made. As an airline flight attendant she'd flown to the most fascinating places in the United States and Europe. She might have missed all of that excitement had she remained in Fall River.

The awareness made her even more determined to lift her little girl out of such boredom and show her what the real world was like. The Goodes couldn't provide such luxuries. All they could give Mindy was a Christian education. Alicia could do so much more for her.

She followed the drive around the sanctuary to the back of the church where a wrought iron fence barred trespassers from the academy grounds. She pulled into a parking slot, turned off her car and stared beyond the fencing. In the distance children were swarming around the playground equipment. They were bundled up in winter coats, knitted hats, and mittens, blending together like a collection of overdressed dolls.

She wanted to get a closer look, thinking perhaps she might recognize her daughter. She stepped out of the car and followed the line of fencing as far as she could go, but she was still several yards away from where the children were playing. Squinting, she focused on a few little girls who looked to be about ten years old. Several had blond curls—like hers—sticking out of their woolen hats.

One of them turned and looked in her direction. She had an angelic face, flushed from the nippy air. And eyes as blue as the sky. Alicia caught her breath.

She thought about calling out the girl's name—Mindy—but one of the teachers also was looking in her direction. She froze. Jennifer Goode was there. Instinctively, Jennifer approached the same little girl and placed a hand on her tiny shoulder.

Then, two more workers stopped what they were doing and turned toward her. They exchanged words among themselves.

She stared back at them. *I'm on this side of the fence, for Pete's sake. I can't hurt anybody from here.*

The first teacher broke away from the group and started walking toward her. She didn't want a confrontation. Not now. She gave a friendly wave, turned from the fence, and retreated to her car. She sat in the driver's seat for several minutes, trying to make sense out of what she had witnessed. The little girl looked a lot like she did when she was ten. She had to be Mindy.

Clenching her teeth, she drove away from the school. At the next intersection she turned left in the direction of the downtown area and the law office of Parker Addison.

A half-hour later she was seated in a plush armchair on one side of a broad mahogany desk that separated her from one of the handsomest men she'd ever seen. Until that moment she'd had one phone conversation with Parker Addison. She'd pictured him as a plump, stodgy, old man. But he looked no more than 35. He'd handled her case with a professional air that belied his youth. Perhaps he could bring things to a satisfying end.

His next words dispelled her concerns.

"We're gonna win this thing." He smiled with an air of

assurance. "The Goodes don't have any legal claim to your child," he went on. "No paperwork. No court approval. Just two people who took care of your daughter for a while until you could get on your feet. That's the way we're going to present your case in court. And that's what is going to win it for you."

He opened the file and perused the paperwork for a few minutes, flipping pages and pensively stroking the sides of his mouth. Alicia waited, her heart beating with anticipation. This whole thing was happening so fast. And so easy. She should have pursued custody long ago. So many years lost when she could have been developing a relationship with her daughter. So many missed opportunities for bonding and sharing and making a stable home for the girl. There was no telling what kind of treatment Mindy had received at the hands of strangers.

Yes, that's what they were. Strangers who had presumed to make a home for someone else's child. Well, that was going to end.

While Parker continued to leaf through the documents, she looked past the plate glass window that separated his private office from his staff. When she first entered the area, she caught sight of her friend's nameplate—*Judy Cunningham, Executive Assistant.* But her friend was nowhere in sight.

"Where's Judy?" she ventured to ask.

Parker looked up from the file. "Huh?"

"Judy Cunningham. She was my best friend while growing up. I passed her desk out there. Isn't she here?"

"No. She took the day off to tend to her mother's funeral." He went back to the file.

A grip of discomfort seized her. She'd never told Judy anything about the pregnancy or the adoption. She'd wanted to put it all behind her at the time so she could move on with her life. She assumed Judy's mother had kept her word and had refrained from mentioning the situation to anyone, including Judy.

She placed a hand on Parker's desk and caught his attention.

"Judy doesn't know, does she?" she said, aware of the tremor in her voice.

He shook his head. "I did what you asked and kept this transaction between you and me. It will stay that way, unless you yourself change it."

She sat back in the chair. A mix of emotions ran through her. She regretted not having confided in her best friend. At the same time, she was glad she hadn't said anything. In her naive innocence, Judy couldn't possibly understand. No, she needed to move on and live the life that had been doled out to her. She'd dumped it all on her parents and had waited, only to have her father's response leave her cold.

"We have to figure out what to do." He'd immediately taken control. "You heard what the boy's parents said. They want you to have an abortion. They know a doctor, and they're willing to pay for it."

Horrified, she burst from the room and ran the three blocks to the Cunningham home, sobbing and pounding on the front door. Mrs. Cunningham came out wearing an apron over her housedress and her hands covered with flour. Judy was right behind her. Adele took one look at Alicia's tear-stained face and waved her daughter back inside. Then, with a comforting arm, she guided Alicia to the wicker swing on the front porch. For the next half-hour, Adele sat quietly listening, with no sign of judgment on her face, while Alicia poured out her story.

"And the boy?" Mrs. Cunningham said.

"Johnny? He's leaving for college when school lets out."

She told Mrs. Cunningham about his parents' suggestion.

"They know a doctor—"

"Oh my. How do you feel about that, Alicia?"

"It frightens me. I told them no. Then they offered to pay all my medical bills if I give up the baby for adoption."

Mrs. Cunningham nodded and clicked her tongue. "So, their son took the easy way out and left you to deal with this by yourself." It was more of a statement than a question.

Alicia bent over, covered her face in her hands, and sobbed her heart out. Mrs. Cunningham stroked her back and mumbled soft words of comfort.

"We all make mistakes," the older woman said. Then she helped her sit up and looked directly into her eyes. "Listen, child. You can't do anything to change what's happened. All you can do now is deal with the situation. In a few months, people are going to notice there's a baby growing inside you. It's not something you'll be able to hide. I don't listen to gossip, but it's a reality. So, you need to start thinking about what you might do when the time comes."

She pulled a handkerchief out of her apron pocket and handed it to Alicia.

"There's one other option," Alicia said, sobbing softly. "My grandparents live on a small farm in the next county. I can go and live with them until the baby comes. I know they'll agree, that is, once they get over the shock. They're old-fashioned people, but they're also kind and good."

"Have you made up your mind about adoption?" Mrs. Cunningham offered. "It makes sense, doesn't it?"

Alicia nodded. "I'm sixteen years old. When the baby comes I'll be seventeen. I'll have another year of high school. My grandparents are too old to help with a baby, and my parents are too ashamed." More sobs erupted and she wept into the handkerchief.

"Why don't we pray about it, Alicia? God will give you the right answer."

They huddled together then, with Mrs. Cunningham calling on the mercy and wisdom of God. She pled for forgiveness and asked him to provide good health for Alicia and the baby—and guidance, she added, so Alicia could make the right decision for herself and for her unborn child.

"Sleep on it," she'd said then. "Take a couple of days, keep praying, and I will too. Then, let me know what you want to do. And remember, Alicia, if you trust God, he will work good out of it."

Several days later, Alicia telephoned Mrs. Cunningham.

"I'm still not sure," she said. "For now, I want to leave Fall River and stay on my grandparents' farm for a while. They're upset, of course, but they agreed to take me until the baby comes. Then they want me to finish my last year of school at the Christian school near their house. That's part of the deal—a Christian education to straighten me out." She let out a sarcastic chuckle. "They also suggested an adoption agency, but I don't want to do that. If I give up my baby, I want it to go to someone I know. Will you help me do that, Mrs. Cunningham? Will you help me find someone who will give my baby a good home?"

The word *good* must have struck a chord with Mrs. Cunningham, for that's when she suggested Pastor Robert Goode and his wife, Jennifer. Alicia knew them from having attended their church. She also sang in the choir, with Jennifer Goode accompanying on the keyboard. She had to admit, the Goodes were the perfect choice. They couldn't have children of their own. Her baby would grow up in a fine, Christian home with decent parents who honored the Lord. And Alicia could get on with her life, knowing her child was being well-cared for.

When school let out for the summer, she said good-bye to Judy Cunningham. Then her parents drove her off to the country. Her grandparents greeted her at the door, frowning and shaking their heads. What else could she expect from two old people who'd grown up in the church? Alicia wept through the entire lecture. Then, apparently satisfied, they wrapped their arms around her and welcomed her into their home.

"It's going to be all right, child," her grandmother said, at last. "You'll eat good food here. Lots of homegrown vegetables. And, when your granddad kills our fatted calf, we'll have enough meat to last us until the baby comes."

They kept their promise to care for her until she delivered. Several weeks before her due date, she contacted Mrs. Cunningham with her final decision to have the Goodes give her child a home.

The moment the Goodes left her hospital room with her baby snuggled in Jennifer's arms she was overcome with a loss that tore at her heart.

Now, ten years later, the memory brought another ache to her core. Mother's instinct took over once again. This time, instead of suppressing it, she reveled in it. She'd come all this way to find out if she could still be a mother. She'd seen her daughter. She was certain of it. That little girl in the playground was the same child she'd given birth to ten years ago. A fresh burst of determination rose up within her. There was no turning back. She wanted her child, and she was going to fight for her. Now Parker Addison was giving her the chance to do that.

He lifted his head from the paperwork she'd sent him. "There's nothing here that binds you to any kind of agreement," he said at last, a smug smile on his lips. "You say you shook hands?"

She nodded, smiling with hopefulness.

"That may have worked in the dark ages, but not today," he said with a chuckle. "Those people made a huge mistake by not getting the deal in writing." He shook his head in disgust. "Christians," he sputtered. "They put everything in God's hands, then they sit back and trust him to work it all out. Like he cares. Will they ever learn?"

At that moment, Alicia endured her first wave of guilt. She thought about Mrs. Cunningham. And the Goodes.

"They're fine people," she said in their defense. "They've obviously done a good job with my daughter. I'm certain I saw her at the school playground today. She appears to be healthy. And happy."

"You're certain it was her?"

"I'm sure of it."

He leaned back in his chair. "Well then. It's merely a matter of presenting our case before a judge. I doubt the Goodes will have any kind of tangible support. I mean, they could show receipts for what they spent on the child from the time they took her home. They could offer doctors' reports on the condition of her health, maybe a letter from her pre-school teacher, perhaps the testimony of friends and family. But, without a legal document, they don't have a leg to stand on. All you need to say is that you wanted them to take care of—what's her name?" He checked the top sheet. "Mindy? That you wanted them to take care of Mindy until you were ready to raise her yourself. Now you're ready."

Alicia left his office with a mix of emotions running through her head. She wanted her baby so much she could hardly breathe. But then another dagger of guilt struck. Like Butch had cautioned, did she really want to destroy so many lives? Especially that innocent child. There was no telling how Mindy might react when she learned the truth.

ROBERT GOODE

Robert Goode stood at his office window that overlooked the children's playground. He looked passed the kids and the teachers and focused his attention on the wrought iron fence that bordered the property. A short while ago, a woman had been standing there watching the children. She was ten years older now, but he recognized her immediately. Anxiety swept through him like an electric current. He clenched his teeth and tensed the muscles in his jaw.

Jennifer entered his office. "I spotted Alicia," he said. "She was right there, behind the fence."

"I know." Jennifer came up beside him. "I was right there next to Mindy, and I couldn't do anything except place my hand on our daughter's shoulder." She shook her head despondently. "Please tell me this isn't happening," she said with a tremor in her voice.

Robert wrapped an arm around her and pulled her close. He knew the signs. She was about to fall apart again, and he didn't know how to prevent it, not when he also was ready to crumble.

"It's gonna be all right, Jen," he said, though he hardly believed it himself. "I talked to Jack Gibbs this morning. He's one of the best lawyers in town. He agreed to do all he can, but he said we need to take on some of the responsibilities."

"Responsibilities? Like what?" Jennifer's eyebrows went up.

"Well, we can run an ad in different newspapers and try to contact Mindy's biological father. We also can notify the grandparents on both sides. I'd be surprised if they want to get involved. Most of all, we can gather as many documents as possible—receipts for what we've spent on Mindy over the years, her health records, her academic reports, that kind of information. We also need to get some of our friends and parishioners to give testimony about our parenting."

Jennifer's brow wrinkled with concern. "Even if Jack keeps the cost down, he does have his own expenses—staff to pay, overhead bills." Jennifer sounded overwhelmed. "And don't forget, there will be court fees. We need to know exactly how much this is going to cost, Rob. And please tell me, how are we going to pay for everything on your salary?"

She slumped into a nearby chair and hung her head.

"It'll be all right, Jen. I'll take out a second mortgage on the parsonage. The property is in my name. I bought it with my own money. We also can clear out our savings account."

"There's not much in it." Jennifer raised her head and stared at him with sad eyes. "What about Mindy's college fund? I don't think we should touch it."

"You're right. It's her money. Whether she's with us or with Alicia."

She brushed a tear from her cheek. "It's hopeless," she whimpered. "Simply hopeless."

"Hey, listen. We have Jack going to bat for us. He's very good."

"Right. But did you see who *her* lawyer is? *Parker Addison.*" She spat out the name. "He's the best in Fall River."

"He's also the most brutal and the least respected attorney in town."

The letter from Alicia's lawyer had stirred up emotions in Robert that he hadn't experienced since his father turned his back on him. Robert thought he'd put away those feelings of animosity, that as a pastor he could forgive and forget, perhaps even love someone who'd hurt him. Now he wasn't sure.

He looked with compassion at his wife. She leaned forward, lowered her head to the desk, and sobbed out her pain. Robert knelt beside her and placed a hand on her shoulder. His heart was breaking for his dear wife. He could handle anything a person did against him. But his wife and daughter? That was another story. Such a threat stirred within him a violence beyond his control. He said a silent prayer for God to help him overcome it.

When Jennifer's sobbing subsided, he rose to his feet and brushed the moisture from his own cheeks. She looked up at him, her eyes moist and pleading.

"We should have demanded an official contract," she moaned. "If we had, we wouldn't be going through this now."

He shook his head. "We couldn't do anything. Don't you remember? That boy and his parents refused to sign." Robert shrugged. "It didn't make sense at the time. They had no interest in the child. They've never tried to see her. Never even sent her a birthday card."

Jennifer nodded at the reminder. "They paid all the medical bills right up to the delivery. Then, they walked away."

"Still, they're her grandparents, Jen. And, don't forget—Alicia's mom and dad behaved just as abominably."

He walked back to the window. The children were lining up to come inside the building. Mindy gave him a wave. He returned the gesture and managed a smile. "I suppose we should be grateful we've had her this long. We got to raise our little girl the way we wanted to, with no interference from meddling grandparents."

"Do you think their lack of interest might help us in court?"

He turned to look at his wife. "Well, it gives us a better chance. What judge would rule in favor of someone who abandoned such a precious little one? Whoever tries our case will hear how we've cared for Mindy, the money we spent on clothes and doctor bills, her current condition—happy, well-adjusted. All of that has to count for *something*."

She pulled a couple tissues from a box on the desk and blew her nose. He knew how these court cases often went. He needed to prepare Jennifer, just in case. He weighed his next words carefully.

"Okay, say we manage to convince the judge that Johnny and all the grandparents have no claim on our child. What do we do about the mother? The courts often find in favor of the mother."

"*I'm* the mother." Jennifer sobbed. "I'm more of a mother to Mindy than that *stranger* is."

She turned up her chin, her lips trembling. He walked to her side, leaned in, and planted a kiss on her cheek. Her salty tears clung to his lips.

"Don't worry, Jen. I won't give up without a fight."

"I wish Mrs. Cunningham were here," Jennifer moaned. "She'd be praying with us right now. Maybe she'd have a talk with that girl. Her daughter, Judy, was best friends with Alicia. Where did she turn when she got in trouble? She went straight to Adele. If Mrs. Cunningham talked her into giving us the child ten years ago, she could also convince her that Mindy is better off with us. Oh, Robert, why did she have to die? We need her. Mindy needs her."

"I imagine a lot of folks still need Mrs. Cunningham," he replied with a grunt. He pursed his lips then, the way he always did when it looked like he was about to start bawling. He couldn't let himself lose control. Not now. Not when his wife needed him to be strong. The loss of Mrs. Cunningham added to his distress and left him wondering how he was going to get through the next couple of days.

Then her image came to mind, like she was standing right there in front of him, like she had done so many times before.

"How I miss that woman," he said aloud.

Jennifer turned her tear-stained face toward his.

"The young people trusted her," he said, remembering. "They flocked to her whenever they needed to discuss something of importance, something they couldn't tell their parents." A wave of guilt swept through him. "Or their pastor," he added, bowing his head. "That woman had a connection with the youth in our church we could only hope to develop one day."

"She prayed for us." Jennifer smiled through a fresh trickle of tears. "She helped us get Mindy. The process went so smoothly, I knew the hand of God was in it." She released a long, shaky breath. "Now look what's happening. I feel so helpless, Rob, like I did years ago when we found out we couldn't have children of our own. Only this is different. This time we have a child that we love more than our own lives, and we may be about to lose her. I'm at a loss what to do."

"Me too. Here I am, the pastor of a church, and Mrs. Cunningham knew more about getting God's attention than I ever learned in seminary." He paused and looked out the window again. The playground was empty. Gray clouds scudded overhead, dragging the last of winter with them. He spun back around. "Let's do that right now, Jen. Let's pray like Mrs. Cunningham did—with our whole heart, trusting God, believing that he will work everything out, and knowing that whatever the outcome, it will be the right thing for all of us."

He helped Jennifer to her feet and took her hand. Jennifer began praying with a passion that tore at Robert's heart. Then, when her words trailed off amidst a fresh flow of tears, he took over and prayed with more fervor than he had in a long time. He tried to speak to God the way Mrs. Cunningham used to, like the Almighty was right there in the room with them, caring, loving, eager to help. He set aside the cold memorized speeches he'd learned in Bible college. He ignored the elaborate phrasing other preachers spouted. Instead, he drew on the Psalms he'd memorized, paraphrased them and allowed them to pull the pain from the depths of his soul. In the end, he left fragments of his broken heart at the feet of the Father, and followed a final "Amen" with a sigh of utter submission. It was up to God now.

Jennifer looked into his eyes and smiled. "I'm not afraid anymore," she said. "Somehow, I believe God will answer our prayer. I don't know how, but I believe He will carry us through this. And no matter what happens—"

Robert nodded, but a stirring of uncertainty gripped his heart. He loved that little girl and doubted he'd survive losing her. There was one more thing he needed to do, one thing they had neglected for the past ten years.

"We need to tell Mindy," he said. "We need to prepare her." He gazed into Jennifer's frightened eyes. "It's time she knew the truth, darling, that she's adopted, but also that we wanted her and still do."

Jennifer shook her head. "I can't." Her voice broke.

"I'll do it," he resolved. "Tomorrow, at the funeral. I'll let her know how Mrs. Cunningham brought her to us, to raise as our own, to love forever."

"Be gentle, Robert."

"I will. I'll make sure she knows her biological mother loved her enough to let her go, and that we love her as if she had been born to us. I have to make her see how much she is loved by all three of us."

Jennifer gave him a kiss and turned to leave. After she departed, he sat at his desk and tried to concentrate on Mrs. Cunningham's eulogy. There was so much to say. How on earth could he reduce all she did in a twenty-minute speech?

He'd known that woman for years. The unique thing was, she didn't push herself on people. They came to her. She didn't walk around poking her head into other people's business. They sought her out. Early on, Adele Cunningham had developed a reputation as a prayer warrior and a woman of godly wisdom. People knew she could keep a confidence and that she would take a sincere interest in whatever was bothering them. He knew of only one time when she forced herself on someone in need. That Powers boy had gotten into so much trouble, everyone expected him to end up in jail. But not Mrs. Cunningham. She went beyond the call when she reached out to that boy.

Poor Sammy. He was doomed from the start. When he was thirteen, he showed up in town one day with his face bruised and blood still dripping out of his nose. No one had to ask him what happened. His father had laid into him again. For years, the old drunk had beat on Sammy's two older brothers. After they went to jail, he turned his rage on young Sammy.

He wasn't surprised when he found out Adele had taken an interest in the boy.

"He's trouble," he warned her.

But, Mrs. Cunningham didn't listen to him. She prayed for Sammy the same way she did for everyone. It didn't matter to her if a person had a million dollars or only the clothes on his back. She treated everybody the same, maybe even went an extra mile for kids like Sammy.

Regardless, Sammy *did* end up the same way as his brothers. He'd been caught robbing the safe at the newspaper office. Robert shook his head at the memory. For some reason, Mrs. Cunningham didn't give up on the boy. Faithful to the end, she made the two-hour drive to the prison a couple times a month. There was no telling what passed between the two of them during those visits.

He scribbled some notes on a yellow pad, crossed out a few lines, then scratched his head. He couldn't concentrate. He wanted to give examples, but he couldn't talk about Sammy. Or about Alicia. One was a worthless convict, the other was a selfish tramp. He startled himself. How could he, a pastor, think so poorly of his sheep? The wayward needed him as much as—or more than—anyone else in his congregation.

He lunged back in his seat. How was he going to say anything spiritual with such negative thoughts running around in his head? He was supposed to be a preacher, the head of a church, an example to his people. Yet here he was, judging, condemning, even hating. Sadly, the prayer he'd said only fifteen minutes before hadn't affected him in the least. He'd meant those words when he said them. So why couldn't he let go?

He set aside the pen and reached for his Bible. Flipping to the middle, he searched for a Psalm that might draw him out of this state of self-righteous condemnation.

His eyes fell on Psalm 51, verse 10: *Create in me a clean heart, O God; and renew a right spirit within me.*

The words of David brought a flood of conviction to Robert's soul, and he had to admit the truth. He'd been rejecting the very people who needed him most. Didn't Jesus say his true followers should feed and clothe the poor and visit those who were in prison? Not once had he gone to see Sammy. Not once did he try to help the young man. Weeks ago Mrs. Cunningham had come to him asking if he'd visit Sammy. He'd agreed half-heartedly. Now he looked forward to fulfilling that promise.

And Alicia? Instead of fearing and resenting her, he should be reaching out. Instead of letting this thing go to court, he should be communicating with her and helping her see that Mindy was better off with him and Jennifer.

He dropped to his knees on the hard wooden floor. "Oh, Lord," he mumbled. "I have allowed myself to succumb to bitterness and self-preservation. Forgive me. Cleanse my heart. Help me love Alicia. She's Mindy's natural mother. I accepted her baby and selfishly ran from that hospital room hoping never to see that girl again. And Sammy? *There but by the grace of God go I.* Isn't that what John Bradford said when a group of prisoners marched past him on their way to their execution? If not for my wealthy parents and the safe path I had followed, I might have settled for the kind of life young Sammy had. Instead of seminary, I, too, might have gone to prison." He wept into his palms and remained there until his knees began to ache.

Then he struggled to his feet and walked to the window. More grayness had settled on the playground. Now deserted of laughing children, the dismal scene increased his feeling of hopelessness. If he couldn't love others as Christ loved him, what use was he as a pastor?

At that moment he realized he needed more than Mrs. Cunningham's prayers and words of wisdom. He needed a change of heart.

TEN

BEN MICHAELS

Ben's plane landed at the international airport in Albany, the state capital. From there, he rented a car and started on the road to his hometown. He'd lived in the South so long, he'd forgotten about the magnificent rolling hills and the spread of farmlands in upstate New York. Not that Florida didn't have hills. He could find a few, if he searched hard enough. But this was different. This landscape had an old-world aura to it, like the terrain in a foreign country where grapevines and apple orchards dominated the scenery. Now he was enjoying the snow-spattered hills, the barns, the silos, the animal pens, even the leafless trees that promised fruit and more greenery in a couple of months.

While enjoying the drive, he tried to erase the last image he had of his wife, standing in the doorway of their home, a pout on her lips. For the first time since they married, her whining and threats had no effect on his plans. He was going to a funeral service to honor the one person who had influenced his life more than anyone else. Nothing could keep him away. Not Candy. Not his coach. Not even little Billy, the joy of his life. In two days, he'd be returning home, and he hoped with all his heart that the place wouldn't be empty.

He'd risked everything in order to make this trip. Mrs. Cunningham had taught him a long time ago that the right thing was the right thing. This one act of strength helped him realize it was time he took charge of his home, time he stood up to Candy, time he showed his son what the head of the household was supposed to look like. Not domineering or cruel, but strong, loving, making the right decisions for everyone involved.

As he drew closer to Fall River, another image came before him and brought a flutter to his heart. He expected to see Elizabeth Adams again. Maybe Candy had a right to be jealous. Elizabeth was one of the most beautiful girls in school. He couldn't help but wonder what she might be like now. Had she changed much in the years since he left home? Did she still have long, black hair that fell past her shoulders almost to her waist? Had she kept her fresh, Ivory soap complexion? Had she gained weight? Lost weight? Stayed the same?

Swallowing, he turned his attention to the passing scenery mottled with patches of snow. The red barns and silos brought back the Sunday drives with his mom and dad, and the stops for ice cream, when he and his sister chose different flavors, then tasted each other's. And the Burma Shave signs with their catchy jingles posted along the side of the highway. A lot of that was gone now. The ice cream shack had been torn down. And in place of the little signs, big billboards had risen up.

As he entered town, he became aware of more changes. The main street had been widened to four lanes, divided by a tree-lined median. The few shops that once bordered the road had given way to a huge shopping mall, a bank building and a gas station. A massive parking lot had encroached on the old sandlot where he used to play ball with his friends. More buildings surrounded it—a large medical complex, a veterinarian's office, a three-story structure containing a bunch of law offices—all of the new structures altering the landscape of what was once a hometown atmosphere but now resembled any other metropolis.

Ben's throat tightened with sadness. He was different now and so was the town where he'd grown up. The next time he came home—if he ever did—Fall River would feel like just another rural village. Now that Mrs. Cunningham was gone, he doubted he'd ever want to come back.

He turned a corner and smiled. One landmark had remained.

The inn at the far edge of town. It sat on the banks of the river where he and Elizabeth used to go swimming in the summer and ice skating in the winter. Ben pulled into the parking lot and went inside. Midway into the lobby he stopped short and gawked at the familiar face behind the desk. Elizabeth Adams. She still had long, ebony hair and dark, haunting eyes. She'd filled out a little, but the additional weight looked good on her.

She looked up and smiled in recognition, her black eyes sparkling the way they used to whenever they met on the street or in the park, like she was glad to see him.

"Why Ben Michaels, what brings you to our fair little town? I thought you'd forgotten all of us by now."

He approached the desk and set his bag on the floor. His heart did a flip-flop, but he managed to conceal his delight.

"Hi, Elizabeth. I'm here for Mrs. Cunningham's funeral." He worked hard to sound nonchalant, but his voice cracked and he found himself blushing.

Her long lashes fluttered over dark, approving eyes. "Of course," she said, smiling. "You look great, by the way."

He chose not to return the compliment.

"You work here?"

She laughed. "You might say that. I own the place."

"Really?"

"Yeah, my husband invested in it shortly after we married."

"I heard you'd gotten divorced," he blurted out, and was immediately sorry.

Her smile vanished. "Funny. I never thought I could say that word. Divorce. But it's a reality, these days. More and more people are getting them. Anyway, my husband—you remember Matt Jenkins?—he got the house and the car and most of the money in our bank account. I got half the bills, this inn, and the right to go back to my maiden name."

"Did you want the inn?"

"Sure. I was the one who ran it. I kept the books. I built up the business, and I added a restaurant. So, I guess it was mine all along."

"Did you have any kids?"

She shook her head and looked down at the inn's log, scribbled something, then came up with a grimace.

"No time for kids, I'm afraid. Matt didn't want any. He was too busy with other interests—you know, building up a real estate portfolio, hunting, fishing—other women—"

She licked her lips. A sadness filled her eyes. She shrugged and went back to the ledger.

"I'm sorry," he said, fully meaning it.

"Hey, that's water under the bridge, as they say." She stared into his eyes with such intensity he nearly fell over.

"So, Ben, can I sign you in?"

"Please."

"I'll give you the best room in the house. It's in the back and overlooks the river."

"Thanks." He didn't know what to say after that. It had been so long since they'd been together. When they dated they never ran out of things to say. But now, in this unexpected meeting for the first time in ages, he was speechless.

"Our food is pretty good," Elizabeth said. "Why don't you join me for dinner tonight?"

Her eyes were hopeful, inviting, two dark pools that took him back to his teenage years when he couldn't resist her steady gaze. He hesitated, then dismissed the warning in his heart. There was no reason he couldn't have dinner with an old friend.

"Sure." He tried to sound nonchalant. "Seven o'clock?"

"Perfect. My evening clerk comes on at five. It'll give me time to freshen up."

Ben checked into his room, set his bag aside, and opened the drapes. As Elizabeth had promised, his room had a view of the river. The scene invoked more memories. There was the old oak tree with a thick branch that extended out over the water. It was strong enough to hold a whole string of kids who lined up on it and dove off the end. One frosty October afternoon the two of them tore off their clothes and headed for that tree in their underwear. Most of their friends had gone off to a weekend camping retreat, so it was just him and Elizabeth. She climbed up ahead of him and leaped into the river with a shriek. He jumped in after her. Once he hit the icy water, he caught his breath, then plunged under the surface, caught her by the ankles and pulled her down. She didn't fight against him, but wrapped her arms around his neck, and they floated back up together, their faces inches apart. She'd pushed him away then and splashed off to another part of the river, with him following in pursuit.

During the summer months, they'd spent many a Sunday afternoon beside that river. Picnics. Playing checkers. Sharing their naive opinions of Pastor Goode's sermons, or discussing the latest Hollywood scandals. Elizabeth looked like a movie star herself, with her wet hair plastered against her suntanned cheeks, her cool dark eyes inviting him to sit closer. One time, she grasped his fingers and pressed them to her lips.

A lump rose to his throat. *Why didn't she wait? Why did she have to go and marry that awful man? I told her I'd be back. Didn't I?*

Then the truth struck him like a bolt of lightning. He was the one who left. He was the one who stopped writing.

He turned his back on the window and left all those memories there. No sense drumming up the past. He couldn't retrieve it, nor did he want to.

He still had four hours to kill before dinner. He grabbed his overcoat and left the inn, jumped back in the rental car and took a drive around town. After cruising the main street, he turned off a side road and pulled up in front of Adele Cunningham's house. Several cars blocked the driveway and a few more were parked along the curb. The light was on in the front room. Shadows passed back and forth. A lot of activity was going on inside.

They're getting ready for tomorrow. The funeral. The reception. The realization plunged Ben into a wave of sadness.

He considered going inside and offering his help, but thought better of it. He was a celebrity these days. He didn't want all those women gushing over him, not now, not while the focus should be on Mrs. Cunningham. He turned off the motor, reclined his seat, and journeyed back to the last day he visited her, right there on her front porch.

She was sitting in a wicker chair, her blond and silver hair curling about her face like a picture frame. As always, she had a glint in her eyes and a smile on her lips.

"Now, remember what I told you, Ben," she said. "God has blessed you beyond your wildest dreams. Don't disappoint Him. Make right choices. You're going to encounter a lot of temptation when you get to the top. Be ready for it. Take it slow. And pray about everything."

He'd laughed. *Get to the top?* Back then, he couldn't even imagine getting to first base.

"I'm not there yet, Mrs. Cunningham," he told her. "This is the first step—the minor leagues. I've got a long way to go. I don't want to disappoint you, but I may never make it to the top."

She'd narrowed her eyes, but her lips were smiling. "You've shown everyone in this little town what people can do if they set their minds to it. You did that, Ben. You had everything against you—the accident, your injuries. You got started late in baseball, but you made it. Don't you know? To all of us, you're a hero."

He'd never thought of himself as a hero. When he looked in the mirror, he still saw a scruffy little boy who walked with a limp. Back then, he stood behind the chain-link fence during the games, until Mrs. Cunningham got a hold of him and insisted he get out there with the other guys. She prayed for him and convinced him he could accomplish great things. She'd even called him a hero. In his opinion, *she* was the hero, and *he* was the one she had rescued.

He closed his eyes. Mrs. Cunningham's image grew larger, clearer. She'd prayed over him on his last day in town. He'd knelt before her and she'd placed both hands on his head. It was like a biblical anointing. With kind words she sent him out into the world on a mission of his own.

"I'm so proud of you, Ben. Do well in your sport and in your choices, and always remember the Lord who bought you and saved you and gave you a second chance."

What if she could see him now? His marriage in trouble, a little boy in the midst, and Elizabeth Adams on his mind.

A tapping on the window drew him upright. Mrs. Cunningham's daughter, Judy, stood on the curb, a smile on her lips and her eyebrows raised in welcome. He rolled down the window.

"Are you gonna sit there all day, or are you coming into the house?"

He flushed, then regained his composure. "I didn't want to disturb you." He nodded toward the picture window. "It looks like you have a lot going on in there."

"We do, but we can always use an extra hand. Paul's here. He's setting up chairs and tables for tomorrow's reception. Wanna help?"

"Well, I guess I can do *that*."

He got out of the car and gave Judy one of those embraces where both parties pat each other's back to let the other one know it's merely a friendship. They walked together to the house. The ladies looked at him with awe on their faces. A pro baseball player was standing in their midst, and they weren't sure how to act. After a few awkward greetings, everyone got back to what they were doing. Ben spent the better part of the afternoon helping Judy's brother, Paul, and a couple other guys arrange the furniture in the main part of the house. Of course their conversation immediately turned to sports.

By the time he got back to the inn he needed a shower. With a sigh, he stood under the hot spray, glad to have a few minutes to himself before meeting Elizabeth for dinner. A slow disturbance of butterflies began to gather in his stomach. How absurd that a grown man should feel like a teenager getting ready for the prom.

He'd gone with Elizabeth, proud to have the raven-haired

beauty on his arm. Her free spirit also had set her apart from other girls. How sad if an unhappy marriage had destroyed it. Come to think of it, how in the world did her marriage fail? He dispelled the thought with a shake of his head. *It couldn't have been her fault. Didn't she say her husband was a cheat?*

Ben spent the next fifteen minutes in front of the bathroom mirror, grooming, tweezing, shaving, combing, and slapping cologne on his face and neck, aware that his heartbeat had quickened and his palms were sweating.

He arrived at the restaurant ten minutes early. Elizabeth was already there, standing in the doorway, chatting with the hostess. She looked up at him, and his heart leapt. She was stunning in a gray ankle-length skirt and a black tight-fitting jersey top, cinched at the waste with a wide belt. She wore a little jewelry—a pair of gold earrings and a matching chain that drooped to her cleavage. Ben reminded himself he wasn't seventeen anymore. He swallowed nervously and stepped toward her.

Their table was ready, complete with a bottle of champagne and a basket of hot orange biscuits.

He looked up from the menu at the woman across the table. Elizabeth hadn't lost her bubbly charm. The failed marriage hadn't broken her, after all. She gazed back at him, her dark eyes like two pools of chocolate. On the table a flickering candle painted color in her cheeks, and she sat erect in her chair, poised and apparently happy about the reunion.

He was certain his brain had shipped off to another country. He couldn't think of the right thing to say, how to even start a conversation with this woman. The truth was, his former girl-friend had turned into a stranger.

"So," she said, her dark eyes reflecting the flame on the table. "Tell me what you've been doing all these years."

"Well. You know the first part, when I went with the minor league team."

"Yes, you wrote once a week in the beginning." Her smile faded and she stiffened. "Then your letters tapered off. I guess you got busy with all that training and the games and everything. I followed your career for a while. Then you made that giant leap into the majors, and you stopped writing."

There was a sadness in her tone that brought a twinge of guilt to his heart. He struggled for the right words, needed to keep their conversation light.

"Yeah, it was like a tornado picked me up and set me on higher ground," he said, chuckling. "It took a long time for me to adjust to all the changes in my life." He frowned then and softened his voice. "I'm sorry I got so lax about writing."

She sat back in her chair. Her eyes rested on him, waiting. An awkward silence fell over their table.

"Don't forget, your letters tapered off too," he said, at last. "I figured something was up. Then my sister wrote and told me you were dating someone. I thought it was best to leave you alone, you know, with all I had to do, and not being ready to settle down. Then, all of a sudden, you got married. I guess you got tired of waiting."

"I had to let you go, Ben. You had entered a different life. Anyway, I'm not sure I could handle the limelight and all the publicity that follows those sports figures around."

He leaned toward her. "I wanted you with me, Liz. It's just— the timing was bad." He dropped back against the chair. "I messed up, didn't I?"

"Maybe not. You got married too."

He nodded.

"It was no secret," she said. "The last thing your sister told me, before she moved away, was that you had a little boy. He must be about five years old now."

"That's right. He turned five last month. Billy. His name's Billy."

"Got any pictures?" Her eyebrows went up.

"Not a problem." Grateful for the diversion, Ben pulled out his wallet and flipped it open. He tried to bypass Candy's photo, but he wasn't fast enough. Elizabeth leaned toward him to get a better look.

"Your wife?"

"Yep. That's Candy."

"She's beautiful."

"She knows it." He drew back and shook his head. "Sorry."

Elizabeth bit her lip, then peered at his wallet as he flipped to side-by-side photos of his son, one when he was a newborn, the other from his fifth birthday party.

"He's a doll," she said. "You must be proud of him."

"I am. He's already showing signs of being a pro pitcher. You should see him throw a tennis ball for his dog to chase. He's got a powerful arm, even puts spin on the ball. And he's a good boy, never gives me a minute of trouble. He's—"

He stopped short, aware that he'd started rambling. He'd never been that nervous on the pitcher's mound. How on earth had he allowed himself to fall into such a state?

He looked around the restaurant. Aside from a roomful of strangers, he recognized a few of the townsfolk. They smiled in recognition, nodded politely at him, and went back to their meals.

"Shouldn't we order?" he said, turning his attention back to the menu.

"Nope. I took the liberty of ordering our food before you came in."

He looked back at her in a mix of surprise and puzzlement.

She grinned. "Prime rib, fixed medium rare, with a baked potato, plenty of sour cream, and buttered green beans. Am I right?"

Her recitation of his favorite meal brought a smile to his face. After all these years, she wanted him to know she hadn't forgotten. He began to relax.

The rest of their meal had Ben cutting man-size bites of meat, shoveling the vegetables into his mouth, and washing it all down with sips of champagne and gulps of water. Elizabeth had a chef's salad. She picked at her food and never took her eyes off of him.

Afterward, they donned their coats and took a walk on the grounds. Elizabeth pointed out the changes she'd made to the gardens, the addition of a gazebo, and a playground for the children of guests. The setting sun bathed her face in gold and painted a rosy blush on her cheeks.

"Care to take a dip in the river?" she said, a glint in her eye.

He balked. "It's the middle of February."

"So? Did that ever stop us before?"

In a split second, he forgot Mrs. Cunningham's words of caution. He forgot about Candy. He even forgot about Billy. Standing before him was the girl he'd left behind, beckoning him to join her for a swim in the river.

No problem, he decided. But what about the persistent thumping in his heart? And what about all the champagne he'd drunk at dinner? He shrugged.

It's a harmless dip in the river, that's all. Should be fun.

ELEVEN

Frank Peebles

Getting back home generated a whole mess of memories for Frank Peebles. Half awake in his hotel room, he lay on the bed and tried to imagine how different things might have turned out if he'd stayed with George, if he hadn't taken a chunk of their business and moved to a more promising part of New York State, and then, a few years later, transferred all his holdings to Dallas, Texas. In the beginning, just the two of them were the sole owners. No stock holders, no board of directors to trample on their decisions. It was just the two of them, meeting over coffee or discussing their next project while fly-fishing on the river. How he missed those days. How he missed George.

In the beginning it seemed like a good idea, but within three months of settling in Dallas, he could see he'd made a huge mistake. He had landed in unfamiliar territory. His board of directors consisted of overbearing cowpunchers and money-hungry oil drillers. The day he settled into his new office he lost complete control of the company. Those investors swept in like a hurricane. Now he'd turned into one of their cattle, driven to the brink of exhaustion by their incessant demands.

How did all that happen? he brooded. *I spent years building up a business that lots of folks expected to fail. I went against my best friend, set out on my own, ignored the naysayers, and did exactly what I wanted.*

Sure, the business had prospered. But he'd made a huge mistake when he invited investors in. How foolish to assume he'd hang onto most of the stock. But, things had gotten away from him. For one thing, his wife's spending had left him no choice but to sell off a few shares here and a few more there, until one day, he looked at the books and discovered his control of the business had dropped to about a third. The board took ownership and made him CEO, a mere figurehead, a puppet tied to strings wielded by a group of idiots who didn't know the first thing about the plastics industry.

With that kind of pressure, Frank had developed ulcers, high blood pressure, and heart palpitations. Meanwhile, Daphne was never satisfied. She wanted a bigger, more expensive house and a car with all the latest gadgets. She'd purchased so many clothes, shoes, and handbags, he'd ended up moving his own clothes to a closet in one of the spare bedrooms. Had to, if he wanted to keep his suits from wrinkling.

To add to Frank's troubles, the board was constantly breathing down his neck for one thing or another. Either the budget didn't balance to their liking, or the plant had fallen behind in production, or his supervisor had let a shipment go out before it had been checked for flaws. The responsibility always fell on him. After a restless night, he'd awaken to more problems. He usually buried his face back in his pillow, not wanting to face another grueling day at work.

But today he was back in Fall River, and for the first time in years, he didn't mind getting up at the break of dawn. He opened his eyes to a sliver of gray sneaking into his hotel room at one side of the patio curtains, and he smiled. He was miles away from assembly line problems, workers' complaints, and the board's annoying interruptions. He felt free. He could go where he wanted to go, do what he wanted to do, and eat what he wanted to eat.

He sat up in bed and began to plan his day. First, breakfast at Dino's Diner, if it was still there. No more of that bland cereal and soy milk Daphne forced on him every morning, or the insipid, salt-free chicken soup she insisted he eat twice a week. Today, he'd pick his favorites from the menu—crisp bacon, a pile of pancakes slathered in butter and real maple syrup, scrambled eggs, home-fries, and strong black coffee. Yes sir, a man-sized breakfast, comfort food to put meat on his bones.

He found the diner exactly as it had been years ago, filled with an assortment of early risers—businessmen on their way to work, several lumberjacks in wool jackets, and a couple of truck drivers who'd left their rigs at the edge of town. After finishing a breakfast that left him burping and pressing his knuckles against his diaphragm, Frank stopped at the drug store and purchased a pack of antacids. Then he went to the river and arranged to rent a rowboat for the day after the funeral, plus a rod and reel. He figured if he paid for it all in advance, he could head out there the minute he fell out of bed.

He paid the fee and handed the surprised dock man a generous tip, then took a stroll through town and checked out some of his former haunts—the general store where he and George used to buy their fishing gear, the Bait Shop where he could load up on lures for catfish and river trout, then Gabe's Cigar Store, where the old cronies used to congregate with their smokes and their wild stories.

One might assume Frank was trying to relive the past. He didn't care. Maybe that's exactly what he was trying to do, reach back in time and re-experience some of his favorite memories, *the good ol' days*, as people often referred to them. In spite of all his success, his healthy bank account, and his thriving business, he missed that time in his life, the carefree, devil-may-care moments, when he and his best buddy, George Cunningham, shared their wildest dreams while fishing on the river. It was during one of those lazy mornings, when they lay back against the inside of a row boat, their lines dangling in the water, that they concocted their plan to open a plastics business. A week later, they pooled their resources. The project took off the first day they opened their doors, and it didn't slow down until Frank divided their assets and ran off with a big chunk of the business, including more than half their workers.

A dagger of guilt pierced his heart. He shrugged it away and set his mind on more pleasant thoughts. He preferred to reminisce over the positive moments in his life and forget about the mistakes he'd made.

Tomorrow, he'd attend Adele's funeral. For her sake, he could put up with the angry stares from her son and daughter and maybe from lots of other folks who hadn't forgotten how he jilted his best friend. All he knew was, Adele Cunningham had forgiven him, and that was good enough for him. In her graciousness, that woman had shown him the true meaning of Christianity, that there was no place for grudge-holding in a Christian's life, and that no one had the right to judge anyone else.

That was a mere fraction of what Adele Cunningham had taught him. She also had shown him how to pray for someone with heartfelt sincerity. She had done that for him the day they stood together, far from the crowd at George's gravesite. To this day, he hadn't forgotten how she'd placed a hand on his shoulder and, even in her grief, she uttered a prayer on *his* behalf.

Her kind words had impacted Frank in a way he never expected.

"Heavenly Father," she'd said. *"Let Frank understand that George and I never held a grudge toward him. Whenever my husband mentioned Frank Peebles' name, it was always with admiration in his voice. George never wished Frank any harm, and he made it a point to pray for him on a regular basis. Most of all, help Frank see that the same Jesus who moved us to love and forgive him can also show him how to love and forgive others. Bless him, Lord, and allow him to prosper beyond his wildest dreams."*

Even now, as he strolled around his hometown, Adele's prayer came back to him, word-for-word. He'd written it down—as much of it as he could remember—and had tucked it in his wallet along with George's memorial card.

Now he'd come back for another funeral. Adele's. He pulled the frayed slip of paper out of his wallet, unfolded it, and read her words again. How he wished he had fully grasped her message the first time. To think that she'd expected him to forgive others the way she had forgiven him. In his mind, lots of people deserved his wrath—his clients, pestering him for their orders. His employees, taking their dear old time to complete a simple job. His board of directors, pressuring him to fix all the things that went wrong. Oh yes, and his wife, nagging the heck out of him. He couldn't imagine loving and forgiving all those people the way Mrs. Cunningham had done. She was unlike anyone he'd ever known.

He made a slow tour of the village and ended up at Gabe's Cigar Store. Sure enough, a circle of old cronies were sitting in a cloud of smoke in a corner, puffing on cigars and gossiping about who-knows-what. Frank didn't know or care. He stayed with them through one cigar, then, bored to tears, he said his farewells and headed out the door. He was a total stranger in his own hometown. If only Mrs. Cunningham were still alive, he'd head straight for her front porch for one of their chats. But he'd let those opportunities slip right past him, and now he wished with all his heart that he'd stayed with George, settled for the good life, and put family over fame and fortune, like his best friend had done.

Frank spent the rest of the day in a rented sedan, driving around town, allowing the familiar places to bring back memories. For years he had put Fall River and all its hometown trappings at the back of his mind. Now he was reminiscing, and it felt good.

Plunging further into the past, he headed straight for the property he and George had purchased years ago and the old barn they'd converted into a warehouse. He laughed out loud. What a ramshackle building it was. Weathered boards, a leaky roof, and floors that buckled under his boots. But it served its purpose in those early days of their business. Their first crew was as ill-equipped as the building. A bunch of high school graduates who didn't know a screwdriver from a butter knife. But he trained them well and they worked out fine.

The old barn has been gone for years. The two of them tore it down and built a larger factory in its place. He gazed at the structure and hardly recognized it. Though still in operation, another name graced the front—Bleeker and Sons, Auto Detailing and Repair Services. Lights glowed yellow behind the row of windows set high on the wall. The double garage doors were raised and a loud whirring noise poured from somewhere inside. It sounded like someone was grinding metal. Frank shook his head. Sure was a far cry from putting out a sleek new piece of plastic.

So, the business had changed hands. No more plastics. The smell of melting synthetics had been supplanted by the odor of grease and oil. Frank screwed up his mouth in disgust. Adele must have sold the plant after George died. Whoever took it over didn't know a thing about manufacturing plastics. Instead of keeping a lucrative business going, a bunch of grease monkeys had set up shop there. He could picture a beat up old jalopy going through some sort of transformation, hardly worth the effort or the expense.

He sat in his car for a while and recalled the first time he and George stepped foot on that property. George wanted to pray over it. Frank closed his eyes, but his friend's prayer went in one ear and out the other. He was busy counting the money the two of them were going to make.

As nostalgia turned to sadness, Frank started up his rental car and pulled away from the site. It was better not to dwell on that period in his life. Too many sorrowful memories. Too many regrets.

He headed into town and cruised down Main Street. The scene had changed a bit. He began to imagine how different his life might have been if he had stayed in that miserable Podunk town, like George had. If he'd been content with a measly few thousand dollars a month, he'd have had time to go fishing on the weekends. And what if he'd accepted George's invitations to go to church with him every Sunday? What if he'd settled down, like his best friend had, raised a family, read the Bible instead of all those business magazines that changed a person's goals from one month to the next? Try as he might, he couldn't imagine such a boring lifestyle, tempting as it was.

Without planning it, he ended up driving past the Cunningham house, slowed the car a bit and came to a stop out front. A lot of activity was going on inside those walls. Shadows moved past the picture window and he imagined the family and friends were setting up for a get-together after the funeral tomorrow.

He would have liked to go inside, would have wanted to tell Paul and Judy how sorry he was. *Sorry for what?* they might say. Then he'd have to go into a long-winded explanation about why he split the business so many years ago. *They were kids back then. Wouldn't make no difference to them.* He flicked a tear away from his eye. Then, he put the car in gear and drove away.

TWELVE

BRENDA SCHWARTZ

Brenda paced back-and-forth in her bedroom. It was the same bedroom where she'd spent many lonely hours as a teenager. Her parents had willed the house to her before they died. She'd settled into it as a single lady, aware that people had begun to refer to her as *an old maid*. How unfair. Single men were called *bachelors* no matter what age they were. But once a woman passed a certain age—and only God knows what age that must be to deserve the title *old maid*—she'd accepted the inevitable. She would never marry.

She stopped pacing and looked out the window. More than 40 years ago, she'd sat on this same window seat, hoping to catch a glimpse of George Cunningham. Most of the time, he scurried past her house and headed for Adele Baker's home next door. They'd become a couple, and Brenda had remained in her bedroom nursing a broken heart.

Time passed. Her boyfriend Arthur was gone. So was George. Now it was Adele's turn. Her memorial service had been set for tomorrow. The church will fill up with people who loved and respected that woman. Even in death Adele Cunningham had taken center stage.

She backed away from the window and went to her cedar chest. *Ha! Cedar chest? In my day we called them hope chests.* Every teenage girl received one when she graduated from high school. They held everything a young woman needed to set up house. Bed linens, tablecloths, kitchen gadgets, everyday china, towels, and other frills and extravagances to make a young girl's heart leap for joy. Most of her friends got to use those items within two years after graduation. Some took a little longer. They first went off to college or took jobs in other cities. But, eventually, the majority of the girls she'd grown up with had husbands and, in many cases, children.

Adele Baker was among the first to marry. Brenda stayed as far away from the church as she could that day. She couldn't bear the thought of George Cunningham waiting at the altar for his bride and Adele looking dazzling in her white gown. Instead of attending their wedding, Brenda took a drive in the country. She cried so hard she couldn't see the road and had to pull off the highway until she finished sobbing. No one missed her. No one asked why she wasn't there. They knew why. It was no secret that Brenda disliked Adele Baker.

And so, the dream of a family never came true for Brenda. When Arthur died in Korea, her dream of marrying and having children was shattered for the second time. In her grief, she emptied her hope chest and gave everything to charity. Then she began to fill it with knitted scarves, appliquéd quilts, and embroidered pillowcases and towels—plus plenty of fabrics, yarns, and notions, so she could make more of those creations. She also added a bunch of silk flowers, coils of ribbons in a rainbow of colors, yards of lace, and a huge bundle of floss.

Now she pressed the release button and popped the lid. A burst of color greeted her. It looked like the inventory of a sewing shop. There was enough of an assortment to make something nice for Adele's memorial service. After all, it was the least she could do.

She reached in and sorted through the items, pulled out several silk flowers in different colors, laid them on her bed, and went back for ribbons and ties. A delicate lace streamer caught her eye. *Perfect,* she thought as she held it up to the light.

Next, she retrieved a pair of scissors and a packet of straight pins from her sewing drawer. She sat on the edge of her bed beneath the overhead light and worked well into the afternoon. When she finished, she placed the large, multi-colored bouquet of silk flowers inside a crystal vase, stepped back and admired her handiwork. It was one of the most beautiful flower arrangements she'd ever made. But, something was missing. *Yes.* She returned to her cedar chest and came back with a bright red rose, which she inserted down the middle of the arrangement. *Adele's favorite color.*

She looked at her watch. Three-thirty. Pastor Goode always locked the doors of the church at four o'clock. There was still time to deliver the arrangement.

She donned her wool coat and scarf, and, with her purse in one hand and the vase in the other, she hurried out of the house to her car.

When she walked through the front door of the church, Pastor Goode was coming down the aisle with a bunch of keys in his hand.

"Why, Brenda, what brings you here today?"

He spotted the flower arrangement in her hand and smiled. "How lovely."

She hesitated. More than anyone else, Pastor Goode knew how much Brenda resented Adele. Hadn't she complained to him when he put Adele in charge of the church picnic? Hadn't she made a fuss when Adele got to sing the solo for the Easter pageant. And after Adele and George announced their engagement, hadn't Brenda poured out her heart to that man of God? If anyone had been aware of her bitterness, it was Pastor Goode, yet he never openly judged her for it.

A wave of discomfort rose inside her. She forced a smile.

"What is it, dear? Is everything all right?" His brow wrinkled with sincere concern.

"I–I wanted to do something nice for Adele—I mean, for her service. I put together this flower arrangement." She took a breath and tried to stop stammering. "I don't know, maybe it wasn't the right thing to do." Embarrassed, she started to turn away.

Pastor Goode gently grabbed her arm and reached for the bouquet.

"Brenda, this is beautiful. Just beautiful," he said. "You created this yourself?"

She nodded and released the vase into his hands.

"Why, I don't think a professional florist could have done a better job," he said, still eyeing the arrangement with admiration.

She shrugged. "It's a little gesture of good will."

"And a fine gesture it is," he said. "Tell you what, why don't we take this right up front and place it in a central spot on Adele's table of memories?"

With halting steps, Brenda followed Pastor Goode to the front of the church. Her heart beat with joy as he placed her flower arrangement in the center amidst a huge display of photos and awards.

"You know," Pastor Goode said, turning around to face her. "We could use more of these fine creations of yours. Except for our stained-glass windows, we don't see much color in here. The pews are plain wood. The altar is always covered with white linens. The gray carpet looks lifeless and threadbare. With your creative talent, you might be able to brighten things up in here."

Brenda tilted her head and gave him a half-smile. "Do you want a couple more of these?" she offered.

"More than a couple. How do you feel about making us several of your magnificent arrangements?" he said, his eyes twinkling. "We can place them at different locations throughout the sanctuary. And to be honest, the nursery and children's room can use some color to stimulate those little minds."

Her mind was already racing ahead with some ideas of her own. She'd made several wall hangings in brilliant colors. Some of them had animals embroidered on them.

"I have plenty of homemade crafts to donate," she offered.

"Of course we'll pay you out of our church maintenance budget."

Brenda smiled and shook her head. "I'd be honored to do it. For free."

He frowned in puzzlement. "Really? For free?"

"Of course. I'll consider it my ministry."

"Well then, it's settled," he said. "You come to my office next Monday morning, and we'll get you started."

He wrapped an arm around Brenda's shoulder and guided her toward the exit. "This is wonderful," he said as they walked. "If I remember correctly, you were quite good with a needle and thread. I'm looking forward to seeing what you can do for us."

Brenda left the church with a smile on her lips. As she walked down the church stairway, she heard the front door latch behind her. She paused and turned. *The church. Of course.* At this stage of her life, her talent had purpose again. She continued down the steps, reached the sidewalk, and walked toward the parking lot, her step lighter, her shoulders back, her chin raised. Wasn't this all she'd ever wanted, to be useful and appreciated? Such a project might also fill the void that even George Cunningham hadn't satisfied? Funny, Adele was gone now. Brenda no longer had to stand in the shadows and watch that woman receive another prize. It was her turn to shine.

Yet, ironically, this opportunity had come to her *because* of Adele Cunningham. Even in death, the woman had invited Brenda into the limelight. She had to admit, Adele Cunningham had never really posed a threat to her.

She reached for the door handle of her car, but froze and looked back at the church. A shiver went through her. For some reason, she had a sudden image of Adele Cunningham smiling down on her from heaven.

THIRTEEN

Sammy Powers

Y ou doin' all right, son?"

Even in the black loneliness of solitary confinement, Sammy Powers knew the voice. Tyrone Jackson was standing in the hall, inches away from the iron door that separated him from the rest of the compound. Tyrone was one of the few guards who had shown compassion toward the prisoners. He'd taken a special interest in Sammy.

In time, they'd developed a friendship, albeit a strange friendship—a black prison guard and a white inmate.

"We've got more in common than you think," Tyrone had told him. "I took a peek at your file the other day. The horrible stuff about your brothers. The trouble in your home. That unstable environment you growed up in. I can relate, Sammy. My own growin' up years were a lot like yours."

"Your father beat you?"

"Ha! Beat me? It's a wonder there's anything left. I used-ta get so many bruises, the kids at school started expecting me to show up lookin' all battered. If I didn't have a black eye or a bruise on my arm, they thought somethin' had gone wrong at my house, like my daddy had left us or maybe he'd been dragged off to jail."

Sammy had looked Tyrone in the eye, peering at him between those iron bars, and he knew the man was telling the truth. Of all the men in his pod, guards and prisoners alike, no one understood him. He was relieved to find out Tyrone did. And it wasn't only about the beatings. Like Sammy, Tyrone had two older brothers who'd gotten in one scrape with the law after another. They were both in prison for another ten years.

"How did you manage to keep from following in your brothers' footsteps?" Sammy asked him one day.

"I simply made up my mind I didn't want that kind of life," Tyrone said. "Don't get me wrong, Sammy. I loved my brothers. Still do. But, I didn't want to go the way they done—breakin' into stores in the middle of the night, robbin' people on the street. When I think back, the truth was, they never got away with nothin'. They always got caught. You'd think they'd-a learned somethin' from it, right?"

Sammy reflected on his own past. His two brothers had fallen into crime, yet he'd blindly looked up to them. Why hadn't he seen the truth the way Tyrone had? Why didn't he break the mold too? It wasn't that he didn't want to. He didn't know how.

"So, what did you do?" Sammy asked him. "How did you change your life? I mean, look at you. You're wearing a uniform. You're a prison guard. You must-a done somethin' right. Who set you straight? Your mother?"

"Nah. She was like yours. She drowned her problems in a bottle o' wine. Every day." He paused then and drew closer to the bars. "No, Sammy. It was my Aunt Mimmi who got a hold of me and made me get serious about my life. The first thing she did was help me through my schoolwork. If I had trouble with a subject—usually it was math—she'd come over to the house after she finished her job at the laundromat, and she'd go over the problems with me until bedtime. Then, she'd tuck me in, say a prayer over me, and sing one of her spiritual hymns before she left. My Aunt Mimmi talked to me every day—either face-to-face or over the phone. She told me she was still prayin' for me, even when I wasn't around her." Tyrone laughed. "That woman pestered God about me day and night, constantly beggin' him to keep me straight. If it weren't for my Aunt Mimmi, I'd be on the other side of those bars with you."

"I know someone like your Aunt Mimmi," Sammy confessed.

"There's a woman in my hometown, Mrs. Cunningham—just a friend, but maybe more than that. She prayed with me, talked to me, even helped me get a decent job at the local newspaper. I was doin' great, until one day temptation got the best o' me. I stole from my boss, the same guy who'd given me a break. So, here I am, payin' the price for my stupidity. If I'd-a listened to Mrs. Cunningham, if I'd-a just done my job and kept my hands to myself, I'd be movin' up the corporate ladder right now."

"Really?"

Sammy shrugged and laughed. "Well, maybe not the *corporate* ladder. Maybe more like the ladder of faithful employees who keep gettin' a raise. It's sad, Tyrone. My boss seemed to like me. I feel bad about what I did. I destroyed his trust, lost my job, and threw away my one good chance for a new start in life. Plus, I disappointed the only person who believed in me."

Sammy was uncomfortably aware that his cell mate had been listening to their conversation. But when he turned to look, he was surprised to see the guy perched on the edge of his bunk, his hands folded on top of his knees and his head bowed. Later, the two of them talked, something they hadn't done since they were thrown in there together. The other guy broke down in tears and admitted that he had fallen away from his faith. He, too, had gotten in trouble, and he, too, regretted it.

"When I get out of here, I'm gonna go home, make up with my mom, and start fresh," his cell mate vowed. "And, I'm gonna go back to church. You should do that too, Sammy."

From that day on, Sammy and Tyrone had regular conversations. Now the guard had even come to see him while he was in solitary confinement. He might have spent the time completely alone if Tyrone hadn't been the one to bring him a tray of food.

The big man's shadow filled the tiny opening near the top of the door. He slid the tray in the slot that was barely big enough to pass the food through.

""I saw the newspaper obit on your bunk. I'm sorry about—you know—about your loss," Tyrone said, his voice conveying a tenderness that could only come from a friend.

Sammy drew close to the door. "She was the one I told you about, the lady who prayed for me, like your aunt did." He received the tray and carried it to the lumpy mattress where he'd spent the night. He set it aside, unable to eat anything with Mrs. Cunningham's death on his mind.

"She must-a meant a lot to you."

"She cared. It was obvious. And I–I loved her, Tyrone. Not in a romantic way. She was more like a mother to me than that lush I lived with all my life. This lady was kind, and godly. I didn't deserve to walk on the same side of the street with her."

Tyrone smiled. "I read her obituary. She sure had a long list of accomplishments."

Sammy's throat tightened. His eyes filled up. He blinked several times, spilling a river of tears down his cheeks.

Tyrone's eyes were peering at him through the six-inch opening. "Hey, pal. I know how you feel. The day my Aunt Mimmi died, I fell apart too. It was a huge loss for me."

"Did you go to her funeral?"

"Of course, I wouldn't have missed it for the world."

"Then, you gotta know how I feel. I need to go home—to be there for Mrs. Cunningham. I need to go to her memorial service and pay my respects."

Tyrone's tender eyes delivered a message of true sympathy. "That's such a shame, Sammy. The obituary said the service is tomorrow."

"Right," Sammy said. "You see how it is." He extended his arms, taking in the entire cell. "I'm stuck here, stuck in this hole, with no hope of getting out, even for a couple of hours to attend my friend's funeral."

"They don't do that here. Once you're in, you serve your time, and they don't make no allowances. No time off to go to funerals or weddings or even the bedside of a sick old grandfather."

Sammy bowed his head and swiped away more tears.

The guard in the hall cleared his throat, a signal to the two of them that they weren't supposed to be visiting.

Tyrone let out a disturbed sigh. "I have to go, or we'll both be in trouble."

Sammy nodded in surrender.

"Tell ya what," the big man said. "How about if I make that call for you?"

Sammy raised his head and stared into Tyrone's eyes.

"You–you would do that for me?"

"Why sure. Your hometown is only a couple hours drive from here. In fact, I live in that general direction. Listen. I get off my shift at 7 a.m. It won't cost me nothin' to go out there, spend an hour or two and let the family know I came on your behalf."

Sammy bit his lip as he contemplated the possibility. The first surge of hope he'd had in weeks filled his heart. Except for Mrs. Cunningham, no one else had cared enough to step foot in that jail on his behalf. No one had prayed for him like she did. Even after he got arrested, she didn't stop praying and talking and pounding it in his head that it wasn't too late to change his life.

"Yes," he said, brightening. "If you do that, Tyrone, it'll be the next best thing to my being there."

"You've got it, pal. Don't you worry about a thing. When I step inside that church, I'm gonna let them know I'm there representing Sammy Powers."

After Tyrone left, Sammy sat on his cot and slid back against the wall. He smiled as though he'd just won the New York State lottery. He wasn't all alone in the world, after all. He had a friend. Tyrone. He reached for his tray and started picking at his food. He had a lot to think about while he ate. A whole bunch of memories from his conversations with Mrs. Cunningham. Lectures he could still learn from. Maybe he could turn his life around after all. Maybe he could still make her proud of him.

THE DAY OF THE FUNERAL

FOURTEEN

JUDY CUNNINGHAM

The service had drawn a large crowd of townsfolk, many of them church members, plus an enormous number of people Judy didn't know. Some must have come great distances to pay their respects to her mother.

If Judy had been in charge, it would have been a simple service, a quiet gathering of family and close friends. But Aunt Connie had jumped in like a whirlwind and arranged everything, including mournful hymns and Bible readings and altar decorations.

Judy regretted that she hadn't stepped in and planned things the way her mother wanted it done, with joyful music by some of her favorite recording artists and with everyone wearing bright colors.

"People should go out happy," her mother had insisted. "When I die, I want a party. Let everybody wear red or yellow. Black is too depressing."

But Aunt Connie was old school. She insisted a funeral needed to be—well—respectful—*stodgy* in Judy's mind. To Aunt Connie, it was all about the loss, not about Adele's new home in heaven and the rewards she was likely receiving. It was about the death of a loved one, not about the life that had touched numerous people, as could be seen from the crowd that showed up.

Connie also had insisted on opening up the pulpit to anyone who wanted to share something about her departed sister. It turned out to be the best part of the service. While growing up, Judy knew about the good things her mother did. Now she was hearing the full story from people who'd actually experienced Adele's kindness. The memories that poured from the pulpit that morning gave her a fresh image of the woman she'd lived with all of her life. Apparently, Mrs. Cunningham had been more than a prayer warrior to a lot of those folks. She'd offered each one of them a shoulder to cry on, a guide into the scriptures, and a fountain of good will.

It suddenly made sense to Judy how her mother dropped everything in the midst of cooking dinner to take a phone call or to rush out of the house to help a neighbor. People who received such kindness shared their stories from the pulpit that morning. Funny anecdotes got the audience laughing out loud and tender remembrances invoked weeping and a sad shaking of heads.

Judy turned in her seat and surveyed the gathering, amazed at some of the familiar faces in the crowd. She could understand why Alicia Carter drove 200 miles. As Judy's best friend, she was once like a member of the Cunningham family.

But Frank Peebles? She figured the guy had forgotten all about the Cunninghams. Yet, there he was, in the back of the church, his head bowed in sorrow—or was it embarrassment? After all, he had left town with half of Daddy's business thirty-four years ago.

Close to the front she spotted Ben Michaels. She recognized him from his photos on the covers of sports magazines. Though spring training was right around the corner, Ben had traveled all the way from Florida to upstate New York to say good-bye to Mrs. Cunningham.

Then, there was Brenda Schwartz. That woman had slunk into the back pew that morning and had spent most of the service sobbing into a hankie. Practically everyone in town knew Brenda bore a love-hate relationship with Judy's mother. Some said the feud went back to the day Adele Baker married George Cunningham. Others insisted it started long before that.

She thought about all the notes Mother had left. There was one for Alicia, one for Ben, and even one for Sammy Powers.

Of course, Sammy Powers didn't show up at all. He was in prison. Mrs. Cunningham's one failure, people said.

Nor was Parker Addison there, which was for the best since Judy was still trying to decide what to do about their relationship.

Before the service started, Judy watched with interest as Pastor Goode led his daughter, Mindy, up to the altar and stood for a long time in front of Adele Cunningham's framed portrait. He whispered something in the little girl's ear. Now, what on earth did a ten-year-old girl need to know about a 62-year-old woman who had died?

Then there was Carl Wilson. Judy had caught her breath when he entered the sanctuary in a wheelchair pushed by his wife. He must have come straight from the hospital. His face had turned ash gray. Dark circles framed the hollows of his eyes. And he could barely hold up his head.

Yet, of all the people who attended Adele Cunningham's service that morning, Carl Wilson had the best reason for being there. Because of her mother, Carl Wilson could return to his mission in Mexico. Because of her, he'd be able to finish building the school for blind children. And he'd be able to see his own kids grow up. Yes, Carl Wilson owed Adele Cunningham far more than anyone else who came to the church that day. He owed her his life.

ALICIA CARTER

Alicia Carter arrived at the church early and stood in the back, unsure whether she should find a seat or stay in the shadows. Near the entry door was the Visitors Log. Numerous individuals had scrawled their names on a growing list. She added her own, then stepped away. Also nearby was a receptacle for sympathy cards and a separate little box marked for donations to Mrs. Cunningham's favorite charity, the children's ward at Mercy Hospital. She'd noticed the request in Adele's obituary, *In lieu of flowers ....*

She scanned the long row of floral arrangements on the table down front and snickered. Seventeen vases in all. Obviously, not everyone had paid attention to Adele's *in lieu of flowers* request. She shrugged, shamefully aware that her main reason for being there had nothing to do with flowers or cards or charitable giving, and only a little to do with paying respects to a friend who had passed.

At that moment, her real reason for being there walked into the sanctuary gripping Jennifer Goode's hand. She held her breath as the girl slipped into the second row on the right, then sat very still, like a porcelain doll, while Jennifer took her place at the organ.

Alicia stared at the child's golden tresses, certain it was the same little girl she'd seen in the playground. Mindy raised a finger and started twirling a blond curl the same way Alicia habitually did. How was it possible that her baby could pick up a similar trait when they'd never spent any time together? Two minutes in the delivery room hardly qualified as a bonding session. It had to be genetics, a sign that she and her daughter belonged together. There were probably lots of other quirks they had in common. She could spend the next ten years finding out exactly what they were.

As other people started filing into the church, Alicia blended with the crowd, and glided into the pew beside Mindy. Two large blue eyes looked up at her. Alicia immediately melted. It was like looking into a mirror from her own past.

"Hi," she whispered, drawing a smile from the girl's bow-shaped lips.

She offered her hand. "I'm Alicia."

Without hesitation, the child shook her hand, then pulled away and tucked her fingers under her thigh. Alicia looked her over. Everything about her was pink, from her flushed cheeks to her tiny round knees. Her feet dangled short of the floor. She had on a dark blue dress, appropriate for a child to wear to a memorial service, and patent leather shoes that reflected the overhead lights.

An unfamiliar warmth filled Alicia as she recalled the day she held her newborn baby in her arms. In those few minutes, she'd experienced a softening of her heart and an overpowering desire to hold onto the girl. It could only be one thing—a mother's love for a child—*her* child.

Mindy looked up again, appeared to be uncomfortable, and shifted a few inches away from her. Alicia's first impulse was to slide closer, but she didn't want to scare the girl. After all, she'd come there to win her back.

She allowed her attention to drift to the front of the church. Jennifer was at the organ, her back rigid, her face turned in their direction. Her dark eyes flickered in recognition. Then, with furrowed brow, she turned toward her husband like she was trying to catch his attention. He stood behind the pulpit, sorting through his notes. Alicia stiffened. Surely, they had expected her to be there for Mrs. Cunningham's service. Her lawyer had sent them a letter informing them that she was coming home.

Alicia lifted the memorial card she'd picked up on the way into the church. It bore a color photo of Mrs. Cunningham and, beneath it, a verse of Scripture: *Psalm 116:15, Precious in the sight of the Lord is the death of his saints.* The inside held the order of service, including the hymns, the reading from the Bible, then the pastor's message, followed by a time of public sharing.

All for Mrs. Cunningham. A flicker of guilt pierced her thoughts. What would Mrs. Cunningham say if knew what Alicia was planning now?

She dispelled the guilt, looked again at the girl sitting beside her in the pew, and her heart swelled with emotion. It was all she could do to keep from wrapping her arms around the precious angel and carrying her away.

"You look pretty in your navy blue dress," she said.

Mindy turned her face up and smiled. "Thank you."

So polite. Such an angel. The Goodes had done a marvelous job. "You go to school here, don't you?"

Mindy swung her feet back and forth. "I'm in the fourth grade."

"Oh, that's wonderful. What do you like to do in school?"

"I like to read books," she said with a giggle that brought a smile to Alicia's lips. "And I like math, and science, and—um—recess. And Margie Gibson."

"Margie Gibson? Is she your best friend?"

Mindy bobbed her head. The bounce of her golden curls set Alicia's heart fluttering. She wanted to run a hairbrush through those locks, wanted to pull them back in a French braid, or a pony tale. She longed to buy new dresses for her child. Had dreamed of taking her to the zoo or to a theme park or simply to the mall on a shopping spree.

"Have you ever traveled away from home?" she ventured to ask. "You know, on a vacation?"

Mindy's arched little eyebrows went up and her sky blue eyes widened. "A vacation?"

"Yes, that's when you go on a trip somewhere, maybe to the beach, or to Disney World. Would you like to go to Disney World?"

"Oooh, yeah. My best friend Margie went there last year. She said it was cool."

"Well, maybe someday real soon you'll be able to go there too. Would you like that?"

The organ burst forth with a rendition of "Rock of Ages" and interrupted their little chat. The pronounced chords sounded harsh, even angry. Jennifer's hardened eyes were fastened to them. Not to be intimidated, Alicia took a deep breath and stared back at her, then lowered her gaze as a wave of remorse surfaced.

She'd left Parker Addison's office yesterday, encouraged that she was doing the right thing. But now, sitting in the church beside her daughter, with Jennifer's troubled eyes on her, she wasn't sure. What if she couldn't make Mindy happy? What if the child missed the only mother and father she'd ever known? Worse yet, what if she didn't like Alicia? Or trust her? They must have told her about strangers and how dangerous it was to go off with someone she didn't know.

As Jennifer transitioned to "Amazing Grace," she softened the keys. A hush fell over the audience and all eyes moved to Pastor Goode. He gestured for everyone to stand, then led the congregants in singing. Alicia stood to her feet, thrilled when Mindy rose with her and took her hand.

When the singing ended, they settled back in the pew. Tears came to Alicia's eyes, and she could hardly concentrate as Pastor Goode gave the eulogy.

She couldn't help but wonder what her life might have been like if she hadn't given up her baby. These days, women had children out of wedlock and few people judged them. She should have put up with the wagging tongues for a while, showed the townsfolk what a good mother she could be. Or she could have left town and started fresh somewhere else. She could have gotten a job and made a life for herself and her child.

But, if she'd done that, she would have missed an exciting airline career. And she wouldn't have met Butch or enjoyed the lifestyle he'd provided. Had it been a trade-off? Or simply the right thing to do?

Pastor Goode's next words broke through Alicia's thoughts. "That woman didn't have a selfish bone in her body. She set aside her own desires in order to help others. Every unselfish decision she made came about after a period of intense prayer. Every word that came out of her mouth must have come straight from the heart of God. Her guidance, her counsel, her words of advice— always, without fail—were meant for good and never for evil. Who can judge the heart of a man—or a woman, in this case? We humans can't understand the working of a great God, especially when his directives come through a woman like Adele Cunning- ham. We can only accept them as being true, and right, and honest."

Alicia struggled against another flood of guilt. If she compared herself with Adele Cunningham, she'd come out far short.

At the close of his message, Pastor Goode opened the podium to whoever wanted to share. Alicia slipped out of her pew. She glanced one more time at Mindy, who's attention was on the line of people moving toward the altar. Instead of merging with those who wanted to give testimonies, Alicia turned in the opposite direction and headed for the back of the church. There in the shadows she waited for the service to end. Then she made her way to the front where Judy and her brother, Paul, were receiving visitors. When a path cleared, she stepped up and gave Judy a hug.

"It's so good to see you," Judy said. "You naughty girl. You haven't called in over a month."

Alicia shrugged. "Been busy—you know, traveling and work- ing on projects." She raised her eyebrows in a mock challenge. "It seems you've gotten busy too."

Judy laughed softly. "It's sad that it took my mother's funeral to get us together."

"Yes. I'm truly sorry for your loss, Judy. She was a wonderful woman."

"Yes, she was." Judy paused and held up her hand. "Hold on," she said. "My mother left something for you."

She handed Alicia a card. Alicia stared at the script depicting her name, then slipped it in her purse.

They talked for a couple more minutes about incidentals that vanished from Alicia's mind as soon as they were mentioned. Her mind was still on the little girl in the second pew. Drawing her attention back to Judy, she promised to stay in touch. Though she'd intended to try to arrange a private lunch with her friend, she squashed the idea. As an awkward silence fell on them, she gave Judy another hug. Then she embraced Paul and repeated her condolences.

The three of them were swallowed up by another surge of well-wishers. To Alicia, it was a welcome interruption, for she'd run out of things to say. She retreated down the aisle. When she got to the back of the church, she turned around and searched for little Mindy. Jennifer finished playing the last hymn, "How Great Thou Art." She stepped away from the organ and hurried off the platform straight for Mindy. With a quick glance at Alicia, she grabbed the girl's hand and joined her husband at the front of the church. They looked like a family standing there. A man with his wife and daughter.

Turning away, Alicia fled from the church. Outside on the steps, she raised her face toward the heavens. A sweep of winter clouds converged overhead turning the sky dark. She shivered from the sudden chill. She hadn't expected to change her mind. But now the sight of Mindy with the Goodes had acted like an ice pick, and it was chipping away at the shroud of ice around her heart.

"What am I supposed to do?" she sobbed. "I have the power to change everything, to bring my plea before a judge, and to walk away with my daughter. It's perfectly legal. Perfectly right according to the law. Then why do I have this hesitation? Tell me, God, what is it you're trying to say? Mrs. Cunningham is gone. I can't ask her, so I'm asking you. Please, don't leave me to deal with this on my own. Tell me what to do and then give me the strength to do it."

SIXTEEN

ROBERT GOODE

Pastor Goode tried not to appear ruffled when Alicia Carter entered the church that morning. Though she had matured over the past ten years, she still resembled the teenager who'd stood on the top row of the choir loft, her beautiful soprano soaring over the other voices.

With only an occasional glance in her direction, Robert busied himself with the final touches of Mrs. Cunningham's memorial service. He carefully placed the sheet music for Connie's requested hymns on the organ. He arranged the last of the delivered flowers with a collection of others on a long table amidst multiple photos showing Adele Cunningham in different stages of her life. Then he mounted the stair to the pulpit and went over his notes for her eulogy.

All the while, he was aware of the lone figure in the back of the sanctuary, illuminated by a ray of sunlight spilling through a stained glass window. She looked angelic standing there with her blond hair aglow, the image of what Mindy might look like one day. She'd come there under the guise of attending a funeral, but in reality she was planning to take his daughter away. He whispered a prayer for strength. He didn't want to lose the battle before it had even begun.

He pressed his lips together, confident that his lawyer had come up with a suitable argument—including material proof—that he and Jennifer were the ideal parents for the child.

Robert resolved to move ahead one step at a time, one day

at a time. The main thing was, he and Jennifer were a team. They were going to do everything in their power to keep from losing Mindy.

His family meant the world to him. Jennifer and Mindy provided constant motivation for everything he did, from preaching on Sunday mornings to maintaining the church and school, to planning for the future. No longer were he and Jennifer childless. God had blessed them. *Surely, the Almighty won't take away that blessing.*

Parker Addison's letter was sitting on his desk. Jack Gibbs had read it. The longtime lawyer had shrugged with an air of confidence.

"I think we have a pretty good chance." He'd looked directly at them. "You say the biological mother hasn't tried to contact you until now?"

"That's right," Robert had responded, a sliver of hope rising within him.

Gibbs grunted and shook his head. "A lot depends on which judge we get," he said. "There are a couple in this county who lean in favor of the biological mother. But those cases usually have to do with divorces. Your situation is a little different from a divorce hearing, so there's no telling what our judge will decide. If I were you, I'd pray real hard that we get Judge Kiefer. I know him well. He likes to make decisions that have a shock effect, likes to leave the courtroom audience gaping in awe and the lawyers shaking their heads in shock. Yes sir, if we get Kiefer it could be to our advantage."

"When—when can we expect to have the hearing?" Robert needed to know. "We'd like to get this over with as soon as possible."

"The birth mother's lawyer will schedule it." Gibbs shifted in his chair and released a sigh. "I'll be in touch with you as soon as I have an exact date."

Now Alicia had come into the church and things were moving at a much faster pace.

He was still lamenting this when people started filing into the pews. Jennifer was seated at the organ looking over the hymns he had placed there. He knew she was merely going through the motions, that she also had spotted Alicia standing at the back of the church.

There was one thing he needed to do, one thing he had promised Jennifer he needed to handle before the ceremony began. He descended the steps, approached the second pew, and took Mindy's hand. He led her to the display table and paused before a large portrait of Mrs. Cunningham.

"This was the lady who brought you to us," he whispered. Mindy's little eyebrows went up. "Another woman gave birth to you, Mindy, but she couldn't take care of you. Mrs. Cunningham figured you should come and live with us, so she asked your natural mother to let us raise you."

Mindy frowned and stared into his eyes, the blue of her own eyes shining with questions. "Didn't Mommy bring me home from the hospital? Isn't she my *real* mommy?"

"Yes," he said, chuckling. "She is your real mommy. She's the one who's been taking care of you all these years. But she wasn't the lady who gave birth to you. Someone else did. Someone who was too young to take care of you. So, she chose to give you to us and Mrs. Cunningham helped to arrange it."

"How did Mrs. Cunningham know what to do?" Mindy tilted her head in that whimsical way that always set his heart flipping.

"I'm thinking she talked to Jesus, and he must have told her what to do. Mommy and I were happy to have you come and live with us. We wanted it to be forever."

"I want forever, too," she said, nodding.

Robert suppressed a swell of emotion. He pointed at Mrs. Cunningham's portrait, "This lady prayed for you before you were born. She wanted to make sure you were going to be okay, that you'd always have people in your life who loved you. What do you think about a woman like that?"

Mindy smiled. "She's nice."

Robert's throat tightened, but he managed to choke out what needed to be said. "Mindy, there's a possibility that God may have another plan for you, a plan that will take you far away from us."

She leaned back and frowned at him. Tears welled up in her eyes.

"I don't want to go away," she said, her voice soft. "I want to stay with you. In my own house, and my own school, and my own bed, and my own room."

Robert blinked several times and caught his breath. Alicia might take his child away, but she could never erase the last ten years and all the happy memories. Not from his mind, or Jennifer's, or even little Mindy's. Those memories were there to stay. Still, he had to prepare her.

"Mindy, darling. Mommy and I may need to go to court and ask a judge to let us keep you. Will you pray about it?"

"Sure, Daddy."

Reluctantly, he returned his daughter to her pew and quickly turned his back to her, fearing she might see the tears that were threatening to spill from his eyes. He had to get to the pulpit. Somehow, he had to concentrate on Mrs. Cunningham's service.

The sanctuary was already filling up. Soon it would be standing room only. He swept his eyes over the growing assembly, wasn't prepared when Alicia boldly slipped into the pew next to Mindy. As the last chords of "Rock of Ages" tapered off, he placed both hands on the sides of the podium and looked out at the congregation. All eyes were on him. He had to control his emotions, couldn't allow himself to crumble. He opened his Bible to Proverbs 31 and the passage on "the virtuous woman."

Though he tried to keep his mind on the eulogy, he was painfully aware when Alicia struck up a whispered conversation with Mindy. A defensive prickling of nerves flared at the back of his neck. He fought the urge to rush down and separate them. But, this was not the time or the place for a confrontation. He had to reserve the battle for the courtroom and let the two lawyers go at it.

Most of all, he had to trust God. Had to remain strong in his faith. The Lord could do anything, right? Even the impossible. After all, the same Jesus who stilled the waves and calmed the storm could also calm the tempest that was sure to rage in the courtroom. Partially comforted, he pulled his attention back to the service, but never lost sight of what was happening in that second pew.

He was surprised when, during the time of personal testimonies, Alicia got up and retreated to the back of the church. *So long, bad rubbish,* he thought, shocked at his own bitterness. The realization nearly brought him to his knees. How could he, a man of God, allow such a hateful curse to enter his mind? Was this battle changing him? Or had it exposed who he really was inside? At that moment, he vowed to lay the entire problem at the foot of the cross. He needed to back off and let everything happen as God willed.

SEVENTEEN

BEN MICHAELS

From his seat on the end of the pew, Ben Michaels had a good view of Elizabeth, seated two rows ahead on the other side of the aisle. She slipped out of her coat and let it fall behind her. She wore a form-fitting black dress with a cinched waist and billowing sleeves. Her raven hair hung in long waves down her back. Silver hoops dangled from her earlobes, and a rosy blush colored her cheeks. As he had expected, even during this solemn time she was gorgeous.

He looked away, tried to focus on something else in the church. The array of flowers near the altar. The stained glass windows. The people who were filling the sanctuary. He hardly knew anyone anymore, yet they all knew him. He caught their looks of recognition, their whispered comments to those who were sitting beside them. He tried to set his mind on the service, but he was still pestered by the moonlight swim of the night before.

He and Elizabeth had spent only a couple of minutes in the frigid water, but it had left a piercing dagger of guilt on his conscience. He'd realized too late he didn't have the strength to be alone with her, especially under those conditions. He'd left her there in the water and had lunged up the slope to the pile of blankets she'd placed on the riverbank.

He was appalled at himself. He'd behaved like a reckless teenager, reliving a past that was dead and buried. He was a married man, a father, and most convicting of all, a professing Christian. And she was a beautiful divorcee who hadn't tried to hide her feelings for him. He'd known it immediately. Elizabeth Adams was still in love with him. At one time, that might have sent him on a huge ego trip. But Ben wasn't the same man anymore. He'd grown up and had moved away from Fall River and from his past life.

He was still trying to dismiss from his mind the temptation he'd nearly succumbed to last night. The moonlight had set Elizabeth's face aglow. She'd followed him out of the water. As she came up the riverbank, he'd held up a heavy quilt, partly to shield her from the cold, but also to hide her from his eyes. Then he'd turned his face away and tugged his own blanket around his shoulders. She'd settled on the riverbank beside him. For a brief moment, he'd gazed at her, huddled beneath her quilt, her chin turned upward in his direction. Her lips parted in a half-smile.

In a split second, he'd known what he had to do. He'd leaped to his feet and left her there on the riverbank. Didn't make any apologies or say good-bye.

In the quiet of his darkened hotel room, he fell to his knees beside his bed and begged God to help him stay strong. Even when Elizabeth knocked on his door, he ignored the soft rapping and her voice beckoning him to open the door.

Now, seated in the safety of the church, he was relieved when the music started and everyone rose to sing the words.

Amazing Grace, how sweet the sound that saved a wretch like me ....
His throat constricted, his eyes began to water.
I once was lost but now I'm found, was blind but now I see.
He stopped singing and chewed his lower lip. He'd come close to falling last night. Thank God, Mrs. Cunningham had done more than pray for him and encourage him when he was a boy. She'd led him to Jesus during those sessions in his bedroom. Because of Mrs. Cunningham, he was able to do more than play baseball, he was able to look forward to a heavenly home.

Even so, he'd fallen away more times than he'd like to count. He'd neglected his family, had argued with his wife, and often in front of his impressionable little boy. He'd spent more time away from home than in it. And last night he'd nearly fallen into grievous sin.

When Pastor Goode opened the pulpit to people who wanted to come up and share, Ben was among the first to take the stairs. He kept his message brief, simply told how Mrs. Cunningham had helped him to reach an otherwise impossible goal.

"If not for her, I wouldn't be where I am today," he concluded.

A few people applauded. He wasn't sure if it was because they were honoring Mrs. Cunningham, or if they were impressed that a famous baseball star was in their midst. Embarrassed, he stepped down. He caught Elizabeth gazing at him with the same wistful smile she'd had on the riverbank last night. He turned his eyes away.

Sitting in the church with Elizabeth only a few feet away, he hadn't yet found the strength to stay away from her. He could only run away so many times. He'd done so last night. But now, seeing her again, he wasn't sure he could repeat it.

He knew Satan used people's weaknesses to drag them down. Elizabeth was a weakness for him. He'd never fully recovered from their breakup. Now the devil was dangling her in front of his face. She'd made it clear she was available. He only needed to say the word. A scripture came to mind. *Flee fornication.* Hadn't he done that last night? Then, why was he still struggling?

He kept his eyes on the altar and listened to one speaker after another, one story after another, determined to do what he'd come there to do—honor Mrs. Cunningham.

Afterward, he hurried to the front and met with the family. While standing in the reception line, he caught a whiff of her lavender perfume before he saw her. Elizabeth had come up behind him—close enough to touch.

"Will you come to the house for refreshments?" Judy said to them both.

"Yes, thank you," Elizabeth blurted out.

He looked at Paul, his childhood friend. "Thanks for the invitation," he said, "I might stop by for a minute."

He avoided looking at Elizabeth, though he knew she hadn't budged from his side.

"I can't wait to hear a few more of your baseball war stories," Paul said with a chuckle.

Ben snickered. "They're not as exciting as people might think. Just the usual throwing of a ball and catching it. Boring stuff for most people."

Paul shook his head. "I doubt it's like the humdrum routine I put up with in the office every day. My life doesn't begin to compare with yours."

Judy held out a small envelope to him. "From my mother," she said. "She wrote it while she was in the hospital—before she passed."

He gulped back the powerful emotion that came over him. Even as she lay dying, Mrs. Cunningham had taken the time to write him a note. He forced a smile and accepted the card.

Without saying a word to Elizabeth, he waved good-bye to Paul and Judy, and proceeded up the aisle to the church exit. He picked up his pace, fleeing, like the Bible said to do. Strange, but the farther he got from his former girlfriend the more he imagined Mrs. Cunningham's approval.

Still, his mind kept drifting back to what could have been a night of pleasure on the riverbank. If he had succumbed, who would know? Immediately, his thoughts shifted to his wife and son waiting for him at home. If they were still there. Had Candy left and taken the boy with her? Did he even have a home to go back to?

If he ever needed Mrs. Cunningham's advice, it was right now. His head reeling between thoughts of Elizabeth and a desire to flee, he hurried to the parking lot. Once inside his car, he remembered Mrs. Cunningham's note. He nearly shredded the envelope trying to get to the message inside.

FRANK PEEBLES

Frank Peebles came late to Mrs. Cunningham's funeral. He wanted to remain separated from the crowd, especially those folks who might remember what he'd done to his good friend, George Cunningham. Maybe they've forgotten how he ran off with a huge chunk of the business and most of their bank account. *And maybe they haven't forgotten*. He didn't want any dirt brought up at Adele's service.

Though George had written him several letters over the years, Frank never opened them—just tossed them in the trash, afraid to read whatever was written inside. He should have known better. Should have known that George wasn't the kind of guy to hold a grudge. Frank never knew how forgiving that guy was until he went to George's funeral, five years ago. That was when Adele told him she and George had been praying for him since the day he left town. Now he wished he had saved those letters. They might have eased the guilt he'd carried all those years.

So, it made sense that he should attend Adele's service, too. But, he couldn't strut into the church like he'd never done anything wrong. Today, he wanted to concentrate on Mrs. Cunningham and all the things she did right. She supported her husband, no matter what he wanted to try, even if it cost their entire savings. A far cry from his own wife, Adele was a low-maintenance beauty, more concerned with keeping a happy home than filling up her closet with clothes she didn't wear more than once. And she had a sweet way about her, never nagged at George, as far as Frank could remember. Took care of the kids like a mother hen. And what a great cook.

He couldn't help but compare himself with the Cunninghams. George with his easy-going way and Adele, his faithful supporter. What kind of life might he have had if he'd married someone like Adele Baker? Not only did he regret the choices he'd made, he also regretted what he'd become—a ruthless businessman, a puppet to a board of cowboys, and a sniveling fool with multiple health problems.

At the other end of his pew sat a pitiful woman who'd been bawling like a banshee since he'd arrived. She looked a little like Brenda Schwartz' mother, but it couldn't be her. The old bag had to be in her 90s by now or even dead. Whoever it was buried her face in a handkerchief, sobbing and sniffling and mopping up a gusher of tears. He slid away from her to the other end of the pew.

Then he spotted Adele's son and daughter at the front of the church. It was best if they didn't notice him. After all, he'd cheated their father out of most of his business. Adele had forgiven him. She'd said George had too. But, people's kids look at things under a different magnifying glass. On the one hand, he wanted to watch the service and leave quietly. On the other hand, he felt like walking up front and facing them head-on. He wasn't proud of what he'd done, but it was a legitimate business decision. It had nothing to do with friendship.

He'd sat through the service straining to hear the words of the preacher. If not for that pathetic woman's wailing, he might have enjoyed the testimonies. As it was, he had to lean forward, his ears straining to make out what all the people said.

When the service ended, and most of the crowd dispersed, he stepped out of the pew and walked to the front of the church. Judy and Paul were standing there, talking to a few stragglers.

He stepped closer. "I'm sorry for your loss," he managed to say. Then he bowed his head, ashamed to look them in the eye. "I'm—"

"Frank Peebles, thank you for coming." Judy pumped his hand. "I'd know you anywhere."

He frowned quizzically.

"My dad kept every magazine article ever written about you," she explained, smiling. "And Mom had a photo of the two of you in your fishing gear on our fireplace mantle."

Judy's voice sounded surprisingly sweet, like her mother's. She looked like Adele, too, in her younger days.

To his surprise, she stepped toward him and wrapped her arms around his neck, holding him close.

When she released him, he looked at her face and his heart melted. Though her eyes glistened with tears, she was smiling at him.

"I–I wanted to show my respect for your mother," he mumbled. "She was a wonderful person—a true woman of God."

He hadn't expected his voice to crack, or to have his eyes puddle up like they did.

Judy tilted her head, and her smile grew wider. "We all cherished her too," she said without the least bit of animosity in her tone. She gestured toward the pews, now empty. "Did you see the crowd that came to say goodbye to her? I'm still in awe." She shook her head and eyed him with interest. "I don't know why you traveled all the way from Texas. You're a busy man, Frank."

Adele's son, Paul, extended his hand. "In any case, we're glad you came."

Speechless and still amazed at their kind reception, he nodded. "I can make time for an old friend's family, can't I?" was all he could think of to say.

Judy tilted her head in that way Adele had done whenever she gave her full attention to someone. "My mother spoke about you often and told me how proud she was to have known you. Some time ago, I read an article about you in Time Magazine, how you built a huge empire from scratch."

He dug in his pocket for a handkerchief. Found none, then spotted a box of tissues on the front pew and reached for it. After mopping his face, he sought the words he'd been wanting to say.

"I never meant to hurt your father—or your mother," he said, looking back and forth at the two of them.

"We know that now," Paul said. "After Daddy's funeral, Mom told us everything, how it was my father's choice to remain behind when you went off to build a new business. She said he could have gone with you, but he chose the small-town life. And, don't forget, he had that thing with his heart." He patted Frank on the shoulder. "In any case, they both wished you well, never held the slightest grudge."

"I–I never knew." Frank shook his head, somewhat in shock over all the good will he'd missed by staying away.

Judy stroked his arm. "Well," she said. "Now you know. You didn't lose your friend, Frank. When Daddy didn't hear from you, he assumed you were hard at work. And Mother? Well, she kept looking through business magazines for stories about their old friend, Frank Peebles. She clipped out articles that spoke of your successes. And the Time Magazine story? She framed it and hung it on the wall in Daddy's office."

Paul let out a chuckle. "You're gonna love this, Frank," he said. "Mom used to point at that article and say to me, *Now, that's what you can accomplish in life, if you're willing to step out and take a risk.* Then, she'd place a hand on my dad's shoulder and say, *Or, you can have a different kind of success. The kind your Daddy made for himself, along with plenty of time for relaxation. It's a choice.*" Paul looked at Frank, a quizzical twinkle in his eye. "You do make time for relaxation, don't you, Frank?"

Frank clammed up, knowing he couldn't give the young man a decent answer on that one.

Paul went on as though unaware of Frank's discomfort. "I ended up with something in between the two of you. I went to college, studied architecture, and went to work for a big company at the edge of town. Like you, I'm dedicated to my job. I have a long list of clients, and I take pride in what I do. As a bonus, I'm making out quite well financially. But when I leave the office on Friday, I don't take my work home with me. Like my Dad always did, I spend my evenings with my wife and kids. On Saturday mornings, I play baseball with my friends, and I go to church on Sunday. Thanks to you, Frank, and to my dad, I've managed to acquire the best of both worlds."

Frank pondered the young man's words. *The best of both worlds.* He hadn't done that, hadn't known how to acquire both. Back then, when he made up his mind to leave, he held onto one thought—he wanted to build up his business and become a rich man. He had no kids, didn't even spend evenings with his wife. She made her own fun, which usually involved spending every dime he brought home. And church? Today was the first time in years he'd stepped foot inside a church. And it took a dear friend's funeral to get him there.

"My mother left something for you," Judy said. She reached inside a basket and pulled out an envelope with his name scripted on the front. "She hoped you might come." She pursed her lips, then added, "If you hadn't, we would have mailed this to you."

He eyed the blue envelope with puzzlement. Gingerly, he accepted it and slipped it in his coat pocket.

"Thanks," he said. "I'll read it later."

"You'll come to the house? For refreshments?" Judy offered. Then, a flicker of understanding crossed her eyes. "Unless you have a flight to catch—"

"No, I don't."

He shrugged, half out of embarrassment and half out of excitement about his plans for the next day.

"I'm gonna stay here for a couple of days, look over the town, reminisce on what it was like when your father and I were friends. Maybe look up a couple of old buddies, that is, if they're still around. And I plan to go fishing tomorrow morning."

"What?" Paul said, and his face lit up in surprise.

Frank blushed. "I haven't gone fishing in years. My rod and reel are collecting dust somewhere, probably in my basement. I'm gonna have to rent everything." He let out an embarrassed chuckle.

"It's a great idea," Paul said. "You should kick back and do something fun while you're here."

An idea struck Frank. "Maybe you'd like to join me, Paul?"

"I wish I could, but my son's got a basketball game, and that's a priority." He placed a hand on Frank's shoulder. "But you go ahead and enjoy yourself. You'll find the fish are still biting, even at this time of year. The flow of the river keeps the water from freezing over. The ice has broken up, and it's smooth sailing right now. You shouldn't have any trouble getting a rowboat out there and having a grand old time. But make sure you bundle up. The fish aren't the only thing that will be biting. The brisk morning air has teeth too."

"Come by the house," Judy repeated the invitation. "It's still in the same place."

Frank nodded and left the church, intending to go straight to the Cunningham house. As he drove away, he thought about the conversation he had with Judy and Paul. He nodded and smiled. Adele and George had done a terrific job with their kids. He maneuvered his car onto the main road, but instead of watching for traffic, he let his mind drift back to yesteryear and the fun he and George used to have.

He forgot he had the wheel of a car in his hands, forgot his foot was pressing against the gas pedal. He wasn't prepared for the flash of metal that came up on his left. There was a screech of wheels and a loud bang. Instinctively, he raised his left arm to protect his face. The driver's door caved into his side. The car spun to the right. He slammed on the brakes, lost his grip on the wheel, and braced for another collision. Sure enough, his rental car slammed into a guard rail. Then everything went still.

He couldn't move. Dazed, he tried to turn his head and look out the window. He fumbled for his seatbelt. He opened his mouth to call for help, but not a sound came out. Footsteps approached on the gravel outside and men's voices rose up outside his window. Though his vehicle had come to a standstill, to him it seemed like it was spinning around in circles, like a runaway carnival ride. He tried to stay awake, but it took too much effort. He gave up trying and succumbed to the comfort of darkness.

NINETEEN

Brenda Schwartz

Brenda Schwartz hadn't cared who heard her noisy sobbing. Not even the scrawny little weirdo at the end of her pew. She was in mourning. Isn't that the way people act when they're in mourning? They cry. They whimper. Sometimes they even blubber. What was she supposed to do? Hide her feelings? Pretend nothing had happened? That she hadn't endured an overwhelming mix of emotions over the death of Adele Cunningham?

Perhaps she had no reason to cry. In fact, she should have been glad their relationship had ended. That part of her life was over and done with. No longer did she have to live in that woman's shadow.

From the time they were teenagers until the present, Brenda had dealt with nearly every negative emotion a person can have. Jealousy, anger, frustration, even hatred. Adele's passing had served as a sort of release from those feelings. Now a different kind of emotion had surfaced. Relief, of course, but also sorrow at having never appreciated Adele for all her kindness to others.

She sat in the last pew, bowed her head and wept unashamedly, still trying to decide if she had come there to release a half-century of pain or to grieve the loss of someone who'd played a major role in her life. She couldn't deny the truth, couldn't think of one time Adele had been nasty to her. Brenda was the one who had set up all the contests between them, both real and in her mind. Most likely, Adele never even knew they were competing.

It was time she stopped blaming Adele for her losses and take responsibility for her own choices. The truth was, Brenda had been dreaming about a life that could never be hers. She'd been living in a fantasy world, pitting herself against Adele, when they were simply two people who lived on the same street and breathed the same air.

A complex web of feelings came over her now as she hunched over and released more tears into an already damp handkerchief. Thank God, the guy at the end of the pew went up front and then left the church.

She pulled more tissues from her purse and blotted her cheeks. The service was over. People had flocked to the front of the sanctuary to give their regards to Judy and Paul. She sat there—alone—as everyone else left the church. She dabbed at her eyes with tissues that were soaked and falling apart, then she searched inside her purse for more hankies but found none. At that moment, a shadow blocked the light coming through the stained-glass window.

"Brenda, what are you doing back here all by yourself?"

Squinting, she tried to focus. Quizzical blue eyes stared back at her. Blonde waves framed the cream-colored face. For a moment, she thought she was looking into the face of Adele Baker. She blinked hard against the mirage.

"Hello, Judy," Brenda managed. "I'm sorry. I–I didn't mean to—"

"It's all right, Brenda. I'm glad you're here. You should come down front and take a look at Mother's photos. You're in a couple of them."

Brenda blinked in surprise. "Are you sure? I'm in them?"

Judy nodded. "Yes. Mother insisted that we use them." She smiled sweetly.

Brenda crumpled up the shredded tissues and stuffed them in her purse. Then she rose from the pew and followed Judy to the front. She spent a few minutes looking at the photos, thrilled that Judy hadn't lied to her. She really was in a couple of them.

"I want to thank you for making this beautiful silk floral

arrangement," Judy said, her fingers stroking the petals. "Pastor Goode told me you brought it to the church yesterday."

"It was nothing," Brenda said with a shrug.

"Well, it meant a great deal to me and my brother. I don't know if you were aware, but you put my Mother's favorite flower right in the center."

Brenda nodded. "The rose."

"Yes, the rose. And it's bright red. We'd like to take your arrangement home and keep it as a memento of her funeral. It was our favorite over all the bouquets that came from the florist shops. It's quite special."

A surge of warmth flowed through Brenda. She'd missed so much joy by staying away from the Cunninghams all those years. Judy was the kind of girl she would have liked to have as a daughter. And Paul. What a fine young man he'd become. She regretted that she hadn't gotten to know Adele's children.

"Here," Judy said. "Mother left something for you."

She handed Brenda an envelope. It bore her name in a flowery script that brought to her mind another talent Adele had mastered. She smiled with remembrance of the calligraphy class they'd taken together. Like everything else, the penmanship came easy to Adele, while Brenda could only produce hen-scratching. She stared at the pale blue note card. Instead of envy for the woman who'd written it, she felt only sadness. She'd lost a dear friend, and she hadn't known it until Adele was gone.

"Come to the house," Judy urged. Her tone was sincere, inviting. "Celebrate my mother's life with us. We'll have something to eat, and we'll reminisce a little. I'd love to hear any stories you might have. After all, you lived right next door to my mother for years. You were thrown together on a lot of projects. I'm sure you have some fond memories. It'll do you good to enjoy some time with us. Please, don't go off and be alone today."

Brenda nodded, but didn't think she could step inside the Cunningham home. It would be too painful. The last time she was there was after George's funeral. She'd been present at the church service and again at his gravesite. Then, she'd gone home and had mourned his death in private. An hour later, she surfaced from her grief. A celebration of life was taking place next door in the house George and Adele had inherited from his parents after they passed. For years, they had lived right under Brenda's nose.

She recalled opening her bedroom window and turning her ear toward the Cunningham house. Music had poured from their windows—George's favorite country tunes—and laughter. She splashed cold water on her face, reapplied her makeup, and then walked over to the Cunningham's carrying an apple pie she'd made the day before. George's death had come as a shock to her. Now she wanted to honor him in some small way.

As always, Adele greeted her with open arms and invited her into the living room where George's friends were congregating. Judy was there. And Paul. They were barely out of their teens back then. And Adele's sister Connie was bustling about making sure everyone had a fresh drink. There was a table of food, of course. But what caught her attention was the display of George's photos, his bowling trophies, his high school yearbooks, fishing awards, and a family portrait. The memory incited another wave of nostalgia and more tears.

"Brenda. Are you all right?" Judy's concerned remark drew her back to the present.

Her next sob brought a hiccup. "I was thinking, that's all. Remembering." She turned Adele's note card over in her hand, fingered the matted finish, looked again at her name scripted on the front.

"I hope you'll join us at the house," Judy repeated the invitation.

After all those years, how might it feel to step inside George's house again, to look at remnants of a past she'd been trying to forget? On the other hand, why should she forget? It hadn't been all doom and gloom. Wonderful moments also filled those years. It was time she set aside all the negativity and focused on the good times.

She looked again at the powder blue envelope in her hand. A tear dropped on her name and blurred the print. More tears fell and she wasn't sure if they were out of regret or out of grief. Perhaps Adele's message might serve as some sort of final reconciliation. Before she ever stepped inside the Cunningham home again, she'd have to read the note.

TWENTY

Tyrone Jackson

Tyrone Jackson was probably the only person at Adele Cunningham's funeral who'd never met the woman. But he wasn't the only dark-skinned individual at the service. The crowd that gathered in the church included a mix of nationalities and races, a sign to him that Mrs. Cunningham had ministered to a broad cross-section of America's diverse population. Of course, the only one he knew personally was Sammy Powers.

After the service ended and most of the visitors had left, he introduced himself to the young couple at the front and learned they were Mrs. Cunningham's son and daughter.

"I work as a guard at the state prison," he told them. "I've come on behalf of Sammy Powers. Do you know the young man?"

Judy frowned. "Yes, I do. My mother tried to help him. Obviously, it didn't work out."

"Well, don't count him as a loss just yet, Ma'am. Mrs. Cunningham may have had more of an effect on Sammy than you might think."

She stared at him, as though unsure of how to respond. Discomfort rose up within him. He shook it off. He was there on a mission for a friend, and he intended to complete it.

"Anyway," he said. "I promised Sammy I'd come and pay his respects. He really wanted to be here himself. I want you to know, the news of your mother's death broke that young man's heart."

"Mother would have been pleased to know he hadn't forgotten her. You can tell him that."

"Yes, Ma'am. I'll be sure to do so." Then, sensing she could benefit from more information, he said, "Sammy took it hard. After reading your mom's obituary, he lost it completely, even got into a brawl with his cellmate and ended up in solitary confinement for a couple of days. I took meals to him and tried to comfort the young man. The obituary came as a real shock to him. He never even knew your mother was sick."

"She wasn't sick." Judy's tone still had a sliver of ice in it. "My mother donated one of her kidneys to a man who needed one. He had a rare blood type, and she was a match. She got an infection. Now she's gone, and he's going to walk away with a fresh start in his life."

Her tone cut the air like a knife. Tyrone was surprised at this sudden rise of bitterness. "Her kidney, huh? My, my. From what Sammy told me about your mother, most people were content with a simple prayer and a word of encouragement. I got that same impression from all the testimonies today. But a kidney. That was quite a sacrifice."

"Yes," Judy said with a softening of her voice. "I tried to stop her, but by the time I knew, she'd already made the arrangements. When my mother made up her mind to do something, nobody could change it." She took a breath and her next words were more tender. "Anyway, thank you for coming, Mr. Jackson, and please, let Sammy know that, even after he was taken to prison, my mother continued to talk favorably about him. For some reason, she never gave up on that boy."

She reached into a nearby basket, searched through a pile of note cards and pulled out an envelope with Sammy's name on it. "Please, give him this. My mother wrote it from her hospital bed."

Tyrone nodded and slipped the note in his pocket. "Thank you, Ma'am," he said. "I'm sure Sammy will be grateful to know she hadn't forgotten him. He's been sufferin' so. Maybe whatever your mama wrote will help him get on the right path again, this time for good."

He shook Judy's outstretched hand.

"Do you want to come to the house?" Judy offered raising her eyebrows. "For refreshments?"

"No, thank you, Ma'am. I think I'll head home. Got a houseful o' kids waitin' for me."

As he left the church, he patted the pocket that held Sammy's note. *Please, God, I pray this note will be the thing that helps that boy get right again. Let Mrs. Cunningham help him one last time.*

TWENTY-ONE

Judy Cunningham

Judy watched after Tyrone Jackson until the church doors closed behind him. With his departure, the church was nearly empty. Pastor Goode had stayed behind and was moving the flower arrangements to other locations in the sanctuary. At her request, he'd left Brenda's silk flowers on the table for Judy to take home.

Immediately after the service, Paul's wife left with their three children. Mrs. Goode also had disappeared with little Mindy..

She thought about the amazing crowd of people who had gathered there that morning. Obviously, Mrs. Cunningham had touched the hearts of a multitude of individuals. How she wished she could have been more like her.

Perhaps all she needed to do was get her mind off her own troubles and start caring for others. Like her brother, Paul, and his wife. Their youngest child had been diagnosed with autism. What had Judy done to help? Other than offering a word of sympathy, she'd done nothing. So little was known about the condition. Yet the needs were obvious. Her mother often gave up a Saturday afternoon to sit with the children while Paul and his wife went hiking or out to lunch.

She left the flower arrangement on the front pew and looked around for her brother. She found him gathering up the photos at the end of the display table. She walked over and helped him place the last of the photos in a box. Paul set the sympathy cards on top, then he handed her the basket that held a few remaining cards.

Judy peeked inside the basket. One more card lay upside down on the bottom. She turned it over and caught her breath. It was addressed to Parker Addison.

Her boss hadn't attended the funeral, and with good reason. The man had been holding her on a shelf, like a well-kept secret, and he'd made no move to bring their relationship to the next level. Week after week, he'd tossed her crumbs, nothing more.

She turned to her brother. He was closing the flaps on the top of the box, sealing the photos inside. His lips parted in a wistful smile.

"It's hard packing away the remnants of our mother," he mused. "I wasn't ready to have her leave us."

She eyed Pastor Goode, who was still moving around the sanctuary, picking up slips of paper, memorial cards, discarded tissues. He gave them a nod.

She turned to her brother. "Paul, let's go outside and talk."

Though he appeared puzzled, he nodded. They grabbed their coats off the pew and slipped out a side door. They headed for the children's playground and settled on a bench under an oak tree. Judy shivered, partly from the cold and partly from the distress in her heart.

Paul wrapped an arm around her and pulled her close. He understood. Even though she hadn't yet said a word, he knew her heart, always had. She buried her face against his wool jacket, grateful for the warmth and the comfort she found there.

"I'm going to miss her so much," Judy murmured, her words muffled by the thick fabric.

"Me too," he said, and his own voice broke.

She looked up at the sad lines on his face.

Then she sat up straight, sucked in a breath of icy air, and turned her eyes toward the web of leafless branches overhead.

"I need Mom, Paul. I need to talk to her one more time. There are some things—difficult things—I need to discuss with her."

He searched her face. "Something I can help with?"

She shook her head. "No. It's—it's woman's talk. Something only another woman could understand."

"What about Aunt Connie? She's loaded with womanly wisdom. Just ask her," he said with a chuckle. Then he grew serious again. "She does have Mom's gentle disposition, though. Far as I'm concerned, she's the next best thing to having Mrs. Cunningham here."

"Thanks, but no thanks," Judy replied with a smirk. "I should have talked to Mom weeks ago. Now she's gone, and I can only guess what she might tell me."

She began to weep, and the tears turned into tiny icicles on her face.

"Judy, it can't be that bad." Paul stroked her hair, his touch so gentle it dispelled any memories of sibling rivalry they'd experienced as kids.

"Let me help," Paul said. "You can tell me anything. I won't judge you. Heaven knows, I've made enough mistakes of my own."

She smiled through tear-filled eyes. "Thanks, Paul, but I'm going to have to deal with this on my own. Hopefully, I'll have enough strength to handle it the way Mom would have wanted me to."

She leaned away from him and studied his face. "What about you, Paul? You look like you haven't gotten a good night's sleep since the day Mom went into the hospital. You have dark circles under your eyes, and I can see by the red streaks that you've been crying."

Coloring, he shook his head. "I'm okay. It's just—well—I couldn't understand why she agreed to do something like that. And for a complete stranger. She never even talked to us about it. Didn't want our opinion, I guess. I found out the day she went into the hospital. If you don't think *that* was a shock—"

"I learned about it after she'd signed the papers." Judy shrugged. "She asked me not to tell you. That was Mom. Whenever she wanted to do something, she just went ahead and did it."

"What in the world was she thinking? Didn't she know the risks?" Paul shook his head. "I tried to stop her. I insisted she think it over. She smiled at me and said she'd already gone through the necessary testing. Then she gave me one of her long-winded *trust in God* messages. 'Of course I trust in God,' I told her. 'But I don't *test* Him.' It didn't make any difference. Mom went ahead with her plan. And now look."

"You were lucky," Paul continued. "You were still living in the same house. You had a few days to adjust. I, on the other hand, didn't find out until it was too late. You should have called me, Judy. Maybe I could have stopped it."

She stiffened. "Don't do that, Paul. I told you, Mom made me promise not to say anything. But, tell me," she said, leaning away from him. "What else could you have done?"

"Well, I could have gotten a lawyer, maybe declared her unfit to make such a decision. I could have delayed the operation long enough for her to come to her senses."

"Right, Mr. Tough Guy," she said with a giggle.

He chuckled with her, and she felt comforted. Paul had been more than a brother to her. Though he was two years younger, they were more like friends than siblings.

"Sorry, Judy," he said, his eyes smiling down at her. "I'm sure, you did what you could."

She nodded. "All's forgiven." Then she thought about the notes her mother had left. "Did Mom give you a card?" she said, fearing that perhaps her mother had not.

To her relief, Paul nodded and drew a familiar envelope out of his pocket. "She gave it to me when I visited her at the hospital before she passed."

"Have you read it yet?"

He nodded again and slid the paper from the envelope. "Here." He held it out to her.

Holding her breath, she opened the card and silently began to read.

My dear Paul,

Heaven knows you have always made me proud. Not only when you won a trophy or a race or a prize of any kind. I was most proud of you when you stepped back to let someone else win. Like the day

I told you Ben Michaels wanted to join the ball team and pitch. We both knew he didn't have a prayer with all the talent you and your friends had. Somehow, you talked the others into playing their worst tryout in history. The coach knew it and so did I. The thing is, I couldn't have been more proud of you and the other guys. The three of you did it all for Ben. The poor kid could barely get around the bases, yet you all cheered him on. He not only got on the team, he got to pitch. Now look. He's a famous ballplayer, and I believe he owes it all to his friends.

My dear son, you didn't stop there. You went on to other sports and did quite well academically too. But that wasn't your greatest accomplishment in life. I'm happy to say, you chose a wonderful girl to be your bride, and the two of you blessed me with the most terrific grandchildren a person could want. Take extra good care of your littlest one. He has potential, and you're going to find out what it is.

My one hope is that you'll tell your kids about me whenever you can. Help them to know me.

And, Paul, be there for your sister, too. Judy's going to need a shoulder to cry on now and then. Women are like that. I won't be there to offer my shoulder, but you can offer yours.

I love you, now and forever. Mom

Judy finished reading through a blur of tears. When she looked at Paul, a river of emotion was running down his face. Words stuck in her throat.

"Well, shall we go back inside?" Paul said, his voice breaking. "Pastor Goode will want to close up the church."

She gave him back his note. "Aunt Connie must be warming up a ham and pulling salads out of the fridge. I suppose I should get over there and help."

Paul grinned. "Don't worry, she's got a whole slew of ladies from the *casserole brigade* helping her."

Judy laughed. She rose to her feet and allowed herself a final smirk. "I told her I wouldn't know half the people who came to the service. I'm sure you know what she said."

"What did she say? I can only imagine."

"She said, *Judy, stop thinking about yourself and think about your mother. She'll be looking down on us and will be thrilled to see so many people coming out to say good-bye to her.* Well, I couldn't argue with *that.*"

He chuckled, sounding an awful lot like George. She looked at his face and saw her father for an instant. Paul had George's compassionate green eyes and his receding hairline, but hopefully not his weak heart. She held her breath, unable to say another word.

He took her hand. "Come on. Let's get inside where it's warm. For now, try to keep your mind on what needs to be done. It will help you get through the day. And let's remain positive. Mom died doing what she did best—helping other people. She's in heaven now, enjoying all the rewards of a life well-lived."

Judy nodded, feeling more at peace than she had in days. She appreciated her brother. His masculine strength combined with gentleness. Meekness personified. If she could meet a man like Paul, she'd marry him in a second. Instead, she had fallen into a pitiful flirtation that was bound to go nowhere.

PART IV
No Greater Gift

TWENTY-TWO

CARL WILSON

During Mrs. Cunningham's service, Carl Wilson had been sitting in the back of the church, slumped forward in his wheelchair. His wife, Adrienne, stood close behind him, gripping the handles, primed to wheel him out of there if needed. With trembling lips he'd mouthed the words to "Amazing Grace," tears filling his eyes and spilling onto his cheeks. Adrienne gently mopped his face with a handkerchief. He turned to smile up at her, then he returned his attention to the service. It was time to forget his aching wound and the weakness in his legs. Time to focus on the woman being honored that morning.

Carl first met Adele Cunningham four months ago while he was on a sabbatical from his missionary work in Mexico. Pastor Robert Goode had invited Carl and Adrienne, along with their three children up to the altar to share their testimony during a Sunday service. Carl described the mission he'd established in a rustic area of Mexico and the school he had founded for blind children. He talked about the needs, both physical and spiritual, and the trusting ways of the people who depended on him.

He felt humbled when the congregation broke into applause. Then the atmosphere grew dismal as he mentioned his long-time struggle with kidney disease. Smiles melted into creases of concern, and a few handkerchiefs appeared in the audience.

"Until recently, I've been able to keep my illness under control with medication," he said, his throat tightening. "Since last summer, I've been having regular dialysis treatments in Mexico

City. But, those treatments bought me only a little time. My condition has declined to the point that my one hope depends on a kidney transplant. The problem is, I have a rare blood type—O negative. My doctor recommended that I return to America to find a match. Please, keep me and my family in your prayers. Thank you for allowing me to share my ministry with you."

Carl descended the stairs and stood with his family at the front of the sanctuary. People rose from the pews and gathered around them for a time of anointing. Carl was surprised when, instead of leading the prayer, Pastor Goode called on a Mrs. Cunningham to take charge.

He bowed his head, humbled by the sweet words that poured from that woman's mouth. She prayed as though she had known Carl for years, mentioned numerous details about his family and their work in Mexico, including information he hadn't given from the pulpit. What's more, she spoke as though she had a personal connection with God himself. Carl had never heard anyone pray with such familiarity, yet with so much reverence.

A warmth encompassed him. In all his years as a missionary, Carl couldn't remember ever having prayed with such intensity. He came away from that five-minute gathering with renewed confidence that, despite the odds against him, God could heal him and make it possible for him to return to his work in Mexico.

Afterward, Pastor Goode took up a collection for the Wilsons. After a pot-luck luncheon in the fellowship hall, Carl met his prayer warrior in the privacy of the church office.

Pastor Goode stood beside Mrs. Cunningham smiling proudly. "If you want to see things happen in your life and in your work, you need to trust this woman with your prayer needs," he said, wrapping an arm around her and pulling her close. "Miracles happen when she prays. Miracles, Carl. I've experienced some of them myself."

Mrs. Cunningham blushed and swept away Pastor Goode's praises with a modest wave of her hand.

"It's not me at all," she objected. "It's God. He's the one you need to rely on, Carl. You have as much access to the throne as I or anyone else. God will hear you. God will listen. Pray believing, and you'll be surprised at what great things will happen."

"You're absolutely right," Carl said with a nod. "But, for weeks—no, for months—I've been falling on my knees before the Lord. I'm concerned for my family. What will happen to them when I'm gone? And my work. I've only begun to make progress with the mission. The school is half built. It's in a remote area, but children are waiting to come there from all over Mexico."

"I don't believe God is done with you, Carl," Mrs. Cunningham said, her voice warm and not the least bit condescending. "If he wants you on the mission field, he's going to bring healing. Nothing is impossible with God."

Until that moment, Carl's wife had stood quietly in his shadow with their three little ones, like a mother hen and her brood. She released a sob.

"It's okay, Adrienne," Carl said, turning. Then, he looked through tear-filled eyes at Mrs. Cunningham. "We've been through a lot," he apologized. "My wife has been a pillar of strength until now. You see, my doctor couldn't guarantee we'd be able to find a perfect match. But—"

Mrs. Cunningham let out a chuckle, which both surprised and offended him. He stared into two blue eyes sparkling with mirth.

"My dear young man," she said. "You've come to the right place. It just so happens *my* blood type is O negative."

"What?" He nearly choked.

"That's right. My blood type is O negative. Now, tell me, Carl, do you believe in miracles, or don't you?"

"Of course, I do, but I never expected—"

"Listen to me, Carl. I'm willing to submit to whatever tests are necessary." She cocked her head with an air of confidence. "My husband is gone. My children are grown. I have few responsibilities these days."

"But there are risks," he warned her. "I can't expect you—"

She shook her head and smiled with a familiarity he'd never

experienced in a complete stranger. "Let's take it one step a time," she said. "I'll get tested, and then we'll see what the doctors say." She shrugged. "I may not have a lot of money to donate to your mission, but I can give what I *do* have. A kidney, perhaps?" With that she raised her eyebrows and tossed her head like she'd merely promised him a plate of brownies.

Carl shook his head in amazement. "I–I don't know what to say."

"How about, *Thanks*, and let's get started?" she said, laughing. "We want to put color in your face again. And soon."

Carl let out a heavy sigh. The truth was, when he glanced in the mirror that morning, he looked like he was at death's door. His skin had turned ash gray and his normally bright eyes had sunk into dark hollows. His weight had plummeted. And, he no longer had the energy to play outdoors with his children. Perhaps it was too late.

Then the faces of the children at the mission came to his mind. What stood out were the cries of the six who had vision problems, with more waiting to come.

"All right, Mrs. Cunningham," he conceded. "But you should first talk to my doctor. Let him fill you in on all the details—what it means for the donor—the risks, the hospital stay, the inconveniences if you're left with one kidney for the rest of your life."

"Set the appointment," Mrs. Cunningham said with an air of determination. "I'll submit to a whole regimen of tests, if necessary. But let me tell you, young man, if this is God's will, then we must not run from it."

When Carl arrived at his doctor's office, Mrs. Cunningham was already there, seated in the waiting room with an open Bible on her lap. He came alone this time.

"My wife and kids went to a local park," he said in response to her quizzical glance at the door. "I didn't want my children sitting around this waiting room with nothing to do but worry about their daddy's health. Adrienne will keep them busy. They'll have fun, and a time of relaxation will keep my wife from fussing over me—something she's done far too much lately."

He took a seat beside her and craned his neck to get a better look at the scripture she'd been reading.

"The Psalms," he said, smiling. "One of my favorite parts of the Bible. I read one every morning."

"David sure knew how to talk to God about his problems, didn't he? And he continued to praise the Lord, even when he was in the midst of trouble."

"So, what kind of encouraging words do the Psalms have for us today?"

She turned her attention to the book. "Well, I kind of like this verse where it says, *O Lord my God, in thee do I put my trust; let me never be ashamed: deliver me in thy righteousness.*" It's from the start of Psalm 31."

He grinned. "I read the Psalms daily, in English and Spanish. But, I haven't personalized them as I should."

Mrs. Cunningham studied his face. "Tell me, what made you choose to become a missionary?"

He had a sudden urge to open up to this woman. "Several years ago, I walked away from my second year in medical school to follow God's call. I attended a missions conference and listened intently while other missionaries spoke about their work. I was hooked. I never suspected that I'd have to drop out of my ministry to go looking for a kidney."

She sat back and shut her Bible. "Listen to me, Carl, God's not finished with you yet. As long as you're still walking around on this earth, still breathing and thinking and praying, he's going to be at work in your life. It's important that you don't forget that. He's not going to remove you from this world until your work is done."

"I'm afraid I haven't offered much of a testimony lately. I'm worried about my family, and I'm afraid of what might come next." He bowed his head and shuddered with emotion. "I have been performing for everyone else, trying to appear strong, hoping they won't see how frightened I am inside."

She shook her head. "For the life of me, I can't understand why people think Christians are some sort of super-humans who jump for joy even when bad news comes. Yes, you're a missionary, a servant of God. But you're also a human being with feelings, hurts, and anxieties. You've received a troubling diagnosis. Why should you mask your fears behind a cloak of false joy? If you're going to be honest, you'll speak what you really feel. First, to God. Then, to those who love you. You're in the arena, Carl. You need the support of others. You need to let them serve you for a change."

Carl ran a hand through his hair and let the reality of her words sink in.

"Oh, yes," he said. "You're right, Mrs. Cunningham."

She patted his knee. "You're on the right track. I think—" she began, but was interrupted when the door to the doctor's office opened and an attendant beckoned them inside.

Doctor Adam Fletcher greeted them with a handshake and a nod toward two empty chairs. Then he sat behind his desk and peered at the two of them through wire-rimmed eyeglasses. He looked old enough to be retired. He had bags under his eyes and his mustache had already turned gray. Was the guy still up to performing an operation?

Doctor Fletcher perused the file in front of him. Carl waited, his heart keeping time with the seconds.

"So," Fletcher said, his eyes now on Carl. "You need a kidney."

"That's why I'm here."

Without cracking a smile, the doctor shifted his gaze to Mrs. Cunningham. "And you want to give him one of yours." He leaned back in his chair and picked up a pen, which he flipped between his fingers as he spoke. "I've taken kidneys from deceased people and planted them in the living. I've also transferred kidneys from live donors to recipients. The outcome is more promising if the donor is related to the patient—that is, if you want to have a perfect match." He leaned forward and leafed through a couple of pages. "I see here that you and Mrs. Cunningham are not related." He looked up, his eyes questioning.

"That's right, Doctor," Carl said. "We're acquaintances. Friends," he corrected.

"You couldn't find a relative to donate?"

"No, Sir. My brother offered but he's a different type."

"And, Mrs.—um—" he glanced at the first page. "Mrs. Cunningham is a good match."

"Yes," Carl responded, feeling a little embarrassed. Here he was, a young man, and he was depending on an older woman to save his life.

Doctor Fletcher shook his head and his eyes darted from one to the other. "Okay," he said. "If that's all we've got, then that's all we've got. You have a willing donor. And, though she's nearly twice your age, from this medical report it looks like she's healthy."

Carl didn't care for the doctor's demeanor. Was it indifference? Boredom? This was serious business. It was a matter of life and death. He suppressed the rise of anger and tried to stay focused. "So...? What's the next step?" He chewed his bottom lip, still uncomfortable about what might happen to Mrs. Cunningham.

Doctor Fletcher removed his eyeglasses. "My staff will run both of you through a series of tests. We'll want to do a tissue test, see how compatible you are. And, Mrs.—um—" He put on his glasses and checked the sheet again. "Mrs. Cunningham, you will have to endure a separate series of tests to make sure you're a viable donor. We need to take all the necessary precautions to ensure your physical well-being, as well."

Carl turned toward Mrs. Cunningham, irritation building inside him. The guy couldn't even remember her name. He expected to see lines of concern on her forehead. She sat there with a confident smile on her lips and her eyes on the doctor, waiting, it seemed, for his next instruction.

Fletcher removed his glasses again and set his attention on Mrs. Cunningham.

"Madam," he said. "Have you looked at the risks? You're going to spend the rest of your life with one kidney. If yours fails, it won't be easy to find a donor for someone your age, especially with your rare blood type."

"I know the risks, and I have *not* changed my mind," she said. She straightened her back and looked directly at the doctor. "I'm here, aren't I? I came to your office today, knowing you'll speak about the risks. I'm telling you, Doctor Fletcher, I do not intend to run away from this. I will do whatever it takes to help this young man get back to his mission. So, let's not waste anymore of your time. Let's move on to the next step."

"All right then." Fletcher closed the file. He leaned back, crossed his arms, and went over the risks that accompany most types of surgery. Infection, complications with anesthesia, bleeding, blood clots, delayed healing, scarring. He looked from one to the other. "Even death," he added.

"Normally, donors don't require as long a hospital stay as recipients need," Fletcher went on. "Mrs. Cunningham, you can expect to be in the hospital for about a week. After your release, your full recovery will take another month or two. Then, depending on the type of work you do, you can return to your job."

She smiled. "I'm a receptionist in a real estate office four days a week. It's hardly taxing. And I spend Fridays and Saturdays getting the church ready for Sunday services—cleaning the bathrooms and the nursery, things like that."

The doctor stroked his chin. "The real estate job is okay, but you should pass the church duties to someone else for the time being. Too much lifting and bending will delay your healing and may cause adhesions to develop. You'll have to wait a month or two after your release from the hospital. We need to guard against pneumonia, infection at the site of the wound, allergic reaction to the antibiotics."

A rush of guilt surged through Carl. He placed his head in his hands and began to weep. "I can't ask you to do this," he murmured. "It's too risky. Too risky."

Mrs. Cunningham placed a hand on his back. "I'm not surprised or shocked at what Doctor Fletcher threw at me. It makes no difference. I still want to do this."

The doctor set aside her folder and picked up the one marked with Carl's name.

"Now," Fletcher said. "Are you ready to hear what you can expect, Mr. Wilson?"

He ran through a similar list of possible side effects and risks. "The incision will be in the stomach area. If your existing kidneys are not infected, they will remain where they are. We'll have to start you on a regimen of immune suppressants to ward off rejection of your new kidney, Carl. You'll likely be on them for life, which means you'll have to guard against contracting other illnesses, even the common cold."

Doctor Fletcher rose from his chair, walked around his desk and sat on the edge, directly in front of them.

"We already know you have compatible blood types. You both will undergo a complete physical exam that will involve tissue typing and blood work to make sure your white blood cells match." He turned his attention to Mrs. Cunningham. "You will have several urine tests over the next twenty-four hours to check your kidney function. You'll have a chest X-ray and an EKG, a gynecological exam, a mammogram, and, finally, another blood test, two days prior to surgery to make sure you have not developed any antibodies that might attack the kidney you'll be donating. And you both need to have separate psychological evaluations. It's mandatory."

Mrs. Cunningham rose to her feet. "Let's get started."

Astonishment flickered in Doctor Fletcher's eyes. He shook his head, stood to his feet, and walked back to his chair. "You're an amazing woman, Mrs. Cunningham," he said with admiration in his voice. He glanced from one to the other, then gathered up the paperwork and placed it back in the folder. "All right then. If you have no questions, I'll set things up."

The testing period took several weeks. Results from each test came in slowly. Days passed like centuries to Carl. To his chagrin, Mrs. Cunningham never wavered. She remained committed to her decision.

Then, one morning at the end of January, Doctor Fletcher phoned him with the final decision. "It's a go," he said. "I've arranged for an operating room for next Friday. Come in Wednesday at nine for your final blood work and exam."

Carl didn't try to hold back the upheaval of emotions that overtook him. He dropped to his knees and choked out his gratitude to God. His death sentence had been commuted. He no longer faced the grave. Mrs. Cunningham and Doctor Fletcher were handing him back his life.

Of course, like Mrs. Cunningham, he'd be living with one kidney. There'd be follow-up tests and maybe treatments, but the medical team in Mexico City could handle them all.

The day of the surgery, Paul and Judy Cunningham hovered over their mother. When the two gurneys were wheeled into the hall, they caught sight of Carl and eyed him with distaste.

"Don't worry about them," Mrs. Cunningham told him as her gurney passed his. "It's *my* kidney. If I want to give it away, I don't need their permission."

As he was rolled into the operating room, he took one last look at his donor, overcome with admiration for her. Later, in ICU, he struggled to awaken. His eyelids felt like they were glued shut. He tried to blink, opened his mouth to speak, but his tongue felt thick and clumsy and terribly dry. He couldn't lift his hands, or his feet.

Then he remembered. His last prayer had been for Mrs. Cunningham's well-being. Now as he rose from the darkness, he wanted to ask about her. He forced his eyes open. He mumbled something incoherent. A nurse leaned over him, blocking the glare of the overhead light. He shuddered.

"Cold—I'm cold..."

The nurse hurried away and returned with a warm blanket. He opened his parched lips to speak.

"How—how Marses Cunham?" he managed.

The nurse hovered close, her soft brown eyes peering at him over a surgical mask. She didn't speak, just pulled the blanket up to his chin, straightened his pillow, and pressed a cool palm against his forehead.

"You have a slight fever," she said. "I added some medicine to your IV. Your temperature should return to normal soon. You'll have to remain in ICU for the next twenty-four hours, for observation. Then, we'll move you to a regular hospital room. Now, relax. Don't try to talk. The doctor will be come in shortly. "

"Missers Cunning—" He hated that he couldn't get her name out, that his mind and his mouth had somehow been disconnected. "Please," he begged. "I need to know."

She patted his arm. "Doctor Fletcher will tell you everything. Meanwhile, get some rest. You've come through a major operation, Mr. Wilson. You need to let your body start to heal."

She was gone before he could ask another question. Though he fought it at first, he succumbed to the pull of sleep.

He surfaced again, this time to Doctor Fletcher's voice, urging him awake.

"Carl. Carl. Open your eyes, Carl."

The resurfacing took a while. When he finally had all his senses—the smell of anesthetics, the brightness of the overhead light, the sounds of machinery pulsing all around him. He blinked a few times, then turned his head toward Doctor Fletcher. He took a couple of deep breaths, exhaled, and asked again, this time with more clarity.

"How is Mrs. Cunningham?"

"Mr. Wilson, your surgery went fine. Just fine."

"Doctor—please, how is she?"

Fletcher shook his head. "We're watching her. After being moved to recovery, she developed an infection at the site of the incision. We pumped her full of antibiotics, but the infection seems to be spreading. She's in ICU, right next door. She's awake. I can give her a message, if you like."

Tears flooded into Carl's eyes, and he swallowed hard. "Tell her—tell her I'm praying for her, and that I'm so grateful—Oh, Lord, I'm so grateful...." The rest of his words were lost amidst a barrage of coughing that sent stabbing pains to the tender part of his abdomen.

The nurse rushed over with a small pillow and pressed it to his stomach. "Hold this here," she said. "And please relax."

"Is—is she going to make it?" he said, his eyes on Doctor Fletcher.

The doctor bit his lower lip, then let out a long, labored breath. "I hope so. We're doing all we can. We'll have to wait and see. I'll give her your message, Carl. That should bring her some encouragement."

He headed for the open door, then turned. For the first time since he met him, Doctor Fletcher was grinning. It wasn't a happy-face smile, not joyful or ready for a celebration, but more of a sympathetic smile, like someone gives to a person who is in trouble. Until that moment, the man had behaved like a sterile, robotic hospital machine, mechanically performing what he'd been taught to do in medical school. Now, he actually appeared human.

"You wouldn't believe it," Fletcher said, his face aglow. "That woman asked me for a box of stationery and a pen. Here she is, lying on a hospital bed in ICU, and she wants to write notes."

He shook his head, shrugged his shoulders, and left to make his rounds. Carl looked at the dividing wall between his cubicle and the one Mrs. Cunningham was in. He lifted his hand and blew her a kiss, then he shut his eyes, and drifted off to sleep.

Three days later, Carl was in a regular hospital room, gazing out a window at a rolling hillside and a spectacular grouping of blue spruce trees, their branches weighted by a fresh cover of snow. The scene brought an aura of peace to his bedside.

Doctor Fletcher walked in, a grave look on his face, and spoiled the mood. Carl set down the magazine he'd been reading.

"What's wrong?" he said. "Am I rejecting the kidney?"

The doctor sat on the edge of his bed and shook his head. "Your kidney is stable. There are no early signs of rejection, and I'm confident you're going to heal well."

He looked down at his hands, a move that troubled Carl.

"What is it, doctor?"

When Fletcher looked up, Carl was certain there were tears in the man's eyes.

"Doctor—"

He grabbed Carl's hand and held onto it.

"It saddens me to tell you, Carl. Mrs. Cunningham passed away this morning."

Carl jerked his hand back and tried to sit up, but a sharp ache had him dropping back down and clutching the little pillow to his stomach. He tried to inhale, but his breathing came in short, painful gasps. When he found his voice, it was strained, almost a whisper.

"Please, tell me it isn't true. Tell me she's okay."

Doctor Fletcher shook his head. "She never came out of ICU," he said. "I'm so sorry, Carl. We did everything we could, but the infection kept spreading." He grunted. "Even with a delirious fever, she kept on writing those blasted notes. It was like she was on some sort of mission."

"Where are they?"

"Huh?"

"The notes, doctor. Where are the notes?"

"Her daughter came and took them away with the rest of her things."

PART V
THE NOTES

TWENTY-THREE

ALICIA CARTER

Before she left town, Alicia hurried back to Parker Addison's office. "I have concerns," she said as soon as she was seated across from him.

He stuck his thumbs in the sides of his pin-striped vest, leaned back in his chair and tilted his head to one side. His arrogance irked her. Such a display might work in the courtroom, but there, in his office, as they talked about Mindy's future, it made her want to run.

"Really?" he'd said with an air of sarcasm. "You're having doubts at this stage of the game?" He frowned, and the beautiful man disappeared. In his place was something akin to Satan. "I've already filed the papers at the courthouse," he went on. "We only have to wait for a date, and then it's a done deal. You're on your way to being a mommy, Alicia. Isn't that what you wanted?"

"Well, yes, but—"

"Then why don't you trust me and relax?"

"I–I want to do the right thing. To be honest, I'm not sure what that is anymore. I think I need to—"

"What?" In one quick motion, he pulled his thumbs out of his vest and leaned toward her. "You've given me a lot of money to pursue this. Not more than a week ago, you said you wanted your baby back." He shook his head, and she could feel his disgust. "You have a good case, Alicia. There's no paper trail, no proof of legality on their part. I'm confident we can win this, if you'd just let me do–my–job."

He'd said the last three words with such emphasis, she began to tremble. She pulled a tissue from her purse, preparing to catch the tears that had formed in her eyes.

He let out a sigh and leaned back. "Tell me, what changed your mind?"

"I saw her today—at Adele Cunningham's funeral."

"What? Wasn't she the dingbat who convinced you to give up the baby in the first place?"

"Well, yes, I mean, no. She wasn't a dingbat. She was a fine woman, someone I loved and trusted." She glowered at him. "Please, don't call her that."

He jerked his head to one side and gave her a half-smile. "Sorry. But she gave you some bad advice. Look at where that decision has gotten you. Your child, the person you gave birth to, is living with strangers. You don't know if they're treating her right. Why, in my career, I've dealt with all kinds of horrific situations involving kids being raised by abusive foster parents. You've got a chance to rescue your little girl. What bothers me is that you didn't do so sooner. Why didn't you keep the child back then?"

Alicia bowed her head and released the puddle of tears. "I don't know," she sobbed. "I was a teenager. I had no money. My parents had turned their backs on me. They were afraid of gossip. I had no other choice but to let someone else have my baby. Then my grandparents took me in and everything happened so fast. I could give you a ton of reasons why I let my baby go."

Tears were streaming down her face. As fast as she mopped them away, more came.

"And then there were the Goodes. I knew them from going to their church. They seemed like nice people. They couldn't have kids of their own. I assumed they would provide a good home for my child. It all made sense. Can't you see that?"

He pinched his lips together and smirked at her, his arrogance still obvious.

"Look," he said. "Why don't you go home, think it over, and

call me when you're ready to make a decision. I'll let the court document stay where it is. I'm certain once you get inside that big, empty house of yours, you're gonna want to keep going with this."

"Maybe," Alicia said. She blew her nose. Then she rose from her chair. "So, that's it?"

"That's it."

She gathered up her coat and purse, and started for the door.

"Phone me," Parker called after her. "And do it soon."

She left his office with a lump in her throat and a stab of guilt in her heart. She never thought she was the kind of person who hurts others. What right did she have to uproot that little girl's security? What right did she have to judge the Goodes?

She was still suffering from the consequences of her past. She hadn't remained pure and unspoiled. She and Johnny had created another life, one that required more responsibility than two teenagers could handle. He'd left and never looked back. Then she'd walked away from their child too. She'd gone on with her life with a tiny specter gnawing at her maternal instinct. Now she was in a turmoil. Maybe, if Mrs. Cunningham hadn't died, she wouldn't have gone back home. Maybe she would have left Mindy in the only life she knew—with Robert and Jennifer Goode.

During her drive home, she mulled over her dilemma. Should she continue with the lawsuit or drop the whole thing? What was she trying to prove? That the Goodes were unfit parents? That the child appeared to be abused or mistreated? That she'd be a far better mother than Jennifer? She kept shaking her head, aware that she was answering her own questions.

One thing was certain, As the wife of an airline captain, she could provide a far better lifestyle for the girl. Mindy would live in a bigger house. She'd have expensive clothes, a room full of toys, the best schooling, and opportunities beyond what she might find in Fall River. After all, what could an underpaid minister and his wife offer the child? They certainly couldn't love a child more than a natural mother could.

And Alicia *did* love her, with all her heart. Though she hadn't seen her child since that day in the delivery room, the baby's image had haunted her for years. Living 200 miles away didn't matter. In reality, she hadn't been more than a few heartbeats away from her child. It was time to fulfill those biological urges, time to take her baby home.

The radio was pouring out one of her favorite Sinatra songs, "All or Nothing at All." That's about where she stood right then. She could have it all or she could end up with nothing. So could the Goodes. It might depend on her lawyer, but at the present time, she had control. She could keep grabbing onto her past, or she could give it all up and leave those people alone.

Sinatra's velvet voice was singing about half a love. She felt the impact of those words. Over the last ten years, she'd endured half of a love. She loved a child, and the child couldn't love her back.

How ironic. Her child *had* loved someone, but it wasn't her. It was a different mother and a different father.

The next words of the song sent a dagger into her heart. The lyrics claimed if a person didn't have it all, then he—or she— had nothing. Were those the only options? All or nothing? Wasn't there something in between, some sort of compromise that might work? Tears filled her eyes, and she could barely see through the windshield. She blinked them away and tried to concentrate on the road ahead. Patches of ice dotted the highway. She carefully averted them, turned the wheel back and forth and slowed her speed.

She thought about the Goodes, tried to put herself in their shoes. She didn't doubt that couple loved her daughter. She could see it in their eyes the day they cuddled her baby for the first time. She was aware of it that morning, too, when they wrapped protective arms around Mindy. She'd done the right thing, hadn't she, allowing them to raise her child? No one understood her pain—not her parents or her grandparents—no one, except for Mrs. Cunningham.

Adele wrote her often. For the first couple years she'd kept her informed about her daughter's progress. The Goodes had named the child Melinda and had given her the nickname *Mindy*. Mrs. Cunningham kept writing what a terrific job Jennifer and Robert had done, how her daughter appeared healthy and happy.

As she drove, she thought about the round, innocent eyes that had peered up at her during the service. Once again, she enjoyed the sweet, melodic voice, reveled in the girl's shy smile, chuckled over the swinging foot, the nervous giggle, and the gentle fluttering of her eyelashes.

Mindy didn't look at all like the sad, ill-clad orphan she'd expected to find there. She was well-dressed, poised, and as carefree as any other contented ten-year-old. Did she really want to disrupt the girl's life?

She had to admit, her motives had been selfish. She'd come there wanting to fill a void in her own life, believing only Mindy could fill it. But if she wanted to be honest, that morning she'd looked into the face of a stranger. Sure the girl had her golden hair and blue eyes, her porcelain complexion, and even her turned-up nose. But she didn't know Mindy, not really. And Mindy didn't know her, maybe didn't even know *about* her.

What if, instead of offering Mindy a brighter future, she ended up breaking the girl's heart? What if her child rebelled against her?

She glanced at the odometer. Still another eighty miles to go. She had avoided going to the Cunningham house after the service. Judy had invited her, but that wasn't the time or the place for old friends to catch up. She'll contact Judy later, or do like they always had done over the last ten years, talk for ten minutes on the phone and avoid the serious issues. They had moved on. Alicia to her new life and new friends. And Judy stuck in that antiquated little town, doing a boring job, and still unmarried.

While the other guests were filling up on Aunt Connie's good cooking, Alicia had hit the highway, hungry, tired, and struggling with the decision of a lifetime. Up ahead she spotted a diner, *Mike's Place*, the kind of eatery that offered the best-tasting, greasiest hamburgers and fries around, and had a full parking lot to prove it. Her stomach started to rumble. She thought about getting something to eat. Butch wouldn't be home until late. *Might as well stop for a bite,* she mused.

She went inside and slid into a red vinyl booth. Every counter stool was occupied by men in heavy wool jackets and baseball caps. A family of four looked over menus at the opposite side of the aisle, and one booth was crammed with teenagers who'd managed to fit six people at a table meant for four.

She turned her attention to the coin-operated box of music selections on the wall beside her. The teenagers already had taken control. "Rebel, Rebel" was just finishing up, and they were already inserting more coins. Alicia scanned the selections. One struck her hard. Paul Anka's "You're Having My Baby." Then she spotted "Always on My Mind" by Willie Nelson, and searched for a quarter in her bag. Instead, she came up with Mrs. Cunningham's note. She'd forgotten it was there. She started to open the envelope when a gum-cracking waitress came up to her booth and interrupted her.

The woman had a full head of coppery red hair, and she wore a nametag that said *Bunny.* She placed a glass of water and a menu in front of Alicia, then stood back, cracking her gum and waiting.

Alicia hesitated.

"Need a few minutes?" Bunny said. She didn't bother to remove the pencil from over her ear.

"Yes, please." Alicia set aside the note and turned her attention to the menu.

Bunny did a brisk pivot and walked away. Alicia scanned the list of possibilities. It had been a long time since she'd had a hamburger. She'd turned vegetarian two years ago, thinking it might make her healthy enough to carry a baby full-term. Her mouth began to water, but she turned her attention to the salad options. When Bunny returned a few minutes later, she was ready to order.

"I'd like a chef's salad and a glass of ice tea."

Bunny nodded, didn't bother to write anything down, but stared at Alicia for an uncomfortable moment. Then she turned away, a thoughtful expression on her face.

While waiting for her order, Alicia picked up Mrs. Cunningham's note. What had Adele written to her at this stage of her life? Ten years before, that woman had stood beside her in the delivery room, and had remained there, even after the Goodes left with her baby. Adele had placed a gentle hand on Alicia's shoulder. She didn't speak, didn't shower Alicia with trite condolences. She stayed there for the longest time, like a comforting angel.

After a while, she looked at her watch. "The Goodes are waiting in the car," she said, at last. "I'll have to join them now." She bent forward and kissed Alicia on the forehead. "I'm only a phone call away, if you need anything."

Alicia never called, never returned to her hometown, never again visited the Cunningham home. She walked away, severing everything that reminded her of how she'd failed and hoping the distance would help ease the terrible pain of giving up her child.

She attended the Christian school her grandparents had selected and after graduation, she left their farm and didn't look back. She had embarked on a new life, one that offered adventure and a certain amount of stability. Her parents had moved to Florida. No longer did she have any reason to go home. No reason at all—until Mrs. Cunningham died. While the word of Adele's passing had stirred up a longing to return to Fall River, it also conjured up all the pain and trauma of the past. Now, more pronounced than ever before was the emptiness that still awaited her at home.

She turned Mrs. Cunningham's note over and over in her hand. What would Adele say to her now? She couldn't have known what Alicia had been wanting to do. She slid her fingernail under the flap and pulled out a single sheet of blue stationery.

My dear Alicia,

Though you've been away these many years, and though we stopped communicating, my thoughts and prayers have always been with you. I kept up with your life through my daughter, Judy, and was glad you two continued to correspond, though less and less over the years.

It seems my prayers for you have been answered. You've had a full life. You've enjoyed a wonderful career, traveling, seeing the world, doing things you might have missed had you chosen to raise your child on your own. What a difficult burden for one so young.

But then, you married well. You have everything a young woman could hope for—a successful, loving husband, a magnificent home, and the freedom to pursue your dreams. Yes, you have everything— everything except a child.

I was sorry to hear about your miscarriages. Did you ever wonder if maybe God wanted something else for your life? Your inability to have more children tells me that maybe he has other plans. Some people remain childless and get involved in other things that make a difference. However, if your biological clock is still ticking, perhaps you'll want to reach out to another child in need. There are plenty of youngsters out there who hop from one foster home to another and never have the stability a permanent home life can offer.

I want to encourage you to go to the Lord in prayer. Seek his guidance. Like it says in Proverbs 3:5-6, the Lord can direct your path. You merely need to trust in him.

Ten years ago you lost something precious. If you let go of the past, you'll be able to step with confidence into the future. It's been said, you can't drive a car while looking in the rearview mirror. Keep focused on the road ahead. When you least expect it, something new will come up right in front of you. Grab onto it. Take a risk. Step out in faith. You may be in for a wonderful adventure.

With much love and good will,

Adele Cunningham

Something new? A wonderful adventure? What on earth was Mrs. Cunningham talking about? How did that woman know she was still holding onto the past? She hadn't said a thing about it to Judy.

She started to tear up the note, but stopped and shoved it back in her purse. At that moment, Bunny showed up with her salad.

The strange, red-haired woman stood there staring at Alicia for an awkward minute, then her eyes widened with recognition.

"I know you," Bunny said. "We were in the same class back at St. John High."

Alicia looked at the round, cheerful face, the coppery red hair, then at the name tag. Nothing about that woman stirred a memory.

"I'm afraid I don't recognize you," she said, blinking. "I never knew anybody named Bunny."

"Oh that?" The waitress poked a finger at her name tag. "That's a nickname my kids gave me. My real name is Barbara Bunting."

A vague memory flashed before Alicia with an image of a bouncy, red-headed beauty in her social studies class. "Oh, yes. I do remember you, Barb. You were queen of the prom."

Alicia tried to hide her shock. What on earth had happened to Barbara Bunting? She was now about fifty pounds overweight, wore way too much makeup, and she'd colored her hair with some kind of metallic dye. She glanced at the woman's left hand. There was no wedding ring.

"What did you mean, your kids? Are you married?"

"Married? Not me. Look at me. Who would want me now?" She broke the tension with a hearty laugh.

At a loss for words, Alicia smiled back at her.

"My kids— " Bunny pulled a wallet from her apron pocket. "Do you wanna see my kids?"

Alicia nodded, surprised when Bunny unraveled an accordion of photos out of her hand. "Here they are—all seventeen of 'em."

"Seventeen?" Alicia gasped.

With a proud smile on her lips, Bunny flipped through the chain of smiling faces, some white, some black, a couple of Asian children, and one that looked to be Hispanic.

Alicia furrowed her brow and gazed at Bunny with questioning eyes. "I don't understand. Seventeen kids?"

"They're foster kids. I take one or two for a couple of months or so, keep them until they get placed in regular foster care or when they go home to rehabilitated parents." She glanced at the ceiling as if she doubted the rationality of all that. "Or," she said with a lilt in her voice, "they get adopted by some nice couple. Then I take one or two more, and the cycle continues."

"If you're not married, how do you qualify for something like that? Don't you need to have a husband?"

"Oh, no, you don't have to be married. Not these days. There are too many kids in the system. Applicants have to pass a background check and a home study. I'll tell you what, if I hadn't turned my life over to Jesus several years ago, I might not have done something like this." She shook her head, and her metallic red curls bounced. "It's been very rewarding. Sometimes, I think those kids help *me* more than I help *them*."

"Why do you take them for only a couple of months? Doesn't it hurt to give them back? I mean, doesn't it make sense to keep a child for, say, a year or two, or maybe for good?"

"Not me. The regular foster parents do that. I give them a place to stay when they first come into the system. That way, they don't have to live in a shelter. That can traumatize a poor kid. A decent home life is far better.

Alicia's initial impression, that the woman was a lunatic, now turned to admiration.

"When I need a break," Bunny went on. "I tell the agency I'm not available for a couple of weeks. Then, I get to do a few things for myself. I take a mini vacation, regroup, and get ready for my next visitors. I'll tell you what, though, it is hard to say good-bye to my kids. Every one of them has a special place in my heart."

"Bunny!" The gruff shout came from the kitchen window. "Your orders are sittin' here gettin' cold."

"Sorry," Bunny apologized to Alicia. "Gotta go." Then she

hesitated. "Look, here's my phone number." She jotted it on the back of a blank receipt. "If you want to hear more, give me a call."

Alicia stared at the number. Had the meeting been a coincidence or was it God-ordained? Hadn't Adele suggested an alternative like the one Bunny had chosen? Alicia was well-aware of the miracles Mrs. Cunningham worked when she was alive. But now? After death?

Bunny had said she was a Christian. Alicia had received Christ, too, a long time ago, while attending the Christian school. But after graduation, she'd forgotten that commitment and had gone on to live a life of adventure with no time for reading the scriptures or attending church. She certainly hadn't been living for God, not the way the Bible said to. Pastors talked about how people should live out their faith. Once they become new creatures in Christ, they should do good works. She was a believer. But what had she done that had any value?

It looked like Bunny had changed her own life. She wasn't married. She hadn't had kids of her own, but she was living for God. Alicia had been living for herself. She hadn't asked God what *he* wanted her to do. She'd been consumed by her own pain, her own desires, her own selfishness. Maybe, like Mrs. Cunningham said, it was time for her to trust God with her future.

She bowed her head and said grace over her meal, then tacked on an additional prayer. *Dear God, I'm not sure anymore whether I should pursue that lawsuit. Help me know what you want me to do. I'm ready to follow you. No matter what the cost.*

At six-thirty that evening, Alicia walked into a dark, empty house. She hit one light switch after another, brightening every room. Then she reached the bedroom and dropped her suitcase on the bed.

She knew her husband's schedule. His trips to Munich. Barring weather delays, his routine stayed pretty much the same, which meant he'd be walking in the front door within the next two hours, tired and ready for a hot shower and a late dinner.

After unpacking her bag, she stripped off her clothes and

headed for her claw-foot tub, a cup of hot tea in her hand. She placed the cup on a side table and eased into the lavender scented water, shut her eyes and mulled over the day's events—the visit with Parker Addison, the funeral service, the lovely child in the pew beside her—a remembrance that lingered for several minutes and included the concern on Jennifer's face and Pastor Goode's anxiety as he fumbled with his notes. She breathed in the lavender scent, sipped her tea, and forced her thoughts back to the little girl and those round, innocent eyes gazing up at her. At that moment, a shower of tears dropped like bullets into the foamy water, as her struggle returned with intensity.

She released the plug and stepped out of the tub. The water spiraled down the drain, dragging her strength with it. Turning away, she padded into the bedroom and slipped into a pair of pajamas. Then, her emotions still shifting from her desire to have Mindy and the unexpected visit with Bunny—plus Mrs. Cunningham's note— she went downstairs to the kitchen and tried to concentrate on putting something edible together for when Butch walked in.

Yet, even as she rooted around in the refrigerator, her dilemma kept surfacing. She pulled out a package of roast beef, another of Swiss cheese, a jar of horse radish, and a jar of pickles. She peeled and chopped a potato, then boiled and blanched the chunks for a salad and put them in the refrigerator to chill.

She checked the clock. *Butch will be walking in the door at any moment.* She poured herself a glass of wine, perched on a kitchen stool, and reached for her purse. She withdrew Mrs. Cunningham's note.

As she reread it, she focused on Adele's positive comments— the comfortable life God had granted her, the possibility that she could help others, like Bunny was doing, that other people's children could perhaps fill the void in her life.

Then she pulled out the paper receipt containing Bunny's number. Was God playing tricks on her? Had he been coordinating this whole thing? And could it be possible that God had his hand in everything that happened? Mrs. Cunningham's funeral? The children having recess at the exact time she reached the school? The empty place on the pew beside Mindy? Then the meeting with Bunny? Was God showing her what she needed to give up to have the life he'd wanted for her all along?

After draining her glass, she pulled the bowl of potatoes from the refrigerator and began to dice the onions and celery. Out of nowhere a message by Pastor Goode came to her mind. Years ago he'd preached about there being no coincidences in life. *No coincidences?* At the time she was a teenager who had discovered she was pregnant. For some reason, she'd filed Pastor Goode's message in the back of her mind. Now it surfaced again, and for the first time, it had meaning for her.

She added the onions and celery to the bowl, along with a couple spoonfuls of pickle relish and a scoop of mayonnaise. Then salt and pepper, a sprinkle of paprika. As she absentmindedly stirred the concoction, she heard the front door click open, and her husband's bags hit the foyer floor.

"I'm in the kitchen," she called out.

"How come all the lights are on?" Butch hollered from the hall.

"The house was too dark when I got home. You know I don't like to enter a dark house. Especially when I'm alone."

On his way to the kitchen, he hit the switches, darkening the path behind him. Then, he stood in the doorway, a questioning look on his face.

"What's going on, Alicia?"

She set the bowl of potato salad on the table, walked over to him and gave him a kiss.

"Welcome home," she said, then turned back toward the table. She clenched her teeth, willing herself not to cry. But the day's events rose up again and she burst into tears.

"I–I saw her," she said, turning to face him. "I saw my daughter. I stopped by the school and caught sight of her in the playground. Later, I sat right beside her in church, and oh, Butch, she's the sweetest little thing."

"Hey, what's the matter, honey?" His voice was gentle. He led her to a chair at the kitchen table and pulled up another for himself. He slipped out of his jacket, loosened his tie, and leaned close to her. "C'mon. It couldn't have been that bad."

She stared into his crystal blue eyes, assured that they were filled with compassion and not judgment.

"It wasn't bad at all. But it was terribly convicting."

He urged her on with a nod.

"She was a stranger," she admitted with a sigh. "I didn't know her, Butch, didn't know her at all. She was someone else's little girl. I mean, my heart still belongs to the baby that left my hospital room ten years ago. But this child—Mindy—was a stranger to me. A beautiful one, I admit, but still, a stranger."

Butch leaned closer and wrapped an arm around her shoulder. The gesture, though comforting, brought more tears.

"What are you telling me, honey?" he said, his voice low. "Have you changed your mind? Are you going to leave well enough alone?"

She leaned back and nodded.

"I can't do it to her—or to them." She shrugged. "They're a family now. My child has a life that doesn't include me."

"So, what does that mean? For you? For us?"

"Well, as you know, I've been wanting to have a child since the day we married. But, Butch, it doesn't seem like it's part of God's plan for me. So many miscarriages. I had to go and see my little girl—had to find out if this was what I'm supposed to do. But, I left that church with more uncertainty than when I arrived there. I've been praying, Butch, praying that God will show me his plan for my life. And I have to tell you, I think he's answered."

She let Butch read Mrs. Cunningham's note. Then she told him about her meeting with Bunny at the diner, and how seeing photos of her *children* had changed her heart in an unexpected way.

"What do you think if we open our big, five-bedroom home

to foster children? You know, little kids who've fallen into the system and come from situations of neglect or abuse."

Butch straightened, a wrinkle of interest on his brow. "Other people's kids?" he said. "You want to take care of other people's kids?"

"I'd like to think we were taking care of God's kids. They happened to be born into the wrong homes. Their parents are on drugs or alcohol, maybe even in prison. Sometimes they come from broken homes, or their parents have died and the children have nowhere else to go."

"God's kids, huh?" He ran a hand through his hair and grinned at her.

Alicia nodded. She was smiling now with amazing confidence. Instead of hurting the Goodes, she'd be helping others.

"We're well off, Butch. We have more money than we know what to do with." She was surprised to find herself smiling. No more tears. No more anxiety. "We should try it," she pressed. "Maybe take a couple of children for a few weeks until their parents are rehabilitated or until they get adopted. We can test it out, see if it's right for us. If it's not," she raised a shoulder, "then we'll stop. But, I have to at least try, Butch. I won't be thinking about myself all the time. I'll be thinking of ways I can make someone else's life comfortable and happy."

She caught a flicker of skepticism in his eyes.

"Believe me, Butch, it won't be like all my unfinished furniture or the kiln that's collecting dust in the basement. This is about real people—people who need a home. I can't think of anything more fulfilling than to help make a child feel safer and happier.

Butch grinned his approval. "If it'll make you happy, I say, let's go for it. I grew up in a big family—four brothers and two sisters—so, to be honest, I never liked living in a big, empty house. It's too quiet around here. I'd love to be greeted by a bunch of little voices when I walk through the front door after a trip."

Alicia began to cry again, but this time they were tears of relief.

"So, what's next?" Butch asked, his eyebrows arched in anticipation.

"Well, there's a process. We have to pass a background check, a home visit, and whatever else the officials need from us."

Butch shrugged. "I have nothing to hide." He hesitated and gave her a whimsical smile. "Do you?"

She punched his arm playfully. "Of course not. I'm as clean as a—as a—"

"Sinner, cleansed by the blood of Christ?"

"Boy, that's exactly how I feel, right now. Like God has gotten a hold of me and turned me in the right direction. There's one more thing I have to do."

He frowned. "What is that?"

"I have to call my lawyer back home and cancel the lawsuit."

"Lawsuit? You started court proceedings without telling me?"

She shook her head and flushed with shame. "I didn't know how it was going to turn out. I thought I should start—"

"Listen, Alicia. We do things together or not at all. Now, what else haven't you told me? What do you need to do to wipe that slate clean?"

She released a sigh. "Well, I have to send a letter to the Goodes—a thank you letter, telling them what a great job they've done with Mindy and how I appreciate their love and care of her. I want to contribute some money to her college fund, and I want to ask them if I can visit now and then." He was about to protest. She raised her hand. "A friend of the family, nothing more. There's no need to tell her I'm her biological mother, not until she's older—and only with her parents' permission."

Butch was grinning broadly now. "Wow, this is a completely different Alicia than the one I left behind a couple of days ago."

She smiled back at him. "Get used to her, Butch. She's here to stay."

TWENTY-FOUR

ROBERT GOODE

Pastor Goode locked up the church but didn't leave right away. He remained in the sanctuary under dimmed lights that created a quiet haven for prayer and meditation. He knelt in the second pew where his little Mindy had been sitting only an hour before. He pressed his forehead to the rail. For the hundredth time in the past few days, he uttered the same petition. *Please, don't let that woman take my little angel away. Please stop her, Lord.*

It was that simple. Prayers didn't have to be long-winded. They didn't have to be filled with a lot of flowery words. *Help me, Lord, is sufficient, isn't it?* Robert mused. *In fact, can't a person speak to God without uttering a single word—perhaps depend on the Holy Spirit to convey the message? The Bible says so. It also said a person should come to God like a little child—innocent and seeking the Father's help.* At that moment, Robert felt like a child—small, helpless, unable to fight his battle alone.

Through most of his ministry, he'd fallen into a pattern of repetitious prayers. His early-morning meetings with the God of the Universe were scheduled, and if he wanted to be honest, they were downright boring. He kept a list of prayer requests, named names, mentioned needs, a tiresome recitation of petitions. They fell flat. If they were that mundane to him, how must God be receiving them?

Somewhere along the way, between his ordination when he was on fire for the things of God and the last few years of tireless ministry, he'd drifted into an apathetic routine. But in recent days, a different kind of fire had kindled within him. His situation had grown desperate. Someone had threatened to destroy his family. Alicia Davis—or Carter, or whatever she was calling herself these days—had decided to go back on her word. She wanted her daughter back, and she'd already started legal proceedings.

Since receiving the letter from Alicia's lawyer, a renewed spirit had formed within him. He began to pray again like he used to, from the heart. These weren't vain repetitions. They were sincere conversations between a humble servant and his God. He fell to his knees and even to his face, flat on the floor the way John did before the vision of Jesus in the Book of Revelation. And he wept with such intensity he suspected the Father's heart was breaking along with his.

Alicia came to town anyway, and he began to wonder if God had heard him at all. What made things worse was how all this was affecting his wife. She had fallen into a terrible state of despair. That was when his anguish turned to discouragement and then to fear and ultimately to a bitterness he couldn't control. That's when he admitted to himself and to Jennifer that he despised Alicia Carter. He hated her with a vengeance he didn't know resided within him until now. It scared him to think he was capable of such intense hostility.

So why should God answer any of his prayers? Didn't God also see through his hypocrisy? In the end, he had come full circle until he didn't know how to pray anymore.

So he knelt in the church, speechless. He gazed at the wooden cross beyond the altar, above the choir loft. There was no figure to remind him of Christ's sacrifice. No hand-carved message like some churches displayed. Only an empty wooden cross, the emblem of his faith. He sought in vain for the right words. Surely, God knew his heart was breaking. And God knew that as long as he insisted on carrying a grudge against Alicia, he shouldn't be coming to the altar with a petition.

He knew what he had to do. Forgive. But how?

At that moment he remembered the envelope Judy had given him. It was still unopened in his jacket pocket. He drew it out and stared at it for a minute. While he needed to know what Adele had written, he wasn't sure he could handle the truth. For that's what Mrs. Cunningham always spoke. Truth. Even when it was painful.

Summoning courage, he slid the note out of the envelope, and began to read.

Dear Pastor Goode,

How appropriate that you should have such a name. I have seen your goodness displayed time and time again. I've seen how faithfully you ministered to your congregation. Your kind words could draw the worst heathen in the world to God's feet. I've seen the way you love your wife, how you sometimes hold back your rightful authority in favor of her needs and desires. And I've observed your sacrificial care of the child you took into your home, how you've worn the same tattered jacket and scuffed loafers for years while clothing that little girl in pretty frocks and new shoes.

We all have treasures—some tangible, some hidden inside our hearts. Sadly, in a moment of time, we can lose those blessings. Someone stronger—or wiser—can take it all away. I experienced this with the loss of my husband, George. He died unexpectedly, leaving me with an emptiness I was never able to fill. Through such losses, we need to remember that we have a God who is in control, a God who sees it all, can stop it all, and sometimes chooses not to.

As humans, we often hold onto things with a tight fist. If we hold them too tight, they can slip through our fingers. But, if we loosen our grip and hold an open hand before God, sometimes the treasure remains, or God fills our palm with something else.

Having studied in seminary, you know the scriptures far better than I do. But I leave you with these words from the first chapter of Job: "The Lord gave, and the Lord hath taken away; blessed be the name of the Lord."

No matter what happens, never let your trust in the Lord falter.

Remain strong in your faith. Develop the heart of God. Put away all bitterness and anxiety, and trust him. Your people depend on you to be their example. There is no better way to teach them to trust the Lord than to trust him yourself.

With much fondness,
Adele Cunningham

Pastor Goode crumpled up the note and pressed it to his chest. He remained there for several minutes, weeping softly. Then, he smoothed out the note and reread it. As he repeated Job's words, an attitude of submission tore the stubbornness out of his heart and left him with a peace he hadn't expected.

Until that moment, he'd succumbed to his human emotions. A terrible hostility had germinated within his heart. Alicia Carter had come there to see Mindy. She was planning to take his child away. Since receiving that letter from her attorney and learning her plan, he'd allowed hatred to boil up inside of him. He'd even wanted to call down God's wrath on her. The truth was, he'd fallen into Satan's trap. Though God's word said that a man was supposed to love his neighbor as himself, he'd developed an intense animosity toward Alicia and had been prepared to fight her, publicly if necessary.

So what did God expect of him? He already knew the answer. God wanted him to lay down his life for his enemy. And how could he do that? Perhaps, by getting outside of himself and into the heart of his adversary.

With some difficulty, he struggled to understand Alicia. Here was a woman who'd made a mistake as a young girl. The consequences were severe. Pregnancy. Shame. Heartbreak. And she had given up the most precious gift a woman could give—her own child. Now she'd somehow changed her mind. She wanted her baby. Could it be that, in her desire to satisfy her motherly instinct, she hadn't thought about how such a decision might affect others? Could it be that she was acting out of love and not out of cruelty?

Though he had planned to fight against her in court, he now

acknowledged he had one responsibility—to be right with God. This should be his testimony before his congregation. This should be his attitude before a righteous God.

Once again, he mentally recited the words of Job. *The Lord gave, and the Lord hath taken away. Blessed be the name of the Lord.*

He rose to his feet and turned his eyes toward the ceiling and the rainbow of colors painted there by the afternoon light streaming through stained glass windows.

"The Lord gave and the Lord hath taken away. Blessed be the name of the Lord," he said aloud, his voice breaking. He repeated the words again, affixed them to his heart, so he would not falter.

In that instant, he knew what he had to do. He would go to Jack Gibbs' office tomorrow morning and drop the counter suit. It was time he trusted the Lord—in everything—even if it meant losing Mindy.

When he walked out of the church, the spirit of hatred had been lifted from his heart. He no longer resented Alicia, but pitied her and empathized with her. They had one thing in common, an undying love for a little girl they both wanted to call their own. No longer did their case depend on a human judge. The Judge of all the earth will decide.

TWENTY-FIVE

BEN MICHAELS

There was no doubt in Ben's mind that his marriage had spiraled out of control. Though he hadn't thought about Elizabeth for years, seeing her again had revived a lot of pleasant memories. Like when they were young, she'd let him know she had feelings for him. She'd pretty much thrown herself at him last night. Though he'd resisted, he'd come dangerously close to throwing caution to the wind.

Now she expected him to show up at the Cunningham's house. And what would happen after that? He figured she'd invite him back to the inn.

His mind shifted between knowing the right thing to do and his desire to do something else. The wrong choice could end his marriage and perhaps destroy his career. He tugged the blue paper out of the envelope, hoping that whatever Mrs. Cunningham had written might be exactly what he needed. He caught his breath and began to read.

Dear Ben,

I've been following your career, the newspaper reports, the ballgames, your successes, and your marriage, and I'm so proud to be able to call you my friend. Our connection goes back to those days when you first struggled to walk.

But, those were baby steps. Bigger steps followed, taking you to new and wonderful places—places that offered challenges you never encountered before.

And so, because of our relationship, I feel obligated to warn you that, with fame and fortune also comes temptation. In the midst of all your successes, Satan will try to drag you down. But, be aware, the devil is not your only adversary. There is a part of you, the flesh, that will trouble you for the rest of your life. You cannot allow anything but God to have power over you. And remember, fame is something you have. It shouldn't have you.

I remember seeing you as a young boy in leg braces. What stands out for me most at this time was the day you limped down the aisle in church and received Jesus Christ as your Savior. Your decision thrilled me beyond anything you can imagine. It was then that you joined God's team. You weren't playing ball on the sandlot anymore. You were pitching for God.

From that moment on, you needed to put on a different uniform. You needed to put on the armor of God. Ephesians 13–18 talks about truth, righteousness, peace, the shield of faith, the helmet of salvation, and the sword of the spirit, which is the word of God. Without them you will remain vulnerable to Satan's attacks.

Keep applying those crucial pieces of armor to your life. You won't regret it. And pray, Ben, pray with all your heart, because prayer is your lifeline to God as you face the battle of worldly temptations.

With deepest love and admiration,
Adele Cunningham

Tears streamed down his face as he folded Mrs. Cunningham's note and returned it to his jacket pocket. He knew the verses she'd referred to. He'd memorized them as a child. Tonight, before going to bed, he wanted to recite that passage again. In fact, it wouldn't be a bad idea to do the same at the end of every day, until those verses became a part of his life.

The armor of God, huh? he thought. *I should have recited those verses last night before my time with Elizabeth. If I'd recalled them before seeing her again, I never would have accepted her invitation to go swimming. Wouldn't even have agreed to dinner.*

Now he had no desire to get within ten feet of that vixen. What he knew for sure was that he needed to help Candy see that he did love her. He'd almost failed last night. In one fleeting moment of weakness, he could have lost everything—his marriage, his son, his reputation.

He drove away from the church, and as he maneuvered his car onto the highway, he thought over some changes that needed to take place. First of all, he needed to spend more time at home, needed to plan some fun things for his family to do, needed to take Billy to Disney World, like he'd promised. He smiled. And he needed to invite his wife on a moonlight swim. Hadn't she been saying she wanted another child, a daughter maybe?

Instead of going to the Cunningham's house, he was leaving his hometown and everything in it. But, in reality, he wasn't leaving something behind, he was going toward something else. He was going home.

The drive to the Albany airport took a couple of hours. The flight to Orlando was going to take two or three hours more. Then, he'd have to retrieve his car from the parking garage and make the last half-hour drive to his house, all the while wondering if he still had a home and a family. While waiting to board at the airport, he phoned Candy. There was no answer. A chill struck his heart. Where was she? Had she done what she'd threatened? Had she left him and taken Billy with her?

Disappointed, he settled for leaving a message. "I'm on my way, honey. Just so you know, I didn't hang around after the funeral. Elizabeth means nothing to me. You need to know that. I love you and Billy more than anything on earth. And, Candy. I have plans for us that will make you very happy. Please, be there."

Then he got on the plane and looked out the window at the baggage loaders. They seemed to be taking longer than usual. He looked at his watch. The flight was already six minutes late departing.

The man in the seat next to him was busy reading a book. Maybe he should do the same; keep his mind occupied to calm his nerves. He grabbed the in-flight magazine from the seat pocket and flipped through the pages, unaware of what he was looking at.

"First time flying?" the guy next to him said.

"No, why do you ask?"

"You appear nervous, that's all."

He shook his head and returned the magazine to the seat pocket.

"No, I'm not nervous. I have something on my mind is all."

"Oh." And the man went back to his book.

Funny. The guy never even recognized him. Probably for the best. He wasn't in the mood to talk about baseball and his latest award. All he could think about was Candy and Billy. They meant more to him than the game. More to him than life itself.

He was relieved when the flight attendants shut the front door and started their spiel. Relieved again when the plane taxied to the runway and took off.

He stared out the window as the snow-patched fields diminished into a brown and white tapestry below. The plane broke through the overcast with a few bumps, banked 45 degrees to the south, then glided like a giant eagle toward Florida.

The flight was uneventful. He gazed at the clouds drifting below the plane, ate the sandwich and coffee offered by a smiling flight attendant, and pondered a number of scenarios he might expect when he got home. Perhaps a dark, empty house. Perhaps a fretful, sleepless night making phone calls to friends and family. No Candy. No Billy. No future to speak of.

When the plane began its descent, the lights of the city had already started coming on. Trails of vehicles lined the streets in every direction, their headlights strung together and looping over one another.

He wanted to stop at the airport gift shop and pick up a bouquet of flowers and a toy for Billy. He hadn't done something like that in a long time, hadn't considered his family when he'd been away at a game or off somewhere meeting with coaches and trainers. It was time he started thinking about someone else besides himself. Maybe it wasn't too late to put his marriage over his career, his wife and son over golf and card games with the guys. He'd walked away from Elizabeth Adams, or Jenkins, or whatever last name she was using these days. Walked away and it hadn't bothered him in the least.

The thought struck him like a wrecking ball. Even if Candy divorced him, he wouldn't go back to his former girlfriend. Those few hours he'd spent in her company promised nothing but a momentary fling. It wasn't like before, when he left town to go into the minor leagues. He didn't think about her for a long time after that, but concentrated on playing ball. Something inside had told him, even back then, that she didn't offer any stability. There was something flirtatious about her. Chances are she'd been like that with other guys. The fact that she had hit on him, a married man, told him enough about her character to make him want to run from her.

He was alerted to the groan of the flaps extending and the crunch of the landing gear locking in place. One of the flight attendants gave the usual pre-landing announcement. The guy next to him closed up his book. He ignored the man and stared out the window. Flat-roofed hangars grew larger and swept by. Runway lights flew past in a glittery strand of white and blue. The macadam swept beneath the aircraft, there was a tiny bump, the roar of the engines reversing, and then an easy glide to the terminal. Ben Michaels was going home.

A half-hour later, he stepped from the Orlando terminal, his suitcase in one hand and in his other hand, his overcoat and a plastic bag bearing gifts for his wife and son. He tossed them in the back seat of his car, paid the parking fee, and headed out on the highway.

As he drove toward home, the truth struck him like a hammer. If he were to be honest, he'd have to admit *he* was the one who was responsible for the growing tension in their marriage. *He* was the one who'd put a wedge between himself and his wife. *He* was the one who was neglecting Billy.

Instead of doing whatever he wanted and everyone else had to go along, he needed to set aside his own desires and fix whatever was wrong with his marriage. According to the Bible, the husband was supposed to be the head of the home. He was supposed to love his wife like God loved the church. He was supposed to watch over his family, make sure they're safe and well-cared for. Didn't the scriptures say that a man who didn't care for his own was worse than an unbeliever?

He thought about some of the older players, men who were close to 35 and getting ready to retire. They were the ones who spent the majority of their time with their families. Their conversations centered around school plays, kids' sports, and business investments for when they left the game.

One day he'd retire too. Retire? He hadn't imagined doing that. Baseball was his life, his passion. But sports careers had a short lifespan. Most athletes retired around 30 instead of 65. Maybe it was time he, too, faced reality. Maybe it was time he grew up. Maybe it wasn't too late.

A myriad of thoughts ran through his head. With every turn of a corner, every pause at a stoplight, his heartbeat quickened. His hands gripped the steering wheel like a vise. His life might change this very night.

He'd been away for only two days but that could have been long enough for Candy to clean out the house, change the locks, and go to her mother's with Billy.

His entire body tensed up. He shouldn't have gone swimming with Elizabeth. He knew she was trouble even before he went. And what about the dinner? It seemed harmless at the time. In his mind, he had merely shared a meal with an old friend. Yet, he had to admit, Candy would not have approved.

How could he convince his wife that Elizabeth meant nothing to him? He hadn't shed one tear when his sister wrote and told him his former girlfriend had gotten married. Nor had he jumped for joy when she got divorced. Much like the leg braces he'd discarded as a boy, he'd also discarded Elizabeth from his life. Those leg braces no longer had a grip on him. And neither did she.

Elizabeth was fun for a while, but she was too much of a flirt and definitely too much of a free spirit. Once he'd moved on with his career, he hadn't given her a passing thought.

Then there was Candy. She was beautiful too, in her own way. But he couldn't think of one time when she tried to make him jealous by flirting with other men, even though she could have done that. And free spirit? Not a chance. Candy was more of a hometown girl, a beauty queen who'd won multiple small town pageants but never went on to the big contests.

He never doubted her love for him. When he walked in the door at the end of a long day of practice, he could count on her being there, in the kitchen making one of her tantalizing Southern dishes. After Billy came along, she became even more domestic. She learned to sew, did more baking, and spent every waking hour taking care of her *two men* as she called them.

Come to think about it, the only aggravating thing about Candy was when she pleaded with him to stay home more. He'd ignored her pleas, so in recent months, she'd stopped nagging and had settled for slamming doors and stomping around the house. She wasn't the happy homemaker anymore. And whose fault was it? The truth hit him like a ball bat. *He* was responsible for the atmosphere in his home. Now he hoped it wasn't too late for him to fix it.

As he pulled into his driveway, his tension eased. Candy's Buick Century was parked in its usual spot, leaving room on the left for his car. He relaxed and loosened his grip on the steering wheel. His pulse slowed to a normal rhythm.

He wanted to lunge through the front door and gather his wife and son in his arms. But he couldn't rush into the house as if nothing had happened. He needed to regroup first. He released his seatbelt, turned on the car's interior light, and held up the slip of blue paper. Once again, Mrs. Cunningham's words reinforced his decision. He'd escaped a pit of destruction. Now, with God's help, he was going to make a better life for his family.

He exited the car and pulled his suitcase and the gift bag

from the backseat. Juggling his armload, he tried his key in the front door. It opened easily. He breathed a sigh of relief. Candy hadn't changed the locks, after all. She hadn't left home. She hadn't taken Billy away from him.

He stepped inside the foyer. The aroma of Southern fried chicken enveloped him. A welcoming light glowed in the kitchen. He heard laughter—Billy's happy giggles, and Candy's musical chuckles blending like a performance in a Disney musical.

"I'm home," he called out.

The voices went silent. Then Billy emerged from the kitchen with a burst of energy and leaped at him. Ben dropped his suitcase and caught his son in midair. After lowering him gently to the floor, he handed him the bag with the Disney toy inside, but quickly retrieved the flowers.

"I bought you something at the airport," he said, grinning.

Billy tore open the bag. "Oh boy! A Mickey Mouse telephone."

He grinned at his father. "Thanks, Daddy." Then he scurried off to the living room, poking the buttons and eliciting the voice of his favorite Disney character.

Candy had been standing there the whole time, a smile on her lips, her eyes on the bouquet in Ben's hand. He stared back at her and took in her loveliness, her flashing blue eyes, her flushed cheeks dusted with flour, and both of her hands dappled with chocolate icing.

"We made a cake," she said. "Billy and I."

For a moment, her former shyness emerged and her instant blush reminded him of the girl who had enticed him from the stands when he was pitching in the minors.

He took a step toward her, then eyed her chocolate-covered hands with caution. He held out the flowers at arm's length. She reached out for them and laughed. The melodic ripple of her voice beckoned to him.

"Oh, the heck with it," he said, and he pulled his wife to him, chocolate and all. She held the flowers in one hand and stretched her other arm around his neck. He didn't care. He hugged her with such intensity, he thought he'd never be able to let her go.

She leaned back and frowned at the flour on his jacket and the chocolate stain on his shirt collar. "Your suit—"

"It doesn't matter. We can send it to the cleaners. I just want to hug my wife."

They wrapped their arms around each other and fell into a series of kisses.

When they drew apart, Ben looked Candy in the eye.

"We're gonna talk," he said. "We're gonna make plans together. Things to do on the weekends when I don't have a game. Fun things for the three of us to do as a family."

Her smile broadened and her eyes sparkled. "What in the world has happened to you?" Before he could answer, a frown washed away her smile. "What about Elizabeth? Was she there?"

He stared intently into her eyes. "Yes, she was there. And I can say for certain, she means nothing to me. I don't love Elizabeth. I could have married her years ago. I married you, Candy. You're the one I chose. I love you." He gently grabbed her shoulders. "Now listen to me, honey. I'm not going anywhere without you ever again. We're gonna make decisions together—where to live, what to do on the weekends, and what kind of business I'll get involved in when my career in baseball is finished."

A quizzical line creased her brow. "Your career? Finished?" He pressed a finger to her lips.

"It's inevitable, Candy. I have maybe another five years or so in baseball. We need to start thinking about what I'll do after that, so I can continue to take care of you and Billy. Maybe we can buy into a self-storage business or a restaurant. Are you with me?"

"Yes, Ben, I am. It's all I've ever wanted. To have you and Billy—and maybe another baby—or two."

He smiled into her angelic face, loving her at that moment more than he'd ever loved any woman, including Elizabeth Adams.

Elizabeth Adams? Who on earth is that?

TWENTY-SIX

Frank Peebles

Frank Peebles regained consciousness while he was still inside the rental car. He looked around. Shattered glass. Bent door frame. Lopsided cab, as if the tires on the right side had deflated.

He gazed out the passenger window, then through the cracked windshield, and, finally, the shattered window on the driver's side, mere inches from his face. Strangers were swarming around the vehicle. Distant sirens undulated, then grew louder, until their ear-piercing screams were inside the car with him. Three emergency trucks barreled down on the scene. One of them was an actual fire engine, long and sleek and blanketed with men in yellow suits who spilled off its sides the moment it came to a stop.

Within seconds, rescuers worked to free him from the crumpled driver's seat. Large metal jaws tore off the top of his car. Gloved hands reached in, unfastened his seatbelt, and carefully lifted him to safety. They lay him on a gurney and whisked it away quicker than he could say, "What happened?"

Once inside the ambulance, he tried to close his mind to the ear-splitting siren and the red swishing rays outside his window. The vehicle swerved through traffic and sent him rocking from side-to-side. Someone drove a needle into a vein in his arm. Someone else placed an oxygen mask on his face. More hands groped his arms and legs, like they were searching for broken bones. The noise, the swirling colors, the shifting, and the constant probing nearly took his breath away. He blacked out again, but only for a few minutes.

When he awoke the second time, he was still on the gurney, but now he was speeding down a long hallway, surrounded on both sides by men and women in white. A series of bright globes rushed past overhead. A metallic voice came from nowhere. "Code Blue. Code Blue. All trauma workers proceed to the ER." It was for him. Had to be. Seconds later, his bed broke through a pair of double doors and lurched to a stop beneath another set of glaring overhead lights. The frigid air settled over him like a blanket of ice. All around the room were metal stands, hoses, monitors, and an assortment of machines that hissed and thumped and beeped.

Someone had hooked him up to a myriad of tubes and wires and had attached a fresh IV bag to the needle in his arm. A nurse checked his vitals and left the room. It all happened so fast, he didn't have a chance to ask any questions. Despite the throbbing ache, he turned his head from side-to-side, frantic for someone to tell him what was going on.

A man with a stethoscope dangling from his neck strolled in, looked over Frank's chart, and mumbled a few orders in medical gibberish to an accompanying nurse, then he ambled out. Moments later, they wheeled an X-ray machine in front of him and took a hundred pictures. He thought about radiation. Somewhere in the middle of all that, he blacked out again.

When he awakened, he found himself in a regular hospital room, clothed in a backless gown, with the IV needle still stuck in his arm and a pair of oxygen prongs up his nose. The first rays of sunlight were appearing at the window. He'd spent the night in the hospital.

He groped for the nurse's call button. The beds in most hospitals had been equipped with such gizmos these days. There had to be a control dangling at the side of the bed somewhere. His index finger made contact with a round button. He pressed it then glued his eyes to the open door and waited for a nurse to come running. When no one did, he pressed the button again and held it this time. The top half of his bed went straight up and flung his head off the pillow. He searched blindly for another button. This time, his feet rose several inches before he had the sense to stop pressing. With trembling fingers, he pushed one button after another, sending his bed in a whole assortment of spasms. Frustrated, he continued to poke buttons, until a voice came over a speaker on the wall next to his bed.

"Do you need something, Mr. Peebles?" The female voice sounded other-worldly, and he began to wonder if he had left earth.

Frank scowled. The room wasn't hot enough to be hell. In fact, it was so icy cold he thought his toes were about to fall off. He struggled to turn his face toward the speaker. His head ached and so did his side.

"Hello?" he called out. "I need help with this dang bed. And it's cold in here. Could I *please* have another blanket?"

He fumbled again with the control box, but got nowhere. Within two minutes, a woman in white was at his bedside. Stifling a grin, she went to work adjusting his bed. After she got him into a comfortable position, she moved to a cupboard and pulled out a thick blanket, then layered it over him like she was tucking in a helpless child.

"Where am I?" he said.

"Mr. Peebles, you're in Mercy Hospital. You had an accident."

"Did I break anything?" he said, wiggling his toes. "Do I have a concussion? I blacked out, you know."

"Yes, several times," she said, pressing her lips together like she was trying to keep from laughing. "I can't tell you anything, Mr. Peebles, but Doctor Grayson will be in soon. He's finishing his morning rounds."

"Morning rounds? How long have I been here?"

"Since yesterday afternoon. We ran a lot of tests and, except for a bump on your head, you came through fine. Now, relax. The doctor will fill in all the details."

The nurse lifted the control box, and pursing her lips, she let out a "Tsk, tsk," while shaking her head. "Mr. Peebles, if I were you, I'd leave the bed adjustments to us."

Before he could respond with an expletive, she slipped from the room and left him to wonder exactly how bad off he was. If he wasn't busted up, why hadn't they released him? And why all the tests? Except for a slight headache and a dull pain in his side, he felt like he was floating on air. *It has to be the drugs*, he thought. T*hat's it. They'd drugged me.* Anything to keep him quiet. He continued fretting over being drugged without his permission. Time passed. A man in a white coat walked in, a chart in one hand, and a pen in the other. His face was an unreadable collection of wrinkles.

"Well?" Frank said. "Give me the bad news, doctor. I can take it."

"Okay. First, I'm Doctor Grayson. I've been overseeing your care since you came in yesterday. You're a lucky man, Mr. Peebles. You survived an accident that totaled your car."

"It's not my car. It's a rental." He smiled to himself. "No skin off my nose."

The doctor ignored his comment. "How do you feel this morning, Mr. Peebles?"

"My side hurts. Did I break some ribs? What kind of internal damage did I suffer? My head aches too. Do I have a concussion? I know I bumped it somewhere. What about my legs? Did I break any bones? Am I gonna walk again? Do I need surgery?"

"Relax, Mr. Peebles." The doctor perused his chart. "You have no broken bones. No internal injuries, no back problems, no concussion. And, no, you don't need surgery."

"Then what's wrong with me? Why did I lose consciousness? What am I doing in this bed? Why am I in this hospi—"

"Please, settle down." The doctor was frowning now and shaking his head.

"Mr. Peebles, you have a couple of bruises on your left side where the car door buckled in on you. And, except for your propensity to faint, you have no other problems."

"Propensity to faint? I never fainted before in my life. I blacked out, that's all. A couple times. Are you sure it's not a concussion? Or brain damage?"

Doctor Grayson chuckled. "No. You don't have anything like that. We ran a lot of tests on you. I'm telling you, you're fine."

"But the blackouts—am I gonna need brain surgery?"

"They weren't blackouts. They were brief episodes of syncope."

"Syncope?" That sounded worse brain surgery. "Am I—am I gonna die, doctor?"

Doctor Grayson screwed up his forehead and pinched his lips together, like he'd just heard a bad joke and was trying not to laugh.

"Syncope simply means fainting, Mr. Peebles. You had a few fainting spells, most likely incited by the trauma you experienced. I have to say, sir, that you are an extremely stressed individual. Your blood pressure went off the charts. I've given you some medication to bring it down. Other than that, you're fine. The aide will bring you some breakfast in a bit. Once you have something in your stomach, we'll take that IV out. I may need to keep you overnight again, for observation."

"No. I need to catch a flight to Dallas. Gotta get home."

"If you insist, I'll release you this afternoon. But I strongly recommend that you see your personal physician the minute you get home."

"Why? Why do I need to see my doctor? What aren't you telling me?"

"Calm down, Mr. Peebles. There's nothing wrong with you except you're like a rubber band that's been stretched beyond its capability. Get a complete checkup and then take a few days to rest up before you go back to work."

He was on the verge of tears. "So—so, I'm gonna live?"

"Yes, my friend, you're gonna live. After breakfast, take a nice hot shower and get yourself dressed. Sit in the chair over there and watch some TV for a while. When you're ready to leave, we'll call a cab to take you to the airport. Oh, and by the way, they tell me you never got the chance to fill out any paperwork. On your way out, you should stop by the front desk and settle up your bill."

With that, the doctor escaped into the hall.

So, Frank thought. *Roll me in and roll me out, like those plastic parts we run through our assembly line at the plant. One more piece of merchandise—out the door. Just make sure you pay the bill.*

The routine went exactly like the doctor had said. Breakfast. Hot shower. Chair by the window. TV. The doctor's recheck. Pay the bill. Then out the door. After that, he took a cab to his hotel, grabbed his bags and checked out of there too. Then another two-hour cab ride to the airport. By the time Frank was settled in an airplane seat, he'd calmed down enough to believe he might make it home.

Too bad he hadn't gotten the chance to go fishing as he'd planned. Even worse, he'd missed Mrs. Cunningham's after service celebration. But, at least he'd gone to the funeral. He'd paid his respects, met with her two children, and left feeling pretty good about himself.

Adele Cunningham had raised the best kids. Like her, they had forgiven him long ago. Then, even on her deathbed, she'd taken the time to write him a note.

He dug through his pockets. It wasn't there. Almost in a panic, he reached for his bag under the seat in front of him. He found the note stashed in a side pocket along with his wallet and car keys.

The envelope was a little beat up, and the flap was part-way open. He tore it the rest of the way and slid the note out. Though he was eager to know what Adele had written, he trembled a little as he started to read.

Dear Frank ... she began. Good. She'd used the word "dear."

George and I followed your accomplishments for many years. We read several business magazine stories about you. And we prayed that you'd continue to have great success. But, there was something else George wanted for you. He also prayed that you would accept Jesus as your Savior, and that you'd be blessed with the peace that comes with such a relationship.

Even after George passed, I continued to follow the news reports about your business. I felt a sense of pride that I had known Frank Peebles.

I can't help but wonder if all that success, all that hard work came with a cost. You've obviously put in a lot of long, hard hours to make your business succeed, maybe denying yourself times of relaxation and the simpler pleasures of life.

I'm not going to lecture you, Frank. After all, you're far more accomplished than I ever hope to be. I want to leave you with a passage from the sixth chapter of the Gospel of Matthew, where the Lord told his followers: "Lay up for yourselves treasures in heaven, where neither moth nor rust doth corrupt, and where thieves do not break through nor steal: For where your treasure is, there will your heart be also."

I want to ask you, before it's too late, where is your treasure? I suggest you examine your priorities. Place your trust in Jesus. You won't be sorry.

Praying for you, my dear friend,
Adele Cunningham

Frank sat for a long time and meditated over Adele's words. She'd spoken about priorities as if he'd gotten things backwards. What was she trying to say? That George had chosen the better life? Was it one of those Mary versus Martha situations like the one in the Bible? Pastor Goode used it in a sermon one Sunday years ago when George dragged him to church. For some reason, he never forgot that message.

So, was that it? Was he a male version of Martha? Too busy to go fishing? To busy to read the Bible or go to church? Too busy for his wife? For his friends? For God?

If that were true, then George exemplified Mary, the one who sat at Jesus' feet. The Lord said she'd chosen the better thing. Maybe George had too. Which meant maybe *he'd* chosen the wrong thing.

The plane lurched and shocked him out of his musings. A

spread of billowing white clouds enveloped the aircraft. They turned gray, then black. Rain streaked his window. He sat upright and knuckle-gripped the armrests.

The pilot's voice came over the loudspeaker. "This is your captain speaking. We're heading into a widespread storm. Please, fasten your seatbelts. Flight attendants: put away the carts and lock up the galleys."

Frank shuddered. If God wanted to take him, he couldn't do a thing about it. He was a captive inside this hunk of metal. He'd faced death in that car accident. Now he was facing it again. How many chances was God going to give him?

Coming that close to the end of his life had gotten him thinking. What had he done of value?

He'd served himself. He'd cheated his best friend, then walked away, convinced he knew better than George Cunningham did.

He'd built a successful business, sure, but how successful was it? He'd created a monster. And that monster had sucked the life out of him. And what had it given him in return? Migraine headaches, ulcers, heart palpitations, and high blood pressure.

The day he left his hometown, he accepted a different life. A life that had no time for fishing trips. No relaxing days on the river with George. No weekends off, no family to come home to. No real future except the business.

Come to think of it, maybe death would be a welcome visitor.

He stared straight ahead at the seatback in front of him. Even his first-class seat didn't promise safety. The plane lurched again. He waited for the next shock, for the flames pouring from one of the engines, the crack in the fuselage, the shudder and the sudden dip toward earth. He'd seen it all in a movie. Now it was about to happen to him.

But none of those things occurred. In fact, the rest of the flight was as smooth as a cruise on a calm sea, the landing as slick as skating across a bed of ice, and the taxi to the gate as unhampered as a drive along a newly paved highway.

He exhaled, grabbed his duffel bag from under the seat, and

waited for the plane to come to a stop at the gate. Then he pulled his suitcase from the overhead rack and exited with the other passengers, like cattle being fed through a slaughter-house gate. By this time, Frank had devised a new plan. He could do nothing about his past, but if he wanted to better his life, he'd have to make some changes. Mrs. Cunningham had given him the incentive to do it.

He ignored Doctor Grayson's instructions to go home, rest, and make an appointment with his regular physician. Instead, he turned his car toward the office.

Holding his left side, he limped into the factory, past the assembly line and his startled employees. They froze and watched him hobble by, their hands holding the various parts they'd been working on. He strode past his supervisors, their brows lined with interest, and past the two board members who were always lurking about, checking on the workers, inspecting the parts as if they knew what they were looking for.

With labored breaths, he grabbed the railing and struggled to take the metal staircase to his second floor office. Then he dropped into his chair and released a long sigh. The plant manager, Burt Rhinehower, walked in and stood in the open doorway with his hands on his hips.

"What's going on, Frank? You look like you got run over by a train."

"Shut the door," he commanded.

Burt did.

"Sit down."

He did that too.

The manager started to open his mouth.

"Shut your trap, Burt, before you swallow a fly. I've got something to say, and I'm gonna say it once. Then you can report it to the board."

Burt sat there, eyes wide, a shocked expression on his face. Though Frank had always been hard on his employees, he'd crumbled like a wimp whenever the board members showed up. They held all the power now. But that was going to change. He still knew the business better than any of them, and he was going to take back what had belonged to him from the beginning.

He leaned back in his chair, propped his feet on his desk, crossed his ankles, and cocked his head with an air of authority.

"Now, as you know, I own thirty percent of the stock in this company. That has left me at a disadvantage. The board knows it, and they've wielded a heavy hand, pushing me to my limit, both physically and mentally. But what they don't know—or maybe they've forgotten—is that my wife, Daphne, owns twenty-two percent. Now, her stock, combined with mine, pushes me right back to the top."

Burt tilted his head and frowned. "Daphne has never voted with you, Frank. She's always sided with the board. So why should she change that now?"

"Don't you worry about Daphne. I'm gonna have a talk with her when I get home. By the time I'm done with Daphne, she's gonna beg me to take her shares."

"You sound pretty sure of yourself. You and I both know how feisty that woman can get."

"If I can't convince my wife to shift those shares into my control, I'll have no other recourse than to turn in my resignation, retire, and live the rest of my life on Social Security. But, let me tell you, Burt, this place will never have another CEO who knows the plastics industry like I do. Why, I grew up with it. I gave Dupont a run for their money back when George Cunningham and I first started, and I've kept this plant in a prime spot in the current market as well. Who knows, maybe I'll start another plant from scratch and run this one out of business. I certainly have the resources and the know-how to do it."

Burt Rhinehower shifted in his seat, his discomfort evident.

"So, what do you want, Frank? What do I tell the board?"

He grinned, lowered his feet with a groan, and leaned across his desk toward Burt.

"First, you tell them I'm changing the plant operating hours.

From now on, we open at eight and close at five. Every day, Monday through Friday. No excuses. No more overtime. No more calling in the workers before the sun comes up in order to make schedule. None of this *come in at six o'clock* business. Our employees will have a regular work schedule they can depend on. That way they can use their off-hours the way they want to. No one, except the janitor and the security guard, will work weekends anymore. If we can't get production done from eight-to-five during the week, then there's something wrong with us, and we'll need to fix it."

"What if we don't meet our deadlines?" Burt pointed out.

"Then, we'll change the deadlines. We'll set reasonable dates for filling a contract, allowing extra days to resolve any problems that might arise. I want our people to spend their free time with their families. And that's another thing. I want to change the benefits program—increase their medical insurance and vacation days. Next week, I'm giving everyone a raise. And we're gonna start one of those matching retirement plans, where the business puts in fifty cents for every dollar the employee invests."

The plant manager was grinning now. "What's happened to you, Frank? I don't recognize you."

He bristled with embarrassment, then dismissed it. "Nothing's happened to me that didn't need to happen," he said. "Now, listen. I want you to start the ball rolling on these things. I'm still in charge of this company, and I'm gonna change the way we're doin' things. Get our attorney to draw up any necessary papers. And start that work schedule immediately. Announce it to the employees over the loud speaker before I leave the building. I want to see their faces light up."

"You're leaving now?"

"That's right, I'm gonna take a few days off and go fishing. And on Sunday, I'm goin' to church. And I'm gonna take my wife with me."

Frank got up and walked to the plate glass window that gave him a view of the plant below. Burt went to the desk, pressed the intercom button and made the announcement. Surprised and smiling faces looked up at the office window. Frank gave his employees a wave and a nod. He then descended the metal stairway to an eruption of applause.

After he got in his car, he thought of one more thing he wanted to do on his way home. Just for fun, he'd stop at the corner store and pick up a gallon of milk.

TWENTY-SEVEN

BRENDA SCHWARTZ

Though Judy Cunningham had invited Brenda to join the family for refreshments after the service, she decided to skip the celebration. After all, what else could she expect? The woman was a saint. More stories were sure to flow about all she'd done. Then there was that roomful of memorabilia, reminders of everything Brenda had missed, including pictures of George.

She pulled into her driveway, allowed only a sideways glance at the Cunningham house, and went upstairs to her sewing room. She shed her coat and dropped it in a chair along with her purse. She needed to keep her mind occupied by doing something positive. Pastor Goode's request for items for the church came to mind.

She opened one of her trunks and pulled out handfuls of silk flowers, lace ribbons, unfinished embroidery projects, and enough pink and blue remnants to make three baby quilts for the church nursery. She spread everything on the guest bed.

Next, she lifted the dust cover off her sewing machine and opened her notions basket, exposing clumps of colored threads, several bobbins, and a packet of pins and needles.

She stood back and eyed her materials, then made a mental note of what she might need to buy—batting for the quilts, of course, and more colored threads, plus several skeins of yarn. She pressed a finger to her cheek, a spirit of excitement mounting within her.

For the first time in years, she was motivated. She had a purpose now, so happy that Pastor Goode had asked her to spruce up the sanctuary and the church annex. She envisioned the drab walls in the nursery and snorted. *Adele Cunningham may have kept everything disinfectant clean, but she'd failed to add bits of color to the room.* With Brenda taking over the nursery, the babies would look at more than blank walls. They'd see colorful tapestries depicting animals and flowers. They'd cuddle under warm, handmade quilts, and the older children will have new nap-time blankets. She could make pillows, dresses for the dolls, stuffed animals, and an assortment of nursing shawls for the new mommies.

As for the sanctuary? Every week, she'd provide a different silk floral arrangement for the altar, with special designs and colors relevant to whatever holiday it was—purple and yellow for Easter, red poinsettias for Christmas, maybe a cornucopia of autumn leaves and hand-stitched vegetables for Thanksgiving. And when somebody died, she could find out their favorite color and make a special arrangement for the altar, something the family could take home as a keepsake, like Judy had done with the arrangement she'd made in honor of Adele.

Her heart raced and her mind swirled with ideas. She didn't expect to get paid—oh no—not with money. Pastor Goode had said the budget could pay for materials, but she wanted to do the work for free. She'd insist on it. Her reward would come from having her creations displayed and appreciated. How sad that he hadn't asked her to do this years ago.

As she sorted through some of the fabrics and embroidery patterns, she came upon a bolt of material covered with bright red roses, Adele Cunningham's favorite flower. Even beyond the grave, that woman was speaking to Brenda. She was telling her she could be useful again, that she could use her talents to bring joy to others.

She'd even left her a note. Brenda walked over to the chair, flung her coat aside, and searched through her purse for the blue envelope. It lay at the bottom beneath a clump of damp tissues, remnants of her bawling session in the church. She pulled out the mess, tossed the tissues in a trash can, and slid the letter out of the limp envelope. Some of the words had blurred, but she could still make out Mrs. Cunningham's message.

My dearest Brenda,

Dearest? A lump came to her throat. She blinked a few times to clear the moisture from her eyes, and then began to read Adele's message.

If you've received my note, it means I've gone home to Jesus. Don't cry for me, dear friend. I know you will, because you've always been a sensitive person. I want you to know that even in my absence, our friendship will endure through all time.

Brenda stared at the page. *Don't cry?* Brenda thought about the pile of tissues she had soaked with her tears during the service. Even now, she hadn't expected more tears to gather. She blinked them away and read on.

I know we have not always seen eye-to-eye on everything, but that is what gave our relationship so much zip. We were thrown into competition many times, and you always behaved graciously, whether you won or lost.

By this time, Brenda was smirking. Apparently, Adele had had a different view of their relationship. Friendship? Brenda a winner? That rarely happened. In fact, she couldn't recall *ever* beating Adele Cunningham at *anything*. So far, Adele had said nothing to dissolve the love-hate struggle she'd been dealing with. Sure, she'd shed a pile of tears this morning. And, yes, she still carried a grudge at times, particularly when she thought about George and how Adele had swept him away from her. For that reason alone, Adele's note didn't make much sense. Didn't that woman know they'd been bitter enemies? Nevertheless, Adele's next words nearly knocked her over.

You never knew this, Brenda, and I'm ashamed to admit it, but I envied you. I envied your sweet spirit, your quiet way of tackling even the most difficult project, and how you never quit whatever you were doing, completing it to the end.

Your ability to create beautiful things gave me the incentive to try harder at those crafts. I doubt I would have completed any of those projects had I not been watching you.

Something else you need to know, George used to talk about you all the time, how the two of you used to play games and do schoolwork together. He followed everything you did. Attended all of your band concerts and raved about your clarinet playing. He also complimented the decorations you did for the school dances and said he wished you could have been there to enjoy them.

And you'll be surprised to know, George once told me if he hadn't married me, he would have considered you. He admired your unpretentious ways and your ability to bring comfort to a home, not to mention your homemade brownies and mulled apple cider.

I could have been extremely jealous, but I liked you, Brenda—like a sister. And so, I leave you with this message from the apostle John's first epistle: "Beloved, if God so loved us, we ought also to love one another. No man hath seen God at any time. If we love one another, God dwells in us, and his love is perfected in us."

In Christ's love,

Adele Cunningham

Brenda barely got to the end when her tears started blurring the ink. She thought she'd emptied her tear ducts at the church, but now a fresh batch was running down her cheeks. She ran for a box of tissues, blew her nose several times, and sat on the edge of her bed in the midst of all her sewing materials.

"Adele Cunningham," she murmured. "You rascal you. Here I've been cursing you for most of my life, while you've thought of me as a friend."

The words of scripture continued to run through her head. *His love is perfected in us.* Love. A simple word, yet packed with so much emotion—and so much responsibility. Yes, she had loved George the way a woman loves a man. But, for the first time, she had to admit she also loved Adele like a sister.

If she could talk to her now, she would tell her how much she had envied her, too, and how that envy had ultimately turned to admiration.

She determined right then to do the best job she could for the church. She may not be praised for good works like Adele Cunningham had been, but she had found her rightful place of service, and that was good enough for her.

She rose from the bed and went to the window. The celebration was still going on at the Cunningham house. More people were mounting the front steps. Music and laughter poured from inside. It was the kind of gathering Mrs. Cunningham would have liked.

Turning from the materials on the bed, she reached for her coat and hurried out of the room and down the stairs. Perhaps there was still time to share some things Mrs. Cunningham had done for her. She could hardly wait to join the celebration.

TWENTY-EIGHT

SAMMY POWERS

Time. That's something Sammy Powers had a lot of. Time to think about the mistakes he'd made, time to decide what to do with the rest of his life. But it wasn't going to be easy. His record was bound to follow him wherever he went, along with the feeling of failure that nagged him day and night. He'd let people down. His boss at the newspaper. And most of all, Mrs. Cunningham.

When everyone else had given up on him, *she* had spoken words of encouragement. She told him he had worth, that he didn't have to settle for the kind of life his brothers had lived. She helped him find a job. She prayed for him—and *with* him. That woman didn't let him quit.

About the time people were celebrating her memorial service, he was being released from solitary confinement. He wished he could have been at the church instead of in prison. He returned to his cell to discover he had a different cellmate. He still had the same bunk. No one had taken his stuff. Not that he owned anything of value—a toothbrush, a deck of cards, and a clean change of underwear. And the newspaper clipping was still there, on his bunk, where he'd left it.

He stepped inside the metal door and acknowledged the other guy with a nod. He grabbed the newspaper and folded it, then he dropped on top of his cot, and rolled over, away from the bars that separated him from freedom. All he could do now was sleep, eat, and wait for Tyrone to return.

He drifted off, awoke long enough for lunch, then sat on the edge of his bed and played a game of Solitaire. *Ha!* he thought. *Released from solitary to play Solitaire. That's one for the books.*

The boredom continued throughout the day, with Sammy intent on winning at cards while trying to ignore the guy in the other bunk. For some reason, the other fellow was in a private world of his own. He kept his nose in a book—looked like a Bible—then he wrote something in a notebook. *What's he doing? Waiting for me to open the conversation? Well, the guy could wait until doomsday.* He was in no mood to talk, especially not with a Bible-thumper.

The next day, after breakfast, he went back to playing Solitaire. He tossed down an ace and shot a glance at his cellmate, surprised to see the guy was still reading his Bible. That tickled him. Mrs. Cunningham would be so happy to see him rooming with someone like that. *Who knows? Maybe from somewhere up there in heaven, she'd even arranged it.*

He continued to play cards, but glanced up now and then at the other guy. As much as he missed Mrs. Cunningham, he didn't want anyone else quoting scripture to him. That was a special thing between the two of them. *She had earned my trust. But don't let anyone else try to shove that stuff down my throat.*

He lost the game, grunted, then shuffled the cards and started another. He was halfway into the new game, and it looked as though he was going to win this time, when a familiar voice called his name from outside the cage. Tyrone was back.

Sammy shoved the cards aside and sprang from his bed. "How'd it go?" He strode to the bars.

"It went fine, son," Tyrone said, a wistful smile on his lips. "They held a beautiful service for your friend. The preacher gave a wonderful eulogy. The hymns nearly got me weeping. And a whole lot of people had somethin' nice to say about her. Your Mrs. Cunningham would have been pleased."

"Did anyone—um—I mean—I don't expect the family remembered me, but—"

"I spoke to her son and daughter and told them I had come

in your place. Judy—the girl—was pleased you hadn't forgotten her mother."

He bowed his head and let Judy's kind words sink in. Then he raised his chin and looked through a blur into Tyrone's tender brown eyes. Tyrone gazed back at him with compassion.

"Hey, look here," Tyrone said. He pulled an envelope out of his pocket and fed it through the bars. "I had to get this cleared up front, but they said I could give it to you. Sorry, but they had to open it. You know, censors and all."

Sammy nodded and accepted the envelope. "Thanks, Tyrone. And thanks for going to Mrs. Cunningham's funeral. I owe you one."

"You go ahead and read that note. Maybe it'll give you some encouragement. I don't know what's in it. I didn't read it, just passed it to the authorities." He shuffled his feet and stuck his hands in his pockets. "Well, I gotta go, kid."

"Okay. Come by later?"

Tyrone nodded, turned from the cage, and disappeared down the hall.

On his way back to his cot, Sammy glanced at his cellmate. The guy had been sitting there watching the entire exchange with Tyrone. He smiled at Sammy. It was the first time the guy had even acknowledge him. It wasn't a sarcastic smile like the one on his last cellmate's mug. It was a friendly, inviting smile, one that troubled Sammy about as much, but for other reasons. He shot an angry glance at the Bible on the guy's lap.

"Looks like you made a friend," the guy said.

Sammy stopped short and narrowed his eyes. "What's your problem? Do you find my private life interesting? Can't mind your own business?"

"Sorry. I just—"

Sammy took a step in his direction. "You just what?" He glowered at him, hoping he'd back off.

The guy shrugged. "I thought we could be friends, that's all. I mean, we're stuck in this cell together and—"

"And what? We can become buddies?"

Sammy glared at the Bible in the guy's hand. "Don't count on it." He turned back toward his bunk, sat on the edge and opened Mrs. Cunningham's note. As he read her message, his anger began to melt away.

My dear Sammy,

Already he could feel her love pouring from that little piece of paper.

When I took you under my wing, it wasn't because I thought you were a hopeless case that needed rescuing, but because I found potential within those troubled eyes of yours. And inside your angry words was a cry for help. How could I not listen to it?

I always prayed for you to rise above your past and overcome all those hurdles of your childhood. I wanted you to make a better life for yourself. Better than the life your two brothers chose. Better than the life your parents handed down to you.

Even after you got in trouble, I continued to hold onto my dream for you. Even now, as you sit in that jail cell and serve your time, I still have high hopes for you. You're paying for your crime, Sammy, but you will leave prison one day and you can start fresh.

Lots of Bible characters had difficulties. Paul once persecuted Christians. Then he accepted a mission from God and he ended up in jail. Multiple times. He could have given up, but a greater power had gotten a hold of him. Instead of an earthly lawyer, he had an advocate with the Father, the Lord Jesus Christ. You can access that same power. With Jesus in your corner, you can do anything.

I want you to know, I've taken the liberty to pay for your GED studies so you can get a diploma. The prison authorities will help you to access the classes. I also included extra cash in case you want to take some college courses. You can begin right now to plan a different future for yourself. Maybe you'd like to counsel young men who find themselves in a similar condition like what you also experienced, kids who suffer at the hands of an angry parent or one who loves the bottle more than their own children.

I'll leave you with one last promise, Sammy. You can read it in 2 Corinthians 5:17.

Let the words speak to your heart. Don't consider yourself a failure. See yourself the way I see you,, and the way God sees you—as a new creature in Christ. All you need to do is trust him. He'll do the rest.

With deep love and affection,

Adele Cunningham

Sammy didn't want to break down in front of his new cellmate. He gnawed at the inside of his cheek until he drew blood, anything to keep from losing it. But Mrs. Cunningham had given him a verse of scripture, and she hadn't written it out. Months ago, she'd given him a Bible, but he never read it. When she didn't come back to see him, he donated it to the prison library. Now, how was he supposed to read that verse without a Bible?

He eyed his cellmate. "Hey, you."

"The name's Chuck."

"Okay. Chuck. I need to look up a verse."

"Ask me nice, and I'll look it up for you."

He fumed for a minute, then he pictured Mrs. Cunningham looking down at him and shaking her head. He swallowed his pride. "Okay, Chuck, will you look up—let's see—" He checked Mrs. Cunningham's note. "Second Corinthians 5:17."

Without hesitation, Chuck flipped to the right page. Sammy was impressed. The guy knew right where to go, no stumbling over a table of contents, no scratching his head, like Sammy and most of the cons in this place might have done. He stared at the guy with interest.

Chuck pointed a finger at the text and began to read. *"Therefore if any man be in Christ, he is a new creature: old things are passed away; behold, all things are become new."* He looked up. "Want me to read on?"

Sammy nodded.

"And all things are of God, who hath reconciled us to himself by Jesus Christ, and hath given to us the ministry of reconciliation."

Sammy frowned, puzzled. "What's that mean? Recon— reconcil—?"

"Reconciliation. It's what happens when a friendship has been broken and one party does something to restore the relationship. In this case, we were separated from God because of our sins. Then, Jesus died on the cross so we could be restored; reconciled to God."

Sammy curled one leg under him and swung his other leg over the side of his cot. He stared at Chuck, this time out of deep appreciation. The guy was like a Bible teacher.

"So, it's kinda like robbin' a bank and then apologizing to the banker?"

Chuck shook his head. "Not quite. It goes deeper than that. It means something happens inside you so you don't want to do that again. You've broken a trust. You want to repair the relationship. Permanently."

"So you're sayin' we break off with God when we do wrong?"

Chuck nodded.

"That's what Mrs. Cunningham used to say."

"Who's Mrs. Cunningham?"

"Just a friend."

"Did she also say you can make things right with God by trusting in his Son, Jesus Christ?"

"Yeah, she did. Lots of times. I even went to church with her and declared it myself. But after a while, I kinda stored all that away in the back of my mind. After all, what would God want with a loser like me? I been in trouble my whole life."

"I can relate to that."

Sammy eyed Chuck with skepticism. "What put *you* in here? If you're supposed to be God's friend, how's come you couldn't stay straight?"

Chuck cocked his head. "It's the usual story, in the wrong place at the wrong time. Some guy was going' after my kid sister. I plowed into him. The guy's in the hospital with a concussion and a broken pelvis. My trial's next week. If he dies, I'm a goner."

Sammy felt a bristling on the back of his neck. "That's so wrong. You were protecting your sister."

"Yeah, but she's my only witness and she's underage. The family doesn't want her to testify—you know, the whole court thing, being embarrassed, and she's so young."

Sammy snickered. "So they're gonna let you sit here, maybe take the rap?"

"I'm praying God will work on my behalf."

"And you think reading the Bible is gonna help you out of this mess? What do you expect? God rushing to your defense, like some kind of lawyer?"

"Maybe. The fact is, I did wrong. But the Bible says I have an advocate—a lawyer, like you said—going to my defense before God. He did it so I'd be forgiven for my sins, and I'm hoping he'll rescue me from this too. But even if he doesn't, the words in this book are giving me peace. The trial may not go my way, but I can go through anything if I hold onto God's promises."

Sammy blinked a few times as he tried to register what Chuck had said. Peace? Promises? Was all that inside that book, and he'd tossed it aside like rubbish? The next time Tyrone came to visit, he'd ask him to go find his Bible in the library. He'd like to take another look at the message Mrs. Cunningham wrote on the first page—words that eluded him now.

Not only that but maybe Tyrone can help him sign up for some of those classes she mentioned.

He leaned back on one elbow and studied Chuck. Then he said something that surprised even him.

"Will you pray for me, Chuck, that I'll get some of that peace?"

"I sure will."

"Something else, do you think a loser like me might be able to turn his life around?"

Chuck smiled. "Seems possible."

He told Chuck about the classes Mrs. Cunningham had paid up for him.

Chuck nodded with encouragement. "Go for it, buddy. What have you got to lose?"

TWENTY-NINE

CARL WILSON

Night shadows were falling. Carl Wilson sat in his wheelchair and stared out his fifth-floor window at the lighted buildings clustered on the hills outside the hospital. In this one town alone there must be more than 7,000 residents. So many people. So many possibilities. He wished he could have found another donor, perhaps someone who'd already died. He'd been on the list, it seemed like forever. But with him having a rare blood type, and Mrs. Cunningham being a match and willing to give—the whole process moved faster than a runaway train. Now it was too late to reverse anything. Mrs. Cunningham was gone.

He slumped forward, sobbing. He pressed his hand protectively to his stomach. If he had it to do over again, knowing how it was going to turn out, he would have refused her gift. He could have gone back to Mexico. He could take his chances with more dialysis treatments. Or he simply could have placed his life in God's hands and begged for a miracle.

A gentle hand on his back told him his wife had entered his hospital room.

"It's not your fault," she repeated for what must have been the twentieth time.

He shook his head.

"I should have stopped it. After hearing about the risks—especially to Mrs. Cunningham—I should have stopped it. What if my body rejects her kidney? It will all have been in vain. I could still die, Adrienne. Doctor Fletcher said there were no guarantees. Now Mrs. Cunningham is dead, and I'm alive."

"Please, Carl. Your doctor told me you might experience some depression following surgery. You mustn't upset yourself. You know as well as I do, God is in control. You've preached it for years. *Confia en Dios.* Trust God, you always said. Now you have to do what you've been telling other people to do."

"So, that's it? Do we go back to Mexico and continue our mission as if nothing has happened? Do we forget about Mrs. Cunningham?"

"No, we'll never forget her or what she did for you. But you need to start seeing God's plan in all of this. Do you think he sat there wringing his hands when you got sick? Do you think he was surprised to find out you both had O negative blood? Or that you would come home to the United States and visit the church Mrs. Cunningham attended? No, Carl. There are no surprises to God. No coincidences."

He turned toward the window. An icy mist had frozen across the lower part of the pane, blurring the traffic below. Automobile lights went on and flowed by, like a chain of diamonds being dragged past his window. Diamonds. That was a laugh. What was his wife wearing on the third finger of her left hand? A zircon. Had she ever complained? No. Nor had she complained about the humble shack they called home in Mexico's countryside. She'd served beside him, day and night, smiling and humming a tune as if she were living in a palace on the banks of the Mediterranean Sea.

He gazed at her face. An aura of peace dwelt there. "You're a good woman, Adrienne," he said. "I don't deserve you."

She chuckled. "None of us deserve anything, dear." She rubbed his back. "Listen to me. God has given you another chance to make your mission a success. You were just getting things started when you got sick. You need to get your act together, otherwise you're tossing Mrs. Cunningham's gift out the window. Let it count for good. Move forward and do what God has called you to do."

"I wish I had the strength," he said, feeling an awful lot like the zircon on his wife's finger—a fake—a washed-up failure of a man, who took away another person's chance to live so he could fulfill his so-called mission.

"Look," Adrienne said, as she reached for her purse. "Before we left the church, someone handed me this card. Apparently, Mrs. Cunningham wrote a bunch of notes to special people—like you. I haven't opened it, but I've been curious about what's inside."

He reached for the note in her hand, then hesitated. "Will you read it to me, honey?"

"Sure." She tore open the envelope with unmasked enthusiasm.

He didn't take his eyes off the window.

"To a wonderful man of God, a servant of the Lord, a new friend..." she read aloud.

If you're reading this note, then it's clear, I didn't make it, but you did. How blessed I've been to have known you and your family, how thrilled to have a small part in helping you get back to your work in Mexico.

You have a tremendous task in front of you, Carl. Adrienne told me about the mission and the progress you've made with the nationals. She shared some of your plans for the expansion. I pray great things will happen there in that remote area.

Thank you for allowing me to offer what little I could. I'm satisfied to be numbered among those who are 'staying by the stuff,' like those Israelites who weren't able to go into the heart of battle, and like so many others who've been supporting your mission with donations and with prayer. We're all staying by the stuff, and you're in the heart of the battle. As I told you before, I'm not a rich person, but I've been able to give a little something toward your mission. And, you, my brave comrade, will charge ahead, filled with the power of the Holy Spirit, to complete the work you began.

Don't let my death discourage you. Keep forging ahead, like a good soldier of the cross. Forget about the past. Think about those villagers who are awaiting your return and keep stepping ahead.

Like it says in Paul's letter to the Philippians, "This one thing I do, forgetting those things which are behind, and reaching forth unto those things which are before, I press toward the mark for the prize of the high calling of God in Christ Jesus."

Reach for the prize, Carl. I've already received mine.

With sincerest regards,

Adele Cunningham

A flood of tears rushed down Carl's cheeks. With the back of his hand, he wiped them away as more spilled out. Adrienne rested her forehead against his.

"Oh my," Carl choked out. "What a strong woman of God Mrs. Cunningham was. To think, she cared that much about me and our mission. While I thought of her gift as a physical contribution—a kidney to get my body working again—she meant it in a spiritual light, a way to serve God and an opportunity to be a part of something worthwhile."

"That's right, Carl." Adrienne stepped back and dabbed at her own tears. "Oh, darling," she whimpered. "Don't you see? If you let Adele's death defeat you, then her gift was all in vain. But if you do as she said—go on and continue to serve—when we return to Mexico, we'll take Mrs. Cunningham with us. Having her kidney inside you has made her a lifelong part of your ministry. Please, Carl, don't quit. Don't let the mission fail. Don't allow Mrs. Cunningham's gift to be given in vain."

He caught his breath and smiled for the first time in days.

"You're right," he said, with mounting conviction. "As soon as I'm well enough to travel, we'll go back to Mexico, and we'll continue the job we started there. I'll try to make it work. Not for myself, but for Mrs. Cunningham and for all those people who are waiting for us to return."

He gazed out the window. "You know what, Adrienne?"

"What?"

"The educational center is almost finished but we haven't named it yet. Why don't we call it *Escuela para Ciegos de Adele?*"

"Adele's School for the Blind," Adrienne murmured. She nodded her agreement. "That's a great idea, Carl. Then Mrs. Cunningham will always be a part of our mission."

Judy Cunningham

Judy clutched the pale blue envelope with her mother's note inside. Aunt Connie and the crowd of guests would simply have to wait a few more minutes.

She ran her finger under the flap and slid the paper out, then pressed it to her breast and squeezed her eyelids against a sudden rise of tears. Then, taking a deep breath, she began to read.

My Dearest Judy,

You were my gift from God, my princess, my prize. I didn't want to leave you this soon, but it seems God had a different plan. Please don't allow your grief to hinder your walk with the Lord. I want to remind you that I am in a wonderful place, with my Savior, and as he promised, there is no pain, no crying, no fear—only pure, unadulterated joy. My time on earth was filled with many blessings. Among them were you and Paul.

Now, to get down to business. You'll find my will in a little strongbox on the top shelf of my bedroom closet. I'm leaving my car to Paul, and the house and all its furnishings to you. There are no debts. Everything is completely paid off. Your father made sure of that before he passed. Let Paul and his wife go through the household items and choose things they want to keep. If you decide to continue living in the house, you can do so, with my blessing. Paul won't contest it. I made him aware of my wishes weeks ago, and he agreed.

I also have a bank account containing $50,000 from your dad's life insurance policy. The paperwork is in the strongbox along with my notarized permission for you and Paul to take possession of it. Please, *donate $10,000 to Carl Wilson's ministry in Mexico. He thinks all I had to give was a kidney. Will he be surprised!*

Use part of what remains to pay for my burial expenses, and divide the rest between the two of you.

Now, to share my heart. I have some concerns about certain happenings in your life. Recently, word came to me through a friend that you may be about to fall into a dangerous trap, one that will surely bring heartache and shame. I want to remind you of a verse of scripture that helped me escape a similar trial when your father left to serve in the military. He was far away from home. I didn't know if he'd come back to me, and I was frightened and feeling very much alone.

In his absence I developed a relationship with another man in town. He was already married to someone else.

Judy caught her breath. She never knew. Had no idea that her mother had succumbed to the same weakness she'd been trying to fight. She read on, unable to believe her eyes.

We hadn't fallen into sin, but we were close. I knew we were heading for a dangerous precipice, and I didn't have the strength to resist on my own. It was then, while in the midst of temptation, that I made a decision. I turned to the scriptures and particularly to Joshua Chapter 24, and this challenge: "Choose you this day whom you will serve .... as for me and my house, we will serve the Lord." Those words helped me to sever that relationship.

After that, I filled the emptiness in my life with ministry to others. I started praying for people and was surprised when they came to me for advice and encouragement. I became more involved in the church. I counseled other women and helped with their children. Joshua's challenge strengthened me spiritually. I learned to trust God in everything, to pray with intensity, and to guide people by using the scriptures. Did you know that you can find the answer to every problem in God's word?

What I've come to see in all of this is that you're a lot like me. You not only look like a younger version of me, but you have my heart. And you apparently have my weaknesses. The good news is, God has blessed you with the same tools he gave to me. You have the gift of helps, my daughter. You merely need to learn how to apply it.

If you follow in my footsteps, people will start to come to you for counsel and prayer. Don't be concerned if you're unsure how to respond. The answer lies in Romans Chapter 12. Memorize that passage of scripture and keep it in your heart. It will surface when you need it most.

Until we meet again,

All my love,

Mother

A gasp escaped from Judy's lips. She must have been holding her breath that whole time. Somehow, her mother had known about Parker, but she'd never mentioned it. And she'd experienced a similar temptation long ago.

Tears fell like big raindrops on the page. Judy tugged the last tissue from the box on the night table, then she reached inside her purse and instead of a handkerchief she came up with Mrs. Cunningham's note addressed to Parker Addison. She stared at it, then looked closer, her eyes widening. The envelope had not been sealed.

With mounting curiosity, Judy eased the sheet of paper out of the envelope and unfolded it. There was no endearing salutation, only a brief message.

Mr. Addison,

I have been covering my daughter with prayers, pleading with God to protect her from the wolves of this world. I am confident that, just as he watches over the sparrows, he's been watching over my Judy. By the time you receive this note, she may have made a decision that will affect both of your lives. If she does what I hope she'll do, you'll never see her again.

In the meantime, make yourself right with God. It's not too late for you to turn to him and repent. As the Bible says, "The wages of sin is death; but the gift of God is eternal life through Jesus Christ our Lord."

Choose life, Parker. You won't regret it.

Adele Cunningham

Judy's initial impulse was to tear up Parker's note and pretend it didn't exist. She took several deep breaths and looked again at the two note cards. Ironically, they bore the same basic message. Her mother loved her dearly and wanted the best for her.

A buzz of voices on the other side of the bedroom door told her the guests had congregated in the kitchen. She slid the note cards back inside her purse and rose from the rocker. She started for the door, then turned around and allowed her gaze to circle her mother's bedroom. If Mrs. Cunningham had been there, wouldn't she have said the exact same things she'd written in the note?

The following morning, Judy rose from her bed before the sun was up. She'd purposely set her alarm clock for 5 a.m. She dressed hurriedly, didn't bother to put on makeup, just ran a brush through her hair, grabbed her coat and bag, and slipped out the front door.

The drive to her office took fifteen minutes. There was very little early morning traffic, and the favorable timing of the street lights allowed her to zip through town without having to stop once. She wasn't expected to return to work for a few days, but there was something she needed to do, and it had to be done right away, before she lost her courage.

She used her key to enter the building. The reception desk stood empty. A lone guard sat in a metal folding chair next to the bank of elevators. He looked up from the magazine he was reading, gave Judy a nod of recognition, then went back to his article.

Judy stepped inside an elevator and pushed the button for the fourth floor. The halls were empty and dimly lit. She went to her desk and filled a cardboard box with her belongings. When she finished, she wrote her resignation on a slip of paper. No apology. No explanation. Simply the words, "I quit," and her signature. Then she went straight to Parker Addison's office, shoved aside the documents on his desk and placed her resignation and her office key there, along with her mother's note addressed to him. Then she turned off the lights and caught the elevator to the lobby.

When she hit the sidewalk, she took a deep breath of the fresh early morning air, squared her shoulders, and headed for her car.

"Well, it's done, Mother. All I can say is, thank you. Because of you, my life is back on the right track. I want more than ever to make you proud of me, 'cause, you know what? I'm proud of *you*. All those note cards you left—I can't help but wonder how many hearts you touched with your words, even after your death

"I want to pattern the rest of my life after yours. People still need prayers and words of encouragement. You're no longer here, but I am. While I was growing up, I watched you. I listened to your prayers. I stood in awe as you dropped everything to run to a hurting neighbor, to counsel young women, to serve friends and strangers however you could. I didn't know it then, but I was in school all my life. And you were my teacher. You were educating me by your example.

"I kind of relate to Elisha grabbing for Elijah's mantle, hoping to receive a double portion. In the same way, I'm going to try to pick up where you left off. Of course, those prophets were far above me, but your example encourages me to get my eyes off myself and onto others, and to do whatever I can.

"To start with, I'm going to offer to watch Paul's children some weekend while he and Marcia take a much needed vacation. I also want to visit Sammy Powers in the jail, like you used to do, twice a month. Maybe I can encourage him to turn his life around. I'm also going to invite Brenda Schwartz to have lunch with me on a weekly schedule. She's all alone, Mother. And she's childless. But she can be a mother to me and I can be the daughter she never had.

"You taught me how to serve others, Mother. You taught me how to love unconditionally. Someday, I hope to teach those same lessons to my own children, and, hopefully, they'll teach them to their children, and so on. Unknowingly, you left me a legacy that can pass from one generation to the next, a legacy that will never die."

ACKNOWLEDGMENTS

Much appreciation goes to my daughter, Joanna Jones, who proof reads all of my manuscripts, also to my friend and neighbor, Denise Miller, who critiqued the section on kidney transplants, and to my friend and fellow writer, Yeny Rowley, who critiqued the passages containing Spanish phrases.

I also want to recognize my daughter, Vicki Christensen, who has Down Syndrome. When I'm in my office, working, she keeps herself busy playing music, singing karaoke, or watching movies and sitcoms on her computer. Her reward? A challenging game of *Candyland* or *Chutes and Ladders* with Mom, both of us vying for a prize of peanut butter M&Ms, winner take all, though we always share with the loser.

Many thanks go to Mike Parker, publisher/editor of Word-Crafts Press, for his exceptional editing skills and for encouraging us writers to excel in our craft. I also have much appreciation for the talents of David Warren, a terrific artist who designs all of my book covers.

None of my works would be possible if not for the Holy Trinity—Our Heavenly Father, who created the resources that make up our writing materials; His Son, Jesus Christ, my Lord and Savior, who encourages me daily in my work; and the Holy Spirit who guides, inspires, and blesses beyond anything I could ever hope or imagine.

MARIAN RIZZO

Pulitzer Prize nominee in the field of journalism, Marian Rizzo has won numerous awards, including the New York Times Chairman's Award and first place in the 2014 Amy Foundation Writing Awards. She worked for the *Ocala Star-Banner* newspaper for 30 years. She also has written articles for the *Gazette*, *Ocala Style Magazine*, and *Billy Graham's Decision Magazine*.

Several of Marian's novels have won awards at conferences and retreats. In 2018, her suspense novel, *Muldovah*, was a finalist in the Genesis competition at the American Christian Fiction Writers Conference.

Marian earned a bachelor's degree in Bible education from Luther Rice Seminary. She trained for jungle missions with New Tribes (now ETHNOS 360), and she served for two semesters at a Youth With A Mission training center in Southern Spain. Several years ago, she made a trip to the Holy Land, a visit that provided much of the backdrop for this novel.

Marian lives in Ocala, Florida, with her daughter, Vicki, who has Down Syndrome. Her other daughter, Joanna, has blessed her with three wonderful grandchildren.